HIDDEN ASSETS

ALAN WATSON

ISBN: 1500216127
ISBN 13: 9781500216122
Library of Congress Control Number: 2014910946
CreateSpace Independent Publishing Platform
North Charleston, South Carolina

This novel is a work of fiction. Names and characters are the product of the authors imagination and any resemblance to actual persons, living or dead, is entirely coincidental

PROLOGUE

Pico Latouch was discovered hanging from a blue climbing rope, fifty metres from the Chateau Montjan. He chose a strong branch from a large cedar tree, six metres above the ground. How he climbed up and made the neck breaking jump was not clear, even to the fire department workers who helped the police lower his body to the ground.

Had he decided on more subtle attire, he could have hung in the small forest for maybe another day or two: it being December, the dark days ensured his neighbours took little interest in the nature surrounding their luxurious residence.

But the early morning departure of a guest via the underground parking caused the car headlights to light up the bright orange ski jacket. The shock of this wake-up call made the man hit his brakes so hard that several of the chateau residents woke to an unaccustomed tyre-screeching alarm.

Despite all sorts of, "why-did-this-happen? Did-we-miss-something?" Enquiry attempts from the chateau owners to the police administrators, the trail died as quickly as the man's neck broke. Vague stories came and went from the French residents.

"His problems stemmed from a long career in Paris, senior manager in the tax office, he was literally pushed from one department to another, always suspicious, a loner, never found his niche, maybe financial problems, and no women in his life.

His advances towards his neighbour, Gerard Crappy, and the imme-diate rebuffs were seen as a potential cause of his demise."

No further reason for or other relevant information on the death was offered from any source.

The loss of a life was put down to a lonely man, who probably could not survive Christmas on his own. No friends or family, if they existed, ever came.

It was only some weeks later that the owners realised the depth of Pico Latouch's real problem. They were now sharing the same nightmare.

1

Jack Rafter was only forty-two, but he looked and felt awful, really Monday-morning slow and heavy. The large mirror above the marble fireplace confirmed his demeanour. His eye's, normally pure blue and alive, were now red and dead. His mouth was dry and the feeling of fatigue was not a condition he easily accepted. The more he stared at the mirror, the more it told him the extra glass was to numb the current problems. He had a negative feeling over this Monday morning. His money-management business was in a downward spiral, caused by an over-investment for most of his clients in a trend-following fund. Unfortunately, the trends went south whilst the fund's managers held positions 180 degrees opposite; 60% was lost during the last quarter; management fees more than halved; clients threatened to redeem all with endless queries of, "what are you doing with my money?"

And it was not over yet.

He recalled the previous night's calming words from his close friend and neighbour one floor below, Arno Van Bommel, a larger-than-life Dutchman.

"Relax Jack, the whole world knows its Monday tomorrow, calm start to the week. I'll even invite you to Waldoes for lunch if you have the time, but remember to turn that darn mobile off... now one for the road?"

Seriously great idea last night, thought Jack.

Even after fifteen minutes pacing his balcony, exercising his stiff neck from side to side and directing his sore head towards the bracing January north wind and the snow-covered Alps in the distance, he was still not ready to take or make a telephone call. He reflected on a line from Dean Martin.

I feel kinda sorry for people who don't drink. When they get up they know that's the best they're gonna feel all day...

He stretched his back, filled his nostrils with the cold air, and decided to concentrate on the positive. He was, after all, living in paradise in the Savoy region of France; a part owner of the Chateau Montjan, an historic monument originally built in the 12th century. He owned, with a certain amount of generous bank funding, the penthouse.

Below his home sat nine other spacious luxury apartments bought by a bizarre mix of French and international residents. They ranged from the extrovert to the introvert, as often happens when a cocktail of races live close together.

The homes offering the old-fashioned class and space of chateau living were equipped with all possible modern luxuries and the best technology money could buy. In a residence of pure natural beauty, twin grey slated towers rose high above the front of the ivory coloured monument, there were discreet balconies for sun lovers on the south-facing side and massive African cedar doors to enter the main building, so polished that they shone from one hundred metres away. The lighting at night gave the chateau an almost mythical air from another time.

It was a residence Americans dream of recreating back home, the Chinese photograph from every conceivable angle, and Brits consider turning into a luxury hotel, not forgetting the gourmet restaurant.

Only in France, thought Jack.

Five hectares of lush private forests made up the owners personal park, surrounding the entire chateau. The views towards the mountains were truly stunning. Some of the world's most famous ski resorts were just one hour away: Megève, Val-d'Isère, Mérabel, and Saint-Tropez only four hours to the south. All positive stuff, but Jack Rafter still felt rough. Surely he would never do this again...

Elsewhere around the chateau owners were on the move, cars coming and going. The daily servicing routine had begun with a multitude of tasks to be carried out. The residence required daily care and attention, the cleaners, the pool specialist, the indispensable IT guy to check yet again on system efficiency-security. Why did his visits create stress? The residents were never totally confident regarding potential data loss or intrusion. The modern tech world could be a headache, but a necessity all the same.

Tiny details mattered to them. Legally they were all part owners of the monument. They had signed a complex contract to guarantee unlimited personal contribution should any aspect of the chateau need servicing, even upgrading. Anything to protect their considerable investment for many years to come.

Jack pondered on a visit to the gym in the basement, maybe a swim in the indoor pool would ease the pressure in his head more effectively, but what if another resident had the same idea? That would mean conversation, the usual polite offers of, "what do you think, maybe a morning skiing together soon? Would be my pleasure to buy lunch at La Cendrée in Courchevel." Or "have you spotted the new boutique in town? Italian shoes to kill for."

In his current state of head trauma, it was maybe better to stay quiet in comfortable, controlled surroundings. Things will improve, they always do. Another trip to the balcony. The large mug of coffee smelt good in the cold winter air.

Jack pulled the body warmer tight around his neck as the bitter north wind started to relieve the pain. He noticed Arno Van Bommel heading for the main gate in his Swiss-plated Cayenne.

Darn that bloody Dutchman, he thought. We both drank a lot last night, finished the bottle of Merlot together, does he soak it up better than a Brit?

Whatever, Jack was going nowhere for the morning. He just hoped that his complex multi-national client bank would leave his mobile dead and respect his low-key approach to the week. He surveyed the grounds once more, smiled at his choice of family residence and pushed stock markets, trend followers and central banks to the back of his aching head.

In the next room, his mobile came to life, ending his momentary peace and announcing a call from Omran Abdulla. Jack immediately knew who was calling; his phone had been programmed to play a specific musical intro for each client, a very handy diversion should someone look over his shoulder in a crowded room. No names, no questions.

But this was not a call he needed on a cold, rather shaky Monday morning. Could he avoid it?

No, not this investor. Omran was a major client, a Saudi and a distant relation of the royal family. They first met at an embassy party in The Hague whilst Omran was putting the finishing touch to a major deal with Shell. Jack's fees had been substantial, but unfortunately the man was difficult, always stressed, rarely listening or answering a question. Jack often reflected about the relationship. Why would this man invest with his relatively small firm?

"Good morning, Omran, how are you this Monday morning?"

"The markets are looking very negative today ... I find it depressing. What the hell am I paying you for? I am losing money. What's happening with that high-performance trend follower that you like so much?"

Jack's head began to feel tight again as the Saudi continued. "Europe's problems are not going away. Every week more negative sentiment from a PMI index to the latest Moody's downgrade, poor trading volumes, unemployment on the rise. Political problems. Already today another bank declares a huge loss, a black hole. Will we ever see the return to upward trends? Seems it's the only sector in the world that doesn't grow. Why am I in Europe, Rafter? Is my money still safe on that little island in the Irish Sea? Why after a rating agency gives upgrades on my bank holdings am I still seeing an early morning loss of twenty-five thousand dollars? Explain, Rafter."

Omran always referred to his advisor as Rafter when the markets were falling, especially if he could not spot the root of the day's problem and as Jack when things were moving in a more rewarding direction.

Jack tried to relieve the growing head pain by moving onto the balcony, not a risk he would normally take for such calls, but on a cold January Monday morning and being in the penthouse, it was unlikely anyone else would be outside at this time and even less likely that they might be interested in a, "what's happening in the stock market," type conversation.

Getting his thoughts together, Jack tried to reassure his client. "Soon the ECB, or IMF, possibly the Fed, will make moves to calm the markets. They're being backed into a corner, they have to act. I can't promise you when, but something will happen. Please give it some time. The banks will always be with us in some form. Tech companies will come and go but banks will always be part of our life. As we bought in so low, time is our friend. I have seen this bank trend happen many times over the years."

Jack attempted to recount his many well-worn stories of how banks had recovered in the past. "They follow the usual pattern, fire a high number of investment staff, close the poor performing part of the bank, and sell off certain sectors ..."

"I've heard all this before, Rafter," said Omran jumping rudely into Jack's best efforts. "I'm leaving for Riyadh, now. Make sure you have some good news next time I call, otherwise I redeem everything. *Bonne journée*, Rafter."

For a reason he didn't really understand, Jack was surprised, he began to feel better, his composure returning. The combination of required concentration and fresh air were showing the right signs; his vision had returned to normal. Maybe lunch with Arno was not such a bad idea. They both enjoyed a G&T to kick off with, so Mondays can have their pleasant side.

After all, with one uneasy client contact survived so far, things could be worse. Another glance at the laptop. Indeed Omran was spot on, a miserable January day in the markets.

"Darling, what're you up to?"

No reply came from the next room.

As Jack walked towards their bedroom, his recovery took a momentary step back. Carly was speaking with Dan Lancaster, sometimes retired ski teacher, Californian and owner of a ground floor apartment. It seems he was being invited on a girls ski trip. Why? Carly and her friends ski very well. Do they really need his cool assistance? It's not as if they are serious off-piste skiers anyway. He thought it best to pretend he missed this conversation. Let her tell her own version. Could be interesting.

"Girls ski trip," he whispered to himself. "Probably more après than ski..."

Waiting on the balcony for Carly's explanation of events and gently sipping his third coffee of the morning, Jack's nervous system jumped. A sudden shower of gravel being blasted from under tyres and a high revving engine caused Jack to stretch quickly but carefully over the metal rail for a clear view of the circular arrival area in front of the chateau.

With that sound it's most likely Arno, he thought, but not in this style. The man can certainly drive and he knows cars as well as anyone Jack had ever met. He never arrived this way, especially in front of the chateau. Such panic. The man had raced cars at Le Mans, and Zandvoort. This was not cool.

Arno Van Bommel slid the Porsche to a crude, almost uncontrolled stop in front of the main chateau doors – it was the first time Jack had ever seen such a stressed arrival since moving in. Normally the residents preferred the subtle descent into the underground garage.

Carly rushed onto the balcony looking worried.

"Did someone crash?"

The Dutchman's body language said a lot. A large guy of almost two metres, slamming the door of one of his beauties. The sound echoed around the chateau forest, a sound peculiar to the still months of winter. He marched through the doors like a football manager approaching a ref who had favoured the opposing team. Something had clearly pissed him off. Maybe the wine had caused more pain than usual thought Jack, but being his closest confident in the chateau he felt compelled to find out just what had messed his friend up on this particular Monday morning.

Descending to the next floor, Jack approached Arno's door in an almost commando like way, ear close to the wall then door, eyes wide, breathing slowly, hoping to hear something, prepare his opening line, but also having second thoughts.

Jack's mind started to race. Maybe it's a personal matter, husband-and-wife type of stuff. Should I be doing this? Come on, he said to himself, don't be half hearted. But what if Stéphanie opens the door?

The previous night he and Arno had shared a great deal of personal background, from the pleasures of visiting Indonesian restaurants in The Hague to walks down Lange Voorhout, without doubt one of Holland's most stunning streets. The old Holland hidden away from the modern-day traffic jams, falling house values and high unemployment. Okay, several bottles of wine can charge the moment, but a bond had been struck, and after many years of living in Holland, Jack knew the difference between a solid Dutchman and a big talker. Arno Van Bommel was not the latter.

Within a second of pressing the bell he heard the big man powering towards the door, and almost expected him to walk through it.

The door was pulled open with a great deal of anger, a surprised look, and raised eyebrows trying to hide his current dark mood. Arno stared at Jack, his face almost frozen. Jack expected the reaction, so stared back with a concerned, almost doctor-like look.

"Hey, my friend, I was on the balcony clearing my head and I saw you arrive, although like never before. Think we both love cars but you slammed that door like it was a broken down thirty-year old Peugeot. You're okay, I hope? No accident, problem...?" Jack tailed off thinking he had said more than enough.

Arno stayed angry.

"Come in."

Jack followed Arno through the long hallway into the lounge, ensuring he remained silent.

"What da fuck could this be for?" Growled Arno, in a heavy Amsterdam accent. For someone who normally spoke with such a balanced and correct English vocabulary his bad mood was clear.

"Why pick on a Dutchman paying so much tax already in this land. Looks like I picked a helluva place to live..."

Jack saw the recorded delivery notice on the table, alongside a very official-looking letter from, Les Impôts, the French Tax Authorities.

"Sorry Arno, I really did not mean to pry. This is nothing to do with me. Just wanted to be sure you were not hurt or had had some sort of accident."

"You're a good friend," Arno replied. "We're both foreigners here. From what I understand, this happens to many of us. My accountant acts like it's a fucking honour to pay the ridiculous social charges in this country, support *La France*. Sort of surprising he forgot to mention it's a contribution-only system. You know, there's one rule for the Frogs and another for us." He looked directly at Jack. "Have you had one?"

Jack felt a tense shot across his stomach. He'd not bothered to check his post box for the last few days. Maybe the same surprise was waiting for him.

A blur of images raced through his mind. The apartment in Spain, the London home off the Fulham road, several undeclared bank accounts, the investment portfolio. For so many years it was worth the risk to flout the rules, but these days... Not to mention his client bank. Most investors came to him with the intention of money management, but tax-free was a tempting extra advantage if available.

Jack shrugged, thinking who the hell brought this Monday morning along?

"Look Arno, I have heard some gossip recently. We are what... fifty minutes from the Swiss border, can you imagine how many people in this area used a Swiss account, dentists, builders, the pool guy who always got paid in cash. Second home owners who pretended they were always on holiday. Now the tax has started the ball rolling, there's a major clean up operation going on, and we live in the middle of this shit storm. The bloody internet is available to them as well as us."

"Yea, but all hell will break loose if they find out. Steph will divorce me. I'll end up killing a tax woman. Got some serious undisclosed matters – you know my car business in Holland. Christ man, we moved cars for three hundred thousand there. I sold the business for a massive sum, German buyers, height of the market. But why the hell should I pass on my hard work to the French tax system? I spread the money around, property, investments in the US, private equity funds, restaurant in

Marbella, I love that place, my brother's the chef, he's making us a for-
tune. He takes a weekly trip to Gibraltar, tops up our joint account. Now
some tax woman wants to interview me. What the hell am I doing here?
I bought this place for pleasure, like you."

Jack was almost tempted to say, "actually my friend, they don't give
a crap if you end up in the gutter." But he struggled with any response.
His mind was too full of his own possible pending problems. Arno's dis-
closures were exactly like his. No wonder they became friends. Now he
was suffering his own, what if-fear attack.

"And ... when is she proposing to meet up?"

"In two weeks, if I understand correctly. She wants to see the last
three years bank statements, invoices, confirm any accounts I hold, a
list of my investments. She's worryingly specific. Why would she ask
these questions? It's as if she knows something, like someone furnished
her with a here-he-is-on-a-plate list. Why did I decide to become a tax
resident in this crap land?"

No misunderstanding could be possible. Arno was a true Dutch
super linguist.

Jack, now descending into the potential stress pit of how his own
situation could unfold, excused himself.

"Look Arno, guess you need to think this over, get a plan formulated
in your mind. But stay calm. This could just be a try-on, nitpicking a
foreigner, that's all. It happens."

"Let's keep in touch on everything."

"Okay, have a real nice day," whispered Arno sarcastically, closing
the brief meeting as Jack eased through the door.

Jack left thinking of only one small item: the whereabouts of his
post box key.

He calmly walked along the winding gravel drive through the
chateau grounds staring towards the main gate. The mountain views
ignored, he could have been in backstreet London, but still attempting
to fill his lungs with the fresh January air.

Take it like a pro, he thought. Whatever they try, you're a money
expert, all is well hidden, nothing mailed to this address, and the computers are secure, all hidden investment paperwork sent to the London

property. Nothing to worry about. But he actually hoped like hell that the same surprise was not inside.

His hand was shaking slightly when he apprehensively tried to put the key in the mailbox

Must be the effects of last night, he hoped. Nothing to do with the moment. My affairs are nothing like Arno's. He dealt in exotic cars. Can you imagine how some people paid for them? Cash from the latest drug deal. I'm a money man, totally different approach to the situation. I have it all covered.

The registered letter notice lay on top of the other usual telecom bills, local-property-agent-seeks-beautiful-apartment-in-this-area-type circulars.

Jack went from being a very fit, positive man to a slightly older one during those brief seconds.

He was so concentrated on the tiny print that he failed to notice the beautiful smiles of Valerie and Nina Osperen, bottom floor neighbours, walking towards him. They immediately took in his demeanour, and opened with a "G'day Jack" in a weird, almost Aussie accent.

"How's your Monday shaping up?"

"Fancy a ski sometime soon? We know how good you move..."

A ski trip was about as far from his mind as had ever been possible, even though he loved the sport. He quickly excused himself.

"Sorry ladies, bad morning on the markets. Got to rush and sort out some client positions."

He jogged back to the chateau, his head not enjoying the experience.

The sisters whispered and confirmed their suspicions.

"How strange the Brits can act on Monday mornings."

"Maybe he has family problems... Always drinking with that vulgar Amsterdammer, Arno van Bommel. Perhaps his wife has had enough. Thank god we left our marriage problems in Holland."

As their black mail box door eased open, they saw two registered letter notices, one for each of them.

Jack rushed to the post office, parked in the invalid zone, reluctantly signed for the letter with an illegible brush of the pen, almost reversed over an ageing postman who was about to berate him, and returned to the sanctuary of his office, cursing his bad luck. He had taken particular care to open a bank account in France with a major high street group. How much more correct and visual can anybody be... At the same time he registered his business with a major accountancy firm. All of this should have kept him immune or at least 99% protected from the possibility of tax problems.

It seemed his strategy was a little flawed.

The letter confirmed that a female inspector, Madame Boustain, would be at the chateau on Friday, the 25th of January at 10 a.m., for an initial meeting, to review the last three years of his accounts, check invoices and verify bank statements. However, she retained the authority to take matters further. From Jack's acceptable French this meant just as far as she wished. No limits for this tax...lady.

Jack immediately placed a call to his accountant, fuming at the possibility of his affairs being brought into question. Stephan Morel listened as if he knew the routine so well.

"Don't worry, Mr Rafter, we have declared all investments, your income and your property as we discussed. She has no possible evidence. Your accounts are normal, all turnover reported."

Jack swallowed hard whilst staring at the letter.

"She will be wasting the tax office's time, but they also have targets which have to be met. Time wasting is not tolerated these days. Even they have to be accountable down to the area budget."

Jack wanted to get this conversation over, as no comfort was derived from Morel's, "don't worry" comments and his mind shot back to the other, darker side of his financial affairs.

"Okay, okay. Let's meet here say an hour before she arrives to talk strategy."

Now his stomach had turned to lead. Jack knew a multitude of issues could come crashing down on him in the near future. In the last few days he had read an article quoting how severe the penalties are in Spain these days: *100% fine over and above the undeclared sum.*

"If the others here are in my position, we could all be ruined. Why the hell did I bring the family here?" Jack had started talking to himself.

Plus, how would he explain this to Carly? She frequently asked questions regarding the new ways of the fiscal authorities such as, "Don't all countries now exchange information on residents, darling?" Jack always gave her the don't worry routine and passed it off with, "Do you think with my twenty five years' experience I've missed something? I watch the developments every day. We're well protected" But deep in his mind this was not a pleasant prospect after the euphoria of moving into the luxury penthouse, some of the world's best skiing one hour away, all undisclosed financial matters, personal investments securely focused on their West London address. Now his focus was directed solely on a meeting on January 25th.

Does the *fisc* know more about us? How could they?

Yet again he changed his computer access code.

Jack called Arno, needing to share his problem with a friend. "Hey, Arno. I have something to show you."

"Don't tell me you got one as well?"

"Um, yeah, I don't know if we're being targeted here."

"Not possible, Jack. Fine conspiracy theory, but the same day, same chateau? Can't be. That's pure bullshit"

"Well, maybe it is bullshit, but it's the same lady who sent your letter, Madame Boustain. Can't wait to meet this leech."

During the afternoon, Dan Lancaster left his apartment for the basement gym. Being a semi-retired ski teacher he was a regular user and always praised his solid judgement for purchasing his new home with a state of the art gym only one floor below. He greeted Annabel Cameron, who was stretching after some serious abdominal work, with the customary quick kiss on each cheek, followed by the usual "how was your weekend, Monday-why-Monday-type jokes."

Then Dan began his workout on the treadmill. A regular marathon runner, this was his favourite piece of equipment.

Jack thought long and hard about his situation, pondering over the decision to hide much of his accumulated wealth away from his new resident country, and at the same time making all the right moves in

France to show his correct intentions. A sort of black and white scenario. Was he making things too complicated?

This area was buzzing with the threat of fiscal checks, possibly due to the proximity with Switzerland. Maybe Madame Boustain had decided to make routine checks on foreign residents. After all, the chateau project had aroused a great deal of discussion in the area, especially when the final mix of owners became known. Not the usual mix, Brit, Dutch, occasional Swiss, maybe odd Russian purchaser, but this time 40% of the buyers being French.

Take the mind to another place, he thought.

With a long history of hard training and success in contact sports, from his early teens swimming for England to attaining his Kempo karate 3rd dan, Jack knew the body under stress needed exercise, good long rhythmic exercise. The best place being three floors below his office.

Jack feigned surprise when he saw Annabel and Dan in the gym, as if to show he wanted the place to himself. With kisses for Annabel and a solid pat on the back for Dan, he felt the urge to share his ugly morning.

Were these guys in the same position? Could he begin a casual chat regarding a tax inspection with, "hey neighbours, received any recorded delivery letters lately? Any problems with the tax on the horizon?" No, not really.

He quickly considered the best route would be Annabel. Her husband, Henry, was a genuinely nice guy, a huge capacity for humour, a fellow Brit who took part in every possible sport, always a dirty joke to tell. No one was safe around Henry. Must be the best way to investigate further. Henry was the chateau's fun guy, probably the wealthiest owner with a history of serious property deals in the UK during the boom years.

"Hey Anna, did Henry take you skiing over the weekend? Hot tubs in Megève, a bottle of chilled Moët? Yes, I do know his routine..."

Annabel did not look at all pleased with Jack's slick comment.

"Well, yes we did ski a little over the weekend. Val actually, he prefers it. Thinks he's a sort of extreme skier, like I said, he thinks... As if that was not pain enough from earlier this morning, he's developed the foulest mood. Not like him really. Came back from the post office and locked himself in his office most of the day, muttered something about the, bloody French admin, it's never enough. Can't think why? He normally get's the admin done when I leave for shopping, girls things. Really not like him."

Jack was relieved, but also challenged. There was something unusual here, not at all the typical Henry. Must be the same problem … must be.

"Maybe I can offer him a quick pastis later. Cheer him up. Tell him what a great off-piste basher he is."

Annabel raised her eyebrows and flicked her hair back in a typical handsome woman pose.

"Whatever, Jack. Girls are far easier about Mondays than guys. Whatever."

Dan had heard enough. Even over the drone of the treadmill, it was clear that other owners were in the same position as he was. Madame Boustain had also demanded he explain the last three years of his financial affairs.

Knowing he had not been totally honest with the IRS or the French tax system whilst ski teaching the world's wealthiest tourists from Arabs to fellow Americans and Russians, all paying ridiculous amounts to have the tall, cool and technically perfect Dan Lancaster take them around some of Europe's most beautiful ski regions. He knew the best and sometimes most scary places, supported by his contact card depicting a picture of Dan as a seriously cute, blue-eyed fifteen year old.

This emotional marketing, suggested by a Swiss image consultant ensured the female clients actually outbid one another to spend the day cruising through the mountains with the Californian boy.

However, at this moment, image was a distant priority as he stared down watching his Nikes thump the running belt, his thoughts slipped back to a Swiss banker who after a long weekend of extreme skiing persuaded him to put all of his money in the bank's care. It did boast a one hundred and fifty year history of private wealth management.

He recalled the banker's solid promise: *"you don't have to worry my friend. We Swiss know how to handle money problems, protect you from the prying European neighbours. It's simply our lifetime speciality. No one will ever be able to harm you or even find it. Problems do not exist for our US friends. Go enjoy the good life in France. We'll keep your money safe."* To deepen his mood further he recalled a recent financial magazine headline: *Switzerland signs tax avoidance deal with US.*

Back in his apartment he poured a large whisky on the rocks. Who cares if he blows the work in the gym; working out could be the least of his pending problems.

Thinking, playing possible scenarios over, and gazing out from his lounge window, Dan noticed the tech man arriving at the chateau. Every owner had made complaints about the tech system. It cut off, stalled, lost emails on a regular basis, sometimes running far too slow for modern internet speeds. Just not reliable. But today another car followed the white van into the parking. A sleek Audi with what appeared to be a seriously attractive lady behind the wheel.

Gerard Crappy, a rather private man, even towards the other French residents, and a retired finance consultant for one of Europe's largest luxury yacht designers, came out of his apartment and greeted the tech specialist who was closely followed by a tall, dark-haired woman. Dan opened his door and watched them climb the stairs. He was visually stunned by the woman's beauty, hardly noticing the two men, apart from a quick *"Bonjour."* He could only imagine what a great ski companion she would make: a true ten.

Dan watched them enter Gerard Crappy's apartment speaking softly and closing the door without a sound.

That night the lights went out early in the chateau. Maybe the residents preferred the candle to electricity, maybe the urge to play down the day's events, but something had shaken many of the owners that cold January Monday. Since they had moved in, the beautiful Chateau Montjan never looked so dark.

2

Light snow was falling from a heavy grey sky on the morning of January 25th, a nature moment Jack usually enjoyed, but on this Friday morning he would come face to face with a person who held the power to change his life forever and throw him into a black hole. A pending tsunami could not have deepened his mood further.

Carly had been made aware of the meeting, also the potential negative reason behind it, but she had never been comfortable with financial matters, leaving all such decisions to Jack. He wondered if Carly had given him too much freedom over their accumulated wealth. On top of his current business problems, was he about to drag the family into a bottomless pit? Could it really go that far?

Carly had already left for the gym, maybe taking a swim. She made it crystal clear she would stay there until Jack came down to confirm the meeting had terminated, reminding him not to bring her face to face with "that woman."

Stay calm, he thought. At the same time, he knew that would be almost impossible. The fear of the unknown was taking over his mind. Give him the most challenging client, "can you do a better job than my bank?" or an anti-equity investor, "never trusted you money managing guys," type. That would be a walk in the park compared with today's meeting. He could give his best presentation but she certainly would not be buying.

He dressed quickly, choosing his favourite black Armani jacket, faded jeans, Church shoes, old but by far the most comfortable. His surroundings would probably blow her mind anyway, so why look humble.

But he knew that the woman arriving at 10 a.m. couldn't care less about the investment world, his, *sort of* good intentions. She would only focus on the negative. Her function would be impossible if she saw bright spots in a day. She probably already had her dirty little plan in place: tear the guts out of Jack Rafter, then ruin his neighbours. She was probably looking forward to the encounter.

"How do these people sleep at night," he muttered. "Maybe better than I do..."

The door bell rang. He checked his Hublot. Jack felt anxious. Not already... It was impossible to enter the chateau grounds without hitting the main gate buzzer, and this was far too early. As his eye lined up with the small security circle on the door, he saw his friend Arno, head cocked to one side, gazing towards him. He sighed.

"Christ, Arno. Come in bud. What's up? You want to do this on my behalf?"

"A quick visit to ask if you can take a crafty picture of this bitch. I want to know just how ugly she is before I have to meet her."

"Ha bloody ha, Arno. We both know this will not be a Hollywood moment. She probably makes my mother-in-law look sexy."

Before Jack could close the door, Henry Cameron arrived. A large guy, who even when trying to appear serious had a smile in his eyes. Henry had cartoon style, along with a sharp business mind.

"Really sorry, Jack. Know you are the first of us to go through this today, but I wanted to wish you all the best. You know I am 100% behind my friends in this place, and the two guys I'm close to at this moment mean the most to me. Sort her out, and then come over to my place. Name your drink and we'll discuss the whole thing. Of course, Arno, you should be with us."

The friends left as quickly as they came.

Jack appreciated this a great deal. He was always the male bonding type and these gestures helped to calm his nerves.

I'm ready for this, he thought; the *Eye of the Tiger* played somewhere in the back of his head. He began to create a mental picture of the meeting.

As he reviewed his local bank statements, again checking for nothing irregular and no links to his other offshore business – the taboo islands that are now under attack from global governments – his mobile rang. Stephan Morel, his accountant, was at the gate, on time. Within five minutes their preparation meeting began.

Morel was a typical Savoyard accountant: always casual dress, colour coordination sadly missing the spot, no tie, nails chewed to the quick, heavy boots worn under a pair of dark trousers. Slow, deliberate, sometimes over-thought-out replies, an almost guarded response to any question put by Jack, as if he needed to keep both sides of the meeting fair. Jack was looking for enthusiasm.

"We can handle her, nothing to worry about."

Over the years, he had arranged so many client meetings that included an accountant, but had difficulty remembering one that lit up the room. Jack wished for a lot but the best he heard was, "the tax office people also have their job to do you know."

Jack was well aware of the mentality in this part of the world. They would often prefer to keep their local contacts happy; the foreign residents were looked upon as tourists, who were sure to leave one day, so the need to build a long-term relationship sometimes lacked motivation.

But Jack needed clear direction. He had never been in front of a tax inspector before. Many in France talked about the *Contrôle Fiscal* where the administrators try their utmost to find the smallest error then build on it, adding interest over the years, linking the error to a smaller amount of taxes paid than should be the case. Penalties applied. They bent the rules in any direction they wished.

"Okay Stephan, talk me through this. What can we expect from her today?"

"Well, this is the start of a process. You must realise that this can go on for years, depending on how she finds your situation. There are many steps to go through before the end but if she finds something suspicious, we can challenge virtually anything she comes up with, use a lawyer if necessary, the later stage being the judge in Grenoble, an independent decision-maker. But please bear in mind this could be four years or more down the road. Even after that we could continue to challenge in Paris..."

"Are you serious? They can screw me around for years?" Four years of potential misery plus... He was not even sure his sagging business would still exist in four years.

"But you have all of my information. Do you see anything suspicious?"

"No, I don't, but she's doing a very different job to me. She's trained to see problems. I'm trained to find solutions and see you pay the least amount of tax."

Jack scratched his head and glanced at Stephan suspiciously whilst rocking from side to side.

"Today is all about hearing her questions, trying our best to answer without giving her any reason for doubt."

Jack raised his eyebrows, he was so tempted to slate the system he was now under, but remembering one of his long-term Brussels-based clients, a lawyer, who also fell foul of a tax inspection, the result of an undeclared inheritance, he recalled their conversation. "You know Jack I knew whatever emotions I had against this situation or the individual, I had to create an immediate understanding, be almost humble, start the relationship off on a pleasant basis. Dare I take the high ground, these people can make your life hell."

Jack was not renowned for his small ego, but this was some of the best free advice ever received over the years. Now was the time to use it to his best advantage; being bitter on this day was a non starter.

He gazed out of the lounge window towards the mountains, reflecting. Why, oh why didn't he choose a different career and become a ski teacher. Even a ski-lift operator seemed a blissful existence compared to this day's atmosphere. Jack simply wanted the best for his wife and boys. Business was getting tougher and Brussels was not helping, heaping legislation on an already difficult climate to survive in.

Stephan was shuffling through his papers, pulling out accounts covering the last three years of Jack's business activity in France, his SARL, Rafter Investments, a French limited company. Jack felt confident no discrepancies would show up there; for the other matters he may need to hold his breath. A quick glance at his laptop still showed fragmented markets. Confidence was indeed lagging.

A second coffee was poured, Jack kept checking his watch.

"If she's on time, we have around ten minutes."

Stephan cleared his throat as if something important needed to be announced.

"These people are generally on time, goes with the job. Not normal for us Frenchies I know."

Jack smiled politely, remembering his Brussels client.

Keep it pleasant, no high ground.

As they both sipped Italian coffee staring at the array of papers on the table, the main gate buzzer sounded.

"Here we go," boomed Jack.

"Yes, this must be her," confirmed Stephan helpfully...

Jack touched the portable video screen to open the main gate. Glancing out of the window he saw the large black gates slide open and a small, almost fragile-looking figure walk through.

"Why not bring the car in? Surely she's not on foot. It's a cold day and snowing..."

Stephan gave a typical French shrug, shoulders high, palms open, chin up. "Could be they prefer to keep the car away, no number plates. These people are hated."

Jack frowned, thinking if this was the mentality, she's a guaranteed pain. As he expected, the one-sided approach had already begun.

Both men stood in silence, hands clasped together, staring at the ivory coloured door. A soft ring sounded, one quick peep, almost as if Madame Sylvie Boustain was uncomfortable in her surroundings.

Jack opened the door slowly; his face displayed a cold almost threatening stare. She was small, even by French standards, dressed in dull colours and flat faded shoes. No smile. Her eyes gave nothing away. Greasy hair pulled back to form a small pony tail. Seemed she'd run out of shampoo some days earlier. Probably emotion and warmth did't exist in this tiny creature.

The introductions were quick.

"Good morning Madame Boustain."

The limp handshake fully supported the visual presentation.

"Mr Rafter?"

"That's me, please come in. Can I take your coat?"

"*Non, merci.* I will keep it next to me."

Stephan Morel offered his hand.

"I look after the fiscal matters for Mr Rafter in France."

"In France," she repeated softly.

Jack looked a little perplexed whilst shooting a quick glance at Morel.

Again the woman showed no emotion. Jack concluded she would have preferred to meet in the personal comfort zone of her office. But it was too late now.

Put up with your surroundings bitch, he thought.

The large glass oblong dining table was the perfect place for the meeting, big enough to retain personal space whilst the little Madame could easily be overlooked. She was placed at the far end. Jack and Stephan either side of her. This was Jack's idea; maybe he could get a chance to view her notes whilst she talked with his accountant.

Obviously the lady was not comfortable in the presence of men: her body language showed severe unease. She touched her neck repeatedly, flicked her pen from finger to finger, head pointing more down than up. Jack had developed a natural talent over the years of warming clients up, getting them to talk, tell all, his relaxed humour always winning over the ladies. This day he felt sure he could not muster the required energy to lift this individual's low-key personality.

It was obvious she would distrust all matters presented to her.

Peering through the glass table Jack could see her nervous twitch; the legs could not keep still.

He kicked off, thinking let's get this over with quickly. Was it worth offering her a coffee? No, be mean. The Brussels advice out of the window so soon.

"I'd like to know what specifically we can help you with today. I'm so surprised, a tax inspection already ..., my business is small in France, and I have only been fiscally resident for something like five years. Is this normal?"

Her voice was weak; she struggled to look into Jack's eyes. "I cannot say some people are never inspected; some several times. It varies." Her first reply sounded nervous, unsure.

"Okay, so the obvious question, why me today? Since arriving here I have done everything to comply correctly with French law. Here is my accountant. My bankers are one of the largest, most visual high street groups in France. Is this not the normal way to do business in this land?"

Madame Boustain did not look up. She was focused on a large file recently pulled from her case. Her eyes flicked nervously above her glasses.

"I am directed by my chief. I have no idea why people are chosen for an inspection. It's my job to gather information and review if the law has been followed. We must follow the law in fiscal matters."

Nice sidestep, thought Jack. This girl could talk for a whole day, hiding behind THE LAW and ending up saying nothing.

Arno's going to love her.

"Tell me, Mr Rafter, I see Mr Morel has brought your accounts, but in France we can check these anyway. Our law allows us to look at a company's financial position online. But how do you invoice for your work here in France? I do not see TVA being charged on your transactions since you created your SARL, and this could be illegal. We could be looking at TVA contributions missed, plus of course penalties since you started your activity here."

Her confidence seemed to have shot up by at least 90%. Jack was starring at a Black Mamba one metre away from his chest. He tried to sustain his composure.

"Stephan..."

Eyes wide, his mouth tight, Morel scrambled to open a file. Papers flicked through as if trying to beat a clock.

"We have researched into this and, on the specific investment advice Mr Rafter gives, the need to charge TVA is not normal under French law."

"We at the tax office do not agree. His activity is general commercial so he must change TVA."

Her calculator had started, and Stephan was not prepared for this issue.

Jack was feeling violated. How could she kick off with such a powerful position? Why the hell does he pay so much for expert accountancy services, which are blown away by this young woman ten minutes into the meeting?

"Do you have any other concerns about my business activity? Something must have guided you or your chief in my direction."

Maybe she knew a lot, maybe a little, but he had to tread so carefully. His normal comfort zone was finding it hard this day.

Madame Boustain coughed like a small animal. Jack twitched and stared directly into her lifeless eyes.

What would she ask now?

"Mr Rafter, we are aware many foreign fiscal residents in this country choose to hide assets in other lands, sort of pretend they do not exist. I hope you are not one of these people?"

Jack swallowed hard, nodding slightly and narrowing his eyes as if being insulted.

"I read that certain French politicians have lately failed to declare bank accounts outside of this country, so it's not only foreign residents is it, Madame?"

Jack knew he should never have made this knee-jerk comment Morel looked as if he would like to sink under the table. But being a proud man, Jack's ego took over his common sense. He found himself detesting someone he'd only known for a few minutes. The instant mutual hatred between himself and Madame would never wane; only war could follow.

"Well, Mr Rafter, I take no position on the French administration. Anyone who breaks the law should pay the price."

"Convenient," whispered Jack.

"But I do want you to understand what a serious matter this could be for you and your family. You appear to be a specialist in hiding money for your clients, using a whole host of offshore centres.

Can you understand we find it suspicious that you choose to live in France, claim to have no French clients, yet run your business from here? A mirror image of the offshore centres. They work for clients who are not resident there, but hide from offices like mine..."

Jack felt two emotions: even more hatred for the person sitting at his dining table, but more worrying, how could she possibly know? This tangled his stomach the most.

Morel remained silent, only occasionally adding an "ummm" to the conversation. Jack began to wish he would just fade away.

She could smell the money but Jack was speechless.

Jack's bankers recently asked.

"What exactly is your role with your International client bank? Do you only work for clients based outside of France?"

In other words, how do you earn your money? Where does it come from? He told the truth.

"It's normal commissions with fees for investment advice. I use these centres because of the expertise and our twenty-year relationships." He knew his bank considered there was a more suspicious angle on his business activity, but this was simply the way it was.

Now it seemed that the doubtful bank manager might have passed this onto the tax office. He became uncomfortable no doubt and decided to protect the bank's rear. Jack's business became fair game.

So much for trying to build the solid, long-term business relationship, he reflected.

Morel looked confused, almost scared that he was caught up in this web. Jack was tempted to berate him. But not in front of Madame. She could surely sense the desperation in the accountant. She was already serving ace after ace. Jack tried a change of tactic.

"Madame Boustain, as you know, my activity here in France is set up in the best way I could possibly find. I even invited my accountant here today to support my good intentions. If I had intended to bend the rules, heaven forbid hide things in the system, why would I do it this way? We are living in modern-day Europe I hope. People do move to new lands and run a business..."

"As you are aware, Mr Rafter, this is only an initial meeting, I have to report to my chief and she will decide if we need to look further into your fiscal affairs in this country. I am sure Mr Morel has explained you will have the opportunity to meet with her during the course of the control. In fact, several meetings could take place. You will always have the possibility to respond."

Jack already detested the words *"contrôle fiscal"* as if it were some sort of checking mechanism. Just to make sure all is running smoothly...

This is a bloody attack, pure and simple, he thought.

Of course her chief will take things further. She already smelt blood, and my accountant needs the bathroom. The recent Happy New Year wishes seemed a decade ago.

Madame Boustain had one more volley to serve.

"Mr Rafter, you claim for an office in your annual accounts. As this is your business address, can I check the space?"

Morel looked worried. Maybe his firm had been claiming for an office space that did not exist.

Jack rose, head and shoulders above his guests with a tense "Follow me."

At the end of a short descending staircase off the lounge, the walls covered with paintings from Ste-Maxime and Saint-Tropez, the sign on the door announced *Serious Business Rafter Investments.*

Jack opened the door with a firm sweep of his hand.

"Here we are. This is my office."

The walls were covered with financial seminar posters, the shelves full of books on bond markets, futures trends and equity performance statistics.

She barely put her head around the door.

Stephan held his hand over his mouth, eyes flicking from Jack to the tax inspector.

"Okay, that's fine."

Jack knew this was a tiny side issue, just to be correct. The real bombs had been used at the dining table, and by the size of her file, Jack imagined she had plenty more where they came from.

In no time, she offered her limp hand to both men, confirmed that she'd be in touch with a decision and left as if the building was on fire.

Jack, wanting to let her leave with a good taste, called down the stairs, "I will open the main gate for you."

She was already down one flight. No reply came from the tiny lady.

Morel stood alone staring towards the Alps, expecting his client to begin his own attack any second. This had not been not a good first meeting.

"I am truly amazed. Having tried to take all steps towards a correct and legal set-up in France, this woman tears it down in forty-five minutes. What do you think, Stephan?"

"It's the normal tactic, she see's money here. This beautiful building, the size of your home. She's trained to think big money, big risk. We must look upon this as a try-on, nothing more at this stage..."

"Really?" said Jack sarcastically. "So what's next, in your experience?"

"Madame Boustain will no doubt send a letter in a few weeks outlining her findings. Then we have the chance to respond. Until we see that letter we have no idea how she or her chief will proceed, but we must cooperate."

"You know, Stephan, it seems we can do no more from this point. As I have learnt in this land, it's preferable to hide behind a recorded delivery letter than a clear and direct face-to-face meeting. The reality is that half-answers are given and they use all the loopholes they can to trap the foreigner. Let's stop now, and react when we have to. She scored some points today. We have to make sure we score the next time."

Morel was visibly relieved at this. He could now return to his office and hide behind the windowless door.

"Good idea, Mr Rafter. Let's do it like this."

Jack was happy to see him go. He could now reflect in peace. Not a great first meeting but at least she appeared to have nothing solid on the matters that worried Jack the most. The assets undeclared outside of the country, property in London and Spain – these had given him the sleepless nights. Time to catch up with Arno and Henry, who had also been set up with a French limited company, the SARL. Better to break the news to them now so they can prepare.

Carly jumped out of the pool as Jack entered the health centre.

"Has she gone? How did it go? Any problems?"

"Hold on, darling, nothing terrible. Usual misery administrator. Tell you all over lunch. Come on up, quick as you can." As usual, Jack played things down.

As he walked back into his lounge, he automatically checked the magnificent view over the forest towards the mountains, now a subconscious habit. But his morning appreciation for the local nature failed to see the only people in the park.

A car had stopped on the main drive. Two figures were standing, almost hiding behind the vehicle. The woman who had left his apartment fifteen minutes earlier appeared to be a deep conversation with one of Jack's French neighbours.

3

As the Range Rover cruised high into the mountains of the Haute Savoie with Jack at the wheel, Arno next to him, and Henry and Dan slumped in the back, the men slipped in and out of an awkward conversation about family, business and the stunning local scenery.

"See that old guy working his farm high on the left. The people in this area live forever. That woman must be close to ninety. She walks uphill faster than we can."

Henry was focused on the car in front. "Watch him Jack. He drives like he overdid it last night..."

But the men knew clearly that the main point of this day was to relax, ski and, most importantly, talk.

The four had each been through an initial interview with Madame Boustain. All had been threatened regarding non payment of TVA, the penalties, plus gestures of "any undeclared holdings, investments outside of France?" But no more at this stage.

With family around and business matters, the men found little time to clear their heads and discuss it with others in the same position who had decided to take the easy route of hiding assets outside of their tax resident country, using the now dreaded offshore centres. These days, even journalists were happily investigating investors.

Jack and his friends had all skied Europe's best resorts for many years and were experienced mountain lovers. So the descent from Avoriaz to Chatel then back around the circuit a couple of times was a pleasure trip, nothing more a boys day out, but an important time away from the stress of their current lives. Later, a lazy lunch at the Bout du

Lac in Montriond, relaxing in the alpine air with the hope of, for a few hours at least, swapping feelings, talking possible strategy and going deeper into *"why us?"* And also maybe forgetting about the potential problems that were developing around their lives at the chateau.

They all knew that the subject would arise sooner or later, the question being who would break first. But for the moment they all respected the long silences, enjoying the rise into the snowline: the passing of village signs – La Verne, Seytroux, Sainte Jean d'Aulps, and long thoughtful periods that allowed Jack to remember his earlier times in the region.

When their two sons were very young, Jack and his wife had decided to introduce them to the local school system. The boys soaked up the French language like a sponge. The Rafter's had had a beautiful Alpine chalet constructed in a small mountain village some years back. It was built by a local man and his team who did their very best to fulfil the buyers main wish, wood, lots of seasoned spruce timber grown in the region. Jack enjoyed the whole project, especially the meetings with the owner. The man knew everything there was to know about chalet building, sometimes providing answers before the questions had been put. A local Savoyard carpenter, he developed an experienced team around him to deal with the quirky wishes of foreign buyers: a tele-command for the garage door, garden lights, Jacuzzi on the balcony, childrens Park!

These requests had amused the builder, but for the right price he could be very accommodating. His local friends often wondered at his patience. Could these people not work out the ground is snow-covered for the winter months?

The builder's bank balance made the provision of all such requests a comforting experience.

As the so familiar small village signs came and went, Jack reflected on how simple the mountain life had been the lack of stress. Local people never expected much from their lives, children often following the parent's professions, ski teacher, carpenter, farmer, their lives impossible not to link together.

If only life had been so simple in Jack's previous city business, when he moved to The Hague after meeting his Dutch dream girl to concentrate on offering his money management services to the vast expatriate community in the West of Holland. There he found a business paradise whilst also living in the beautiful, truly international city of The Hague.

Nearing the Ardent ski-station car park, the men came back to reality; all had been dreaming of the simple mountain life, the scenery at their feet that was some of the best in the world. At that moment, their chateau could have been in Mexico for all they cared.

"Let me arrange the passes," Henry kindly offered as he almost fell out of the back seat. "They'll be my pleasure, but you buy lunch..."

Arno demanded, "Why, yet again, did we forget to invite our gorgeous neighbour Eva. Far better butt to follow than yours, Dan. She also looks kinda cute from the front..."

"You sure about his butt?" asked Jack.

Dan looked confused at this rapid European humour.

"Of course, I'll throw in a chopper to bring us back here if you like," said Jack.

"No need for that, the last piste is my favourite," replied Henry.

Jack knew Henry was joking. Even the local ski teachers were not fans of the last piste descent to Ardent. By a strange quirk of nature, the snow cover was generally good enough but often icy, making the final kilometre less pleasant than higher runs and requiring more concentration.

Arno could only swear about his boots. "After so many years of buying the latest tech, moulded foot comfort, ease of entry, easy-click bindings, I still find these bloody things a pain."

Dan shook his head and laughed. As a ski teacher he practically did it all with one hand. "No stress, Arno. The tech works, but you need to work with it. Your power should be used up top, not in the car park."

As they neared the bubble lift, Jack was greeted by an old friend, Philippe, a resident of Jack's old mountain village. Arno, Henry and Dan could still not get their heads around why French men were happy to kiss. What's wrong with a manly handshake or a slap on the back?

"How's the family?"

"Superb. You too? All good?"

"Okay. *Bon ski.*"

The four hustled into the cabin, making sure it was their private space, Arno's behind blocking two agitated French men from entry. Turning and gazing down from thirty centimetres above them, he decided the next cabin was all theirs, like it or not.

As the doors bumped together, the usual shuffle of adjusting gloves, zippers, cleaning glasses took place. But the pressure was mounting. All knew Jack's idea of a boy's ski-day together was basically a meeting in the mountains, away from the dangerous possibility of being viewed, even overheard at the chateau. Trust was at a serious low; suspicion filled their days. The four men, being friends from the first encounter, had built a sort of guys trust from the first handshake. Now it was time to get some understanding between them, sort out a strategy and maybe derive some comfort from being in this together.

Jack kicked off. "Come on, guys. We have all been interviewed by her. She has monumental problems with my set-up in France, not enough tax paid, TVA not charged. We all seem to be, well ... under attack from the tax system. You could call this financial rape supported by the legal system. Sudden specific threats of declare all or suffer the consequences. Don't you smell a sort of conspiracy here? It's too neat, all of the owners under attack."

Arno chipped in. "Not for sure all of us. That sneak Crappy has not confirmed anything. He for sure is avoiding contact, impossible to get more than a *Bonjour* out of him, pretends he's so busy. Typical fucking frog. And Mardan seems really low key, little sign of him these days. Plus my very own country girls, the Osperen twins, have daddy back in Aalsmeer. He's one of Holland's largest flower producers, so I don't think they have much to worry about. He could buy the whole chateau with any one of his credit cards. Anyway they spend more time in the south, Grimaud; the chateau is just a ski apartment for them."

Jack continued. "With you on Crappy, Arno. Carly and I feel uncomfortable about him. He's just not acting normal. Let's watch him. But the whole thing has been on my mind far too much lately. There are more questions than answers. It's depressing trying to put the pieces together. I can contemplate maybe the odd person getting into trouble, no declaration of the residence in Marbella, messy paperwork, a large foreign transfer into a local account or something like that. But as we are all being hit in one building, I can only guess that we are a seriously hated bunch. Maybe the locals detest what we spent on the project."

Henry made his entry. "It's all our money, and we are paying taxes and social costs. Every month they dream up another tax, company tax, turnover tax, bloody think-of-a-number tax. Is that not enough? You know the French are famous for being anti wealth, anti money, changing the tax system every moment. Only talking about it sends them under cover, hiding behind the shutters. And now a socialist administration. That large scratch on Arno's Porsche, pure jealousy."

As the La Linderet bowl appeared, the sun hit the glass. The chair lifts were already in action towards Avoriaz and Chatel; restaurant workers were busy stocking up from the snow cats parked behind their chalets. Another beautiful alpine day. Henry pointed to the hovering chopper, picking up a stretcher. Someone had had a very short ski experience.

As the men prepared for the exit, skis and sticks in hand, it was obvious to Jack that this conversation had a long way to go. Could this be the day when they all confessed as to the real depth of their own problems; they certainly all respected one another, but would caution step in? Or would they tell all, share the problem and fight it together?

Conditions were perfect: early February, before the major European school holidays began, leaving ample chance to enjoy the space. Nine-fifteen in the morning, minus ten degrees and snow that made that wonderful crunch sound under skis. Negative thoughts were, for the moment, left behind in the lift.

The cruise down towards Chatel on wide perfectly groomed pistes flowed like an early spring river. Dan led with Henry at the back. The French culinary world had always been a weakness for him, he reasoned, okay, I ski a little slower, but I always get there. Plus someone needs to be behind in case a friend falls. Henry almost believed himself.

Jack eased his arms wide, gliding, loving the moment and congratulated himself on his decision to take an early night and get a good long sleep.

After several runs, and making the pass over to Switzerland, the men felt a large Swiss coffee was now well deserved. A mountain chalet came into view, the Swiss appearance different to the French, giving more attention to the authentic mountain look, cowbells above the door, old photos of skiers fifty years or more ago, local wood carvings – even the darker wood confirms you are in another country, but thankfully no passport control, a strange failing for the Swiss. Many travellers remember a different interrogation at the border.

Heading for a corner table that was tucked away behind bronze cow bells, a rack of old wooden skis and a large Swiss flag, the four men eased into the space.

Immediately a young girl arrived at the table, starting in unsure English.

"Good morning..., can I taak your order please?"

This was met by a swift reply in Jack's best French, *"Quatre grands cafés, s'il vous plaît, mademoiselle."*

She left with a giggle.

Henry addressed his friends, clearly rejuvenated by the crisp alpine air. "As we, the neighbours, are, shall we say... special, for sure nobody will give much away, and it must be safe to assume we all have a skeleton here and there, an unfortunate reality of making more money than the norm. Come on, we all took a risk here and there. Can't remember how many shelters I used to avoid property tax over the years. Seriously guys, I think it's fair to say we trust one another. It goes no deeper or broader than that."

Jack felt relieved that his friend and neighbour came so far forward with this comment, a clear let's-be-serious-and-tell-our-own story.

Henry continued, "For sure, we all have a past which is recorded somewhere due to modern technology also being available to the evil administrators. Some dealings are impossible to hide or wipe away. We all know the good old days of hiding the property in a trust, wife's name, brother, etc. don't work as well as they used to."

Arno nodded, his eyes wide as if to say, the good old days.

"When you take an overview of ourselves, as neighbours, we are a pretty unusual bunch. Four very different nationalities living in the same chateau, reasonably happy together, all motivated to utilise above-the-norm security, almost an island guaranteed to attract attention. Maybe we should have been more discreet."

Arno spoke up. "Too late for that option now. We need to fight this before it goes to the next stage. Stephanie is already talking about moving. I think we all have that thought, do we not?"

The other men nodded with pained expressions.

Dan quietly cursed himself. Now it was time to contribute his share, get closer to these European guys, and he was going for full disclosure. He truly respected these men and felt he owed it to them as his friends.

"Well, you know me. Typical Californian boy, love the sport, France, Europe. It all fits perfectly in place – and no real plans to go back. But I made the stupid mistake of being paid very well in a sloppy way – often a wad of cash at the end of a ski day. The type of clients I attracted were also more than happy to transfer direct to my Swiss account. No questions. I gave them a hell of a day; they paid me a hell of a lot of money. An American couple even set me up for a week at a time in Le Fer à Cheval Megève, all expenses paid. Look after our two beautiful daughters and their friends, name your price, they offered. I did, they paid. Not exactly a hard week's work, I well...worked harder through the night than the day."

The guys were looking seriously jealous, awkward smiles appeared. They all shared the same thought. *This ski teacher lives with us in the same chateau, our lives are full of business risk and stress, but he escorted models around the piste. We made a cruel choice of profession.*

"I feel I have to tell you guys this," Dan continued as if he needed to ensure his story hit the right note. "I trust you, and I am not such a dumb blonde to assume you buy the line that a ski teacher earns like you finance guys, and you, Arno, a big time exotic car dealer."

This brought the four heads closer together, almost as if they didn't on any account whatever want to miss a word of this confession. Dan was about to open the flood gates.

Jack surveyed the room: not a possible tax inspector in sight. But the mountain music was becoming irritating.

"My client base was broad. Apart from the usual US visitors, wealthy Brits, Arabs, Russians and lately more from the Far East, I also skied fairly often with an Italian guy and his wife, Tony and Gabriella Conti. They never convinced me that the day was all about the ski experience. They asked so many questions. How long had I lived in Europe? Where did I ski? Who did I know? Family – even got into my military past. I think I mentioned to you guys about my time with the marines, Middle East campaigns, some ugly memories. The guy's wife, Gabriella, loved all this. She complimented me about my height, broad shoulders. You know how Italian women are?"

The three other men nodded but knew little about Italian women, they were hoping like hell that Dan would spill the beans, their eyes wide in anticipation, all shoulders pointed towards the ski teacher.

The second round of coffee arrived. Not another word was spoken until the girl walked away from the table.

"One evening, after an easy day with a Dutch family in Courchevel, I fancied a beer, to spend time alone and take a break away from the constant skier doubts. I heard it every day, *"how did I look on the black piste? My turns are not like yours, will they ever be*?"

"Enough, I thought, time on my own. My mobile rang – you know how it is during high winter season, the craziest calls. *"Come to a party tonight. I wanna do deep powder tomorrow, name your price."*

"Lunatic times, BUT this call was different, a very calm, almost sleepy voice."

"Buona sera Dan, its Gabriella. How are you, my darling?"

Henry smiled at Jack. Arno lifted his head and blinked.

"I felt a need to be equally relaxed," Dan continued. "I told her, really fine. Relaxing after a day up top."

"Nice, hope I'm not disturbing you, darling. You are most likely surrounded by today's admirers?"

"I almost felt proud to tell her that I was alone with not a possible conquest within ten metres, but her voice sounded sleepy, sexy."

"Tell me, I have a small problem. Just arrived in Courchevel."

"I interrupted her.

Huh, excuse me, where?"

"Yes that's right, Courchevel. Tony has been delayed, family business, so I was wondering if you are not occupied, maybe we could get together for a drink, if you don't have an early start tomorrow, maybe dinner?"

"Of course a thousand thoughts ran through my mind, 99% of them the same as those going through your minds right now, guys. Beautiful Italian woman on her own, maybe a kilometre away from me and she likes me. Tell me, guys, what would you do?"

Arno spoke up.

"Call my lawyer. Tell him to prepare a contract and make it iron clad. Italians are complicated. Sold a lot of cars to that bunch, restaurant owners from Amsterdam. Always a hiccup, but I did enjoy the free meals."

Jack laughed shaking his head at his friends.

"Ski teach, Italian woman alone needing company in the mountains. So bloody original, Dan. Is this your high octane story for today?"

Henry sighed and said, "Why the hell don't I have a past like this?"

But Dan sipped his coffee whilst slowly moving his head from side to side, as if he knew things were going wrong. This story had a deeper point. Holding the silence for a few more seconds, he thought about his choice of words before continuing, this had to sound right.

"Look guys, I'm only telling you this because, first, I respect you, and secondly, I think my problem is different to yours, very different. It's only right you know about it. You're all street smart, more than me I guess. I could bore the hair off your heads with dumb ski stories, daft situations, the invites back to a hotel room for a massage ... but my problem is a serious one, very serious."

The men's mood became sombre, more focused than just listening to a guy-and-a-married-woman story, Dan was certainly not joking.

"Of course, we met for dinner, almost hurried through it; never a doubt in either of our minds where the night was going, Gabriella had a room in the hotel – sorry to be boring – but invited me up for a night cap."

Arno chipped in again. "Told you, call that lawyer and keep your pants on until it's sorted."

Dan was now too focused to stop.

"The morning after, all was cosy with breakfast in the room. I had to leave by 8:30 for lessons. We kissed, a long cuddle, gestures of, *see you soon maybe*? I felt strange that day. Something was wrong. I skied with two young British guys, good skiers, but just could not get my mind into gear. These guys noticed and proposed we cancel the planned second day. I was not really surprised. Don't worry, I was not in love, but something about the last twenty-four hours didn't sit comfortable in my stomach. My mind was full of it."

Dan scratching his chin under full concentration.

"That evening I decided to spend a quiet night at the ski firm's only available apartment. Switched the mobile off. Silly really, because if I had left it on I may have been prepared."

By now the usual lunch crowd was arriving at the chalet and tables filled up rapidly. It was a popular place, with magnificent views towards Lac Léman. The new guests made all four men uncomfortable, especially a large German woman who had forgotten to shower that morning, inching her generous bottom along the bench towards Dan. The story could not be continued in this atmosphere.

"Shall we, guys?" Suggested Henry. They all stood up. Arno paid.

With helmets and gloves pulled on and boots locked up they headed towards Avoriaz. Even late morning the February snow still felt good under ski.

Jack, Henry and Arno constantly swapped what-do-you-think-comes-next glances to one another at the chair lift. Dan said nothing, almost as if he was skiing alone.

Descending the last piste of the morning towards Ardent, all were hungry and looking forward to the speciality Savoyard menu at the Bout du Lac. Resting on the car Arno eased his boots off with a look of pure pleasure across his face.

"That's enough skiing for me until the February crowds leave again," he announced. The others nodded in agreement.

The short drive to lunch took barely five minutes.

Jack had brought many clients and friends to this restaurant with never a faintly disappointed comment. The view across the frozen lake was pure mountain magic. Ice climbers could often be seen navigating the frozen mountain face opposite. Meals sometimes became cold as clients watched the amazing display. The lady owner reminded them the plate on the table was more important than any winter sport...

Madame Gaurnier greeted Jack as warmly as ever. She and her husband, Emile, had seen the Rafter boys grow up in the region, and the family were still regular guests.

"Any table you want. Take your pick."

Jack requested the table in the far corner, giving enough space to let Dan continue his increasingly bizarre confession.

It never took long for aperitifs to be delivered. But all eyes were drawn to Dan, waiting for the next instalment. However, he seemed timid, almost reluctant to continue.

Arno tried to inject some humour. "I guess the Italian went home, and the next one arrived. A good old Texan girl this time, maybe?"

Dan looked serious. "No Arno, not as simple as that."

Four glasses of Mondeuse arrived at the table, but they barely noticed. All attention was focused on Dan. Madame Gaurnier sensed the mood, and thought it best to hold off taking the order for a little longer.

"Like I said," Dan continued, "having a quiet night at the apartment, you know through friends, ski firms – I have a good selection of places to crash for the odd night, depending on where I teach during the day.

There was a sudden knock at the door, which I thought strange because who would know I was there, apart from the ski firm? I came face-to-face with Tony Conti. My worry, embarrassment, whatever I was feeling must have showed. He didn't say anything, just gestured his way in with his arms wide open. I thought, my god, after all my adventures, this one blows up in my face.

He kept his back to me a for a good fifteen seconds, then turned to face me, raised his eyebrows and asked,"

"so how was last night with my wife?"

"Fuck me, no," muttered Henry under his breath.

The tension at the table showed. The three friends stared at Dan who suddenly looked pale for a man who spent his life in the mountains.

They were all now staring into the dark eye's of Tony Conti.

"I must have tried to say something quickly but, I mean, what the hell could I say? No not me... you're mistaken, wrong guy.

Tony was staring at me with serious intent. I didn't feel brave enough to try throwing a line at him. My normally reliable legs were tense. I felt like a beginner about to ski a black run for the first time, I just blurted out my defence.

Sorry, what the hell was I thinking of...

Tony looked at me as if he was staring at a small boy, his head to one side, a sour smile on his face. Sorry, but for some unexplainable reason it reminded me of a scene from *The Italian Job*, the put-down line to Michael Caine about his Aston Martin when they were stopped in the mountains by the Mafia.

"Your car? PREEETY car... Then Tony began to smile."

Arno fidgeted with his ski pullover and raised his shoulders. "See, this is what can happen without a contract. Now he wants you to take his wife off his hands instead of a messy divorce, typical bloody Latino."

"Not exactly, Arno," said Dan in a suddenly agitated voice. "Something far sicker. An offer I could not refuse. He told me in slow but very clear English, I would now be his personal mountain delivery boy or, to be more precise, his drug courier. It would be my job to deliver the goods to his contacts all over this part of the Alps. Private chalets, the wealthy with a bad habit. They would be protected from carrying the stuff in and out of the region and I would be the personal delivery boy. In return, he would pay me handsomely and keep me alive. He illustrated this in a sort of graphic way with hand movements across his throat, as if to say *Capisci...*"

Dan sat back looking humble. "So, guys, this is how I got into your league. A big ugly Swiss bank account, delivering small but expensive packages to the no-limit mountain guests."

Jack surveyed the restaurant. No one sitting too close; only families bragging about the morning's exploits and loud children telling how they "beat the teacher" and were the "best in the class." He turned back.

"This is serious stuff Dan. I'm sure I speak for all of us when I say thanks for being so straight and open. We all have a past that is now becoming all too transparent. But you have really been through the ugly side of life. This could involve other forces maybe far more aggressive than Madame Boustain. Is this still your regular winter programme?"

"No, no," muttered Dan. "Please don't think I could still be doing this. I never saw Gabriella again. Maybe that was a good thing, but Tony who was always hands on, never left me alone during the season for more than a couple of days. But one evening he didn't arrive at a planned meet-up in a small parking area just outside Val-d'Isère. I thought this strange - he'd never missed a meeting, even with heavy snowfall he arrived on time, criticizing me if I didn't. I waited fifteen minutes – that was the deal. Too long in one place could look suspicious. I waited for a call. Heard nothing for days. I began to panic. Something was wrong. With every Latin face I came close to it took longer for the glance to turn away, at least that's what I imagined. I had new locks put on the door, slept awfully, skied like an old man. It was driving me mad. Tony's mobile stayed dead. The only logical thing I could come up with was to check via one of the clients. That would be dangerous, but I had no other option. I finally decided on a Russian-owned chalet in Megève. They always treated me with respect, like a business meeting instead of; *here comes the dope delivery boy.*"

I knew where the family skied, but a chance meeting on the slopes could be full of pitfalls – children listening, friends not into the same habits. That could blow up in my face. So thought it best to make a polite visit one evening. The chalet was a blaze of light, easily worth at least ten million euros. I gave a weak tap on the door and a stunning girl opened."

"You here for talk with my daddy?"

"She had a strange accent. She gestured me into the hall where two large men stared at me from the far end of a snooker table. I nodded but they stared straight through me. This idea felt wrong already.

A door opened from somewhere in the back. The man – I think his name was Juri, but I had learnt quickly that names were bad manners in this business. Only, my friend, hey man, the hero is here. This type of greeting was normal."

Juri said in a very heavy accent.

"No meeting planned, why are you here?"

"The large men were still staring at me.

Sorry to come here, but something is wrong. Tony has disappeared. I chocked for using a name. The Russian shook his head looking angry."

"Tony got greedy, like they all do. A greedy businessman is a disaster. Think he had an accident. You need to find new partner. Good luck."

"The eyes from the end of the snooker table guided me quickly towards the door. I needed to get out and forget that address and as rapidly as possible. I walked back up the drive, expecting to be shot any second. That night as I fell in and out of sleep, even with several paracetamol, I dreamt that at least ten bullets hit my back."

The friends looked at each other searchingly: now they were living in the same residence as a former drug courier, who could be approached at any time to continue his winter programme, the possible victim of a revenge killing. There was a new dealer on the block. For their own personal fear factor, the tax office momentarily fell into second place.

4

Eva Critin was an early riser. She took a quick daily trip to the gym for the treadmill, always the same, a cardio-based workout before fruit and yogurt for breakfast, followed by a weird concoction learnt from a Hawaiian tennis pro she met years ago in Oman: coconut, pure lemon juice and grapefruit. Sharp enough to make the eyes water, but as the tennis pro confirmed, a vitamin explosion to help return any shot aimed in your direction that day. Eva thought the current day's required such support.

She scrolled through her emails, sent from a variety of old friends in Paris, keeping in touch, asking about the current snow conditions: admirers who never gave up, plus the occasional old political contact. Eva, a former employee of the *sûreté*, the French security service, knew the shadowy underside of French politics better than most. She looked towards the park. Near one of the small forests, she saw a group of what looked like six, maybe eight people, all dressed in dark suits and long winter coats, walking behind a man who appeared to be carrying a laptop.

As the party criss-crossed in and out of the trees, she pondered as to why such well-dressed individuals were walking in the owner's private park in the middle of winter? Not a sight she had caught before. Maybe someone was selling up and needed a survey? But the interior at this time of the year is a more pleasant place to be viewing. After all a park is a park.

She refocused back on the screen, making a mental reminder to ask the most prolific gossip specialists in the chateau, the Osperen sisters,

Valerie and Nina. If there was a view to be had on this, the self-appointed know-it-alls, the breaking-news providers, would have it.

As Eva prepared to leave for the beauty centre, she picked up her car keys from the office table and gazed down at the letter from Madame Boustain. She was sure this was some sort of mistake. Eva had prospered whilst living in Paris: a truly beautiful woman with a cold career focus from an early age. Free advice from senior bankers had been provided, they organised the most secure, undetectable structures for Eva's respectable investment portfolio.

The Luxembourg managers kept her constantly informed on changes in fiscal law and information exchange. She felt confident no one would have given her away: a person with her contacts could surely cause all sorts of problems for a mere confused administrator from the tax office. The proposed meeting on February 15th would be an impolite waste of time. Eva would treat the tax lady like an irritating gnat, sending her packing in no time. No accounts would be shown. Pick on the real criminals, she thought as she left for the town centre.

Jack had noticed a real downward spiral in the general ambiance of the owners.

Christmas time was usually a period of great pleasure in the chateau. With the suicide of Pico Latouch put behind them, almost all the owners, with the exception of the shifty, almost guarded presence of Gerard Crappy and the generally depressed, even suspicious-looking Bernard and Sophie Mardan, made gestures to, "pop in for a drink, let's open a bottle of champagne to celebrate the New Year". A genuinely positive atmosphere.

But this was now over. Madame Boustain had dropped a depression cloud on the chateau owners, although not all of them had confirmed receiving notice of a tax inspection.

They must have all replayed the same thought, time and time again. Why us? Could it be because we can afford such an elegant home? Because we are from other areas of France, or even other countries, is such extravagance not acceptable under the new French socialist administration?

The biggest problem was the fear factor. Should one owner confirm his dilemma to another? Would this weaken their position? Was there a mole in the chateau?

The owners had arrived at the chateau in such positive form. They had virtually all been cash buyers, with new expensive top-of-the-range cars. The garage was a pleasure to visit: from the Range Rover at one end to the Cayenne at the other, like a personal motor show.

Then there was the arrival of the removal lorries. So much unusual furniture; it sometimes took the workers two days to fully unload.

Now the residents were trying to avoid each other, even becoming suspicious of their neighbours. The mailboxes were emptied with unusual regularity, as if any suspicious documents should be quickly hidden in the safety of the apartment.

Computers were overworked, pass codes changed, files deleted, memories checked and replaced. The owners dug furiously, all seeking the latest updates on tax law enforcement. There were regular headlines in financial journals:

Another offshore financial centre gives into the pressure of providing client identity. Yet another Swiss bank agrees to release its client list to whichever tax authority thinks it's being cheated by the swindling residents in their own country.

Even journalists were taking up the cause, using their vast and sometime dubious resources to expose the wealthy money hiders.

This constant pressure only added to the owners suspicions that someone or something was after them, a massive force with the advantage of employing cold non-caring people whose only mission in life was to take the maximum and leave the minimum. A sort of criminal activity, they thought, with a legal backing, leaving them standing on the edge of a cliff, the ground underneath crumbling by the day.

Lawyers, the best money could buy, were contacted in Geneva. Half truths were told, promises of, "obtain the right result for me and write your own cheque," were offered. Suggestions of, "frankly I believe we're being picked on," were mentioned to little avail, as soon as the lawyers put the dreaded questions:

"Is there anything you might have missed on your tax declaration? Do you have undeclared assets outside of France?"

Suspicions were aroused on both sides.

The owners knew they had been less than truthful. With perfect hindsight, things would have been planned differently: the investments, properties and assets in other countries could have been declared. Now the whole world had gone from ignore the problem, just move to another land, hide it an offshore account at the start of their business lives to the current, go after the last penny tax regime where people could end up behind bars for evasion. Ruined overnight.

Most of the world's tax systems have now agreed to work together, passing on all background checks that any other national authority asks for.

And it was this modern fiscal cooperation that caused sleepless nights for each and every owner in the Chateau Montjan

Bernard Mardan had a soft spot for Eva Critin; he secretly adored her. He had never been unfaithful to his wife, but with Eva … He gazed down as she walked back into the chateau, looking splendid after her daily facial. The other male residents harboured similar interest, but they managed to keep it fairly hidden, although her magnificent chest was a popular talking point for the men of the North. Mardan struggled over this. Maybe his Latin roots made him give into macho gestures. Staring at the wrong place was one of his many weaknesses.

He desperately needed to talk to somebody, to share his insecurity with someone from his own race. The foreign residents could not cut it: they thought in a northern way and he was a southern man. He looked towards Eva, a beautiful sophisticated Parisian who would be the perfect confident. He could tell her everything, like an adulterer to a priest.

His wife was still at least three hours away visiting a cousin in Valence. Making a final check on his watch, he pressed the buzzer on Eva's door. She showed little surprise on seeing him. A small nod offered him entry but her face gave away little emotion, as if this had to happen one day. Mardan's eyes immediately lost control.

She politely gestured towards a green leather couch and invited him to join her for an aperitif: a glass of Sancerre, not a normal choice for a French woman in mid winter. But then Eva never followed the usual etiquette routine. This was probably why she was so appreciated from Paris to Saint-Tropez. Her roots were more Eastern European.

Mardan swallowed almost half the glass in one go. Eva observed he was a man in severe stress: his legs crossing and uncrossing several times. He now complimented Eva for the third time on her choice of décor and appeared as if he was about to make his first parachute jump, but was not sure whether to hang on to the plane door or just go for it and fly.

"Okay," he said, hoping he sounded confident. He stretched his legs ready to go. Eva was calm. "Have you heard the latest whispers about Latouch?"

"Nothing new, I guess. A sad lonely man, a suicide. What more?"

"My wife's sister is married to a judge in Chambéry. His brother is the local police chief and they get together regularly for dinner."

"And?" Eva came across as slightly bored with this revelation.

"The case is not closed. One detective has a theory that it was murder; footprints were found around the tree, maybe two or three different sets other than those of Latouch. We all wondered how he climbed up."

Eva stared towards the lounge window. She was rarely lost for words, but this shocked her. A murder in the chateau grounds, and now a far-reaching tax attack. She thought back to the group that she recently spotted in the park. There was more to this. She snapped out of this thought and returned her gaze to Mardan.

"So, Bernard, whatever the police think, no doubt we will hear from them. They appear to love their work, so let's hope they get to the bottom of this. Anything else on your mind?"

"Yes, actually there is. Seems we have some tax problems in the chateau. I hear everybody is under the spotlight."

"Indeed."

"But maybe some of us are in it a little deeper than others."

"How so?"

"Well, I was a star money manager once. A futures trader, young, hungry, a seriously motivated top performer for the Styer banking group. I could do no wrong. They threw money at me, new clients from the Middle East every week."

"So where is the problem with such a positive past?"

"One day the group director told me to prepare myself for a special meeting. He explained I would not be meeting the client direct, but a middle man. It was actually three middle men, very Middle Eastern appearence and talking in rapid Arabic."

Eva began to wonder why she had become the one privileged to hear this confession.

"They complimented me on my record. The director had praised me to the hilt, the one who assumed the role of *quote big figures;* he informed me that the bank had been selected from a short but specialised list to perform a series of particular complex transactions."

Eva noticed Mardan had slipped into role, as if he was still in the original meeting.

"So good for you." She said softly.

"Not really." Mardan had slid down in the chair, his parachute was flapping. "It was a set-up. The group director put me in control of the clients transactions, which were vast amounts of money transferred from bogus accounts in the Far East, which I later found out was used to supply weapons to various Middle East and African factions. It never occurred to me that problems were on the horizon. I assumed that compliance had checked these guys out from the beginning. Okay, I managed the money, but it came and went so quickly. I lost control of whom, when, and where. My bonus was enormous and my wife thought I was a champion."

"And how did things go wrong?"

Eva knew that this was the only direction such a story could possibly go.

"One day all hell broke loose. The police arrived at the office, our computers were taken, and I was told to go home and wait."

At this stage, Eva was beginning to wonder what Mardan could possibly expect from such a polite listener. She would certainly not enlist her powerful contacts to assist a man like him: she had only known him for a matter of months.

"I will not bore you with the whole story."

Eva appreciated this more than Mardan realised.

"Lawyers interviewed me time and time again. I was banned from any contact with colleagues but expressly the group director. Eventually, after many months, he was convicted and sent to jail."

Finally, thought Eva.

"But, and this is my whole nightmare, I was never asked to return the bonuses. I think they came from an account that was never discovered. The money never entered this country. I kept my share a long way offshore. Places like Singapore, the Caymans. Maybe it was a slush fund to keep the dumb robots like myself out of the loop in case I was investigated. It was so complicated."

Eva smelt a rat, which was talking and growing right in front of her.

"Not normal, Bernard. You may have been the innocent trader in the middle, but the money was dirty, and you knew it. Why did you not offer to do the right thing?"

"Easy to see that side today, but I knew a future career in the same business would be impossible. How long could I hide the past? I thought it best to lie low. We moved to Thailand, tried to forget the mess, and let a few years go by. And now, missing my country, I made the mistake of ending up here. I thought that was a good decoy, surrounding myself with international neighbours, but now we are all under a tax inspection."

"So what are you going to do?"

"Well, we kept the apartment in Thailand, maybe a sixth sense told us to do this. It's going to be home for probably the rest of our lives. We leave in a day or so."

Eva looked surprised. Having heard so many men confess all manner of sins in her presence, this one had a little more depth that she hadn't quite got to yet.

"Not prepared to wait and see if it blows over?"

"Too many bad people involved, the jailed director is out now. He was very bitter that I got off. He set the deal up, no doubt with a massive pay-off, but I stayed free. Maybe he is behind this."

Eva shook her head gently whilst sipping her wine: she thought this an unrealistic possibility. "What on earth has your past got to do with the others here?"

The man was rambling: best he goes home. Eva encouraged him to leave by saying a Skype call was imminent.

Mardan left without finishing his Sancerre. As he walked to the stairs, he was even more convinced that he had no friends or future in the chateau.

Arriving back at the door to his apartment, Bernard felt disappointed. Why did Eva not throw a small branch his way? He was drawn to her but she obviously not to him. He had hoped that she might have offered to speak with an old advocate contact to try and help him. But it had been the polite listening routine, no more than that. However, Mardan consoled himself in the surety that Eva was solid. She would not repeat this conversation in the chateau. Not her style.

Back in his apartment, Bernard poured himself a large pastis and waited for his wife's return. He saw no future life, even in such a beautiful residence. More worrying, he could not contemplate the full discovery of his past by any local hunters. The need to discuss the future with his wife was now paramount. His mind wandered through their apartment in Phuket. Not as large or technically equipped as their home in the chateau, but a safe haven far away. The thought of warmer weather consoled him. But as he sipped his pastis he knew, once the decision was made, he would never visit his beloved homeland again, too risky. They could even be waiting for him at Charles de Gaulle airport.

"Modern technology talks too much," he whispered quietly to himself.

His wife returned carrying a large bouquet of roses, a gift from her cousin in Valence. As she posed the bouquet towards her husband smiling, his face gave away the reality of his morning. No smile came back, more a searching glance to show he expected support for what he was about to propose. This dream was about to end, but he could not begin speaking. His eyes filled with tears.

Sophie gently placed the roses on the dining table. "Tell me; are we about to escape again, my darling?"

Bernard's flickering eyes told it all. The only question was, how soon?

5

THE NORMALLY PLEASANT, well-mannered residents were changing their approach to life. Mood swings were observed; heads normally held high were now directed to the ground; the normal courtesy of interest in another neighbour's health was long forgotten; service personnel once greeted with enthusiasm were now ignored. Faces showed the pale colour of winter. Blinds were closed for most of the day – not an unusual sight in France, but it was for such a private location. Most residents wanted to take full advantage of overlooking the protected forest and the views to the Alps.

Although spring was around the corner, nobody showed enthusiasm for the improving weather, as if a massive storm cloud covered the chateau and the occupants could see no way to disperse it. The pressure was like a great clock ticking their lives away until the ultimate decision was made, a decision none of them had any control over. It was too late to change all the errors of judgment that had led to them to this terrible predicament. Every day that passed led to more sleepless nights, pill popping and extra alcohol consumption, a vicious circle that was getting smaller by the day.

If the lawyers of Geneva were searching for new business, a flow was about to begin from an unexpected source: a collection of several well-heeled owners who had, innocently or constructively, fallen foul of the local tax system.

The firm of Bayer, Merlot & Grass was often the first port of call for big-problem, big-invoice clients. The firm enjoyed the new boutique image of the legal world: their offices were classic Geneva, on the rue François Bellot, filled with a collection of old paintings depicting scenes from the ancient city to Lac Léman, ancient wooden yachts. Clients came like moths to the light, the word-of-mouth circuit that often emanated from the large accountancy firms, and their specialised area of secret bank account holders. *Innocent victims* arrived on a daily basis.

Didier Grass was the front man, often the first partner to greet a worried client. Aged forty-five with a slim build and eye's that rarely blinked. An honours graduate from Lausanne University; he was an experienced professional capable of clearing up some of the most disastrous client situations.

The chateau clients called up, one by one, their stories following a similar pattern usually starting with, "As I am a fiscal resident in France, I would feel more comfortable talking with a tax lawyer who is familiar with the French tax laws and the international banking and investment system, but not too close geographically to individuals who are causing me problems."

For Grass, this simply meant, I need you to work exclusively for me, no inside favours for the powerful administrators who may be behind this. This was the worry of all business-savvy clients: who knows who, and which person at the end of the road was going to really benefit from the process.

The fourth chateau client to visit Rue François Bellot was Arno Van Bommel. He decided a sharp Hugo Boss suit, with matching Armani shirt and tie would be appropriate for the occasion, knowing lawyers in Geneva never took a client seriously if they appeared in a casual manner. After all, a lot was at stake; no small details could be left to chance.

The secretary greeted Van Bommel seconds after he hit the door button.

"Good morning sir, welcome."

It was immediately obvious that she had benefited from the ski season; with her bronzed winter tan and bright blue eyes. The firm must be easy on long weekends, thought Arno.

After accepting the customary offer of coffee and a small selection of Swiss chocolates, Arno relaxed into a large leather chair that was perfectly placed to appreciate the well-lit paintings and the next face to appear at the antique wooden door.

Within two minutes she was back, inviting Arno to follow her up a small flight of stairs to where Didier Grass was waiting at his office door.

Arno always took great interest in the first seconds of any meeting. As this man could potentially save him millions, his concentration was paramount.

"Welcome to our firm, Monsieur Van Bommel." With only a slight trace of a French accent.

"Good to meet you, and thanks for the quick appointment."

"Please make yourself very comfortable."

Arno raised his right eyebrow at the word *very*. Looking at the dark brown leather couches, very comfortable seemed a guarantee.

"So, Mr Van Bommel. You live in a beautiful chateau an hour or so south from here in the Savoie. It sounds special. How is the life in that area?"

Arno was a no nonsense Amsterdammer. He often killed off conversations when they began with too many pleasantries. He thought, yes, it could be pleasant but at this moment it's rather ugly. A hut in back-street Mumbai seemed more appealing than his current home.

"Let me explain my miserable situation."

Arno commenced with a direct stern look that even the past criminal clients of Grass found hard to muster.

"I know you have been contacted by several of my neighbours. We talk together. We are all suffering from what seems to be the same suspicious covert attack from the French tax office. Within a space of days, we all received personal recorded delivery letters. I don't know the specifics of every neighbour, but at least five, maybe six of us have been invited to explain, by the same woman, details of our investments, all bank accounts held and property holdings because we are fiscal residents of France. So my first question is how could this happen to a group of people all living in the same chateau within a space of say, two weeks?"

Grass looked to the ceiling quickly, took a deep breath, focused back on his pad, then looked over his glasses at Van Bommel.

"Strange things are happening these days. The old logic of a person who one day decides to start driving a Ferrari and therefore bring attention to himself, that's over. Now the tax office can examine so much without ever speaking to a potential suspect. You know our banks are under pressure to disclose client accounts. It's happening and it's hurting so many who thought they were safe for life. I am constantly battling on behalf of French people living around the Lac Léman who have been targeted, they thought Switzerland being so close was the perfect haven; now the Swiss have turned on them."

Arno began to lower his head, "if you can't trust a Swiss banker who can you trust?"

Grass ignored Arno's sarcastic comment continuing.

"Just by searching the internet, they find businesses that pretend to have a fiscal base in, say, the UK or Holland, but they are actually operating a full-time business in the Alps. A consultancy sitting on a mountain with a laptop selling property. From this it's a simple matter of time. They run checks with the local bank, the supermarket client records, ski school; you name it, and of course discover daily transactions. The rest is, as they say, history."

Arno was not impressed. "I am not a chalet operator or consultant selling property, and I detest supermarkets, nor do I pretend to live anywhere else. I made the decision to become a tax resident. Okay, I have to pay, but now it seems it's not enough. I may have one or two things outside the country, but that's nothing to do with them, I made the money years ago."

Grass formed a very discreet self-indulgent smile, as if the meeting's outcome was planned before it ever started.

"Do you use an accountant, Mr Van Bommel, one who is registered in France, one who knows the ins and outs of the French system?"

"Yes I do, but my impression is that he works more for the tax office than for me. He only ever produces a list of how much I have to pay, never comes up with any bright moves, save a sum here, declare this in another way, a tax advantageous structure. He just counts for the other side. I feel responsibility to the client does not exist..."

Grass began to feel uneasy. A large Dutchman sitting in his office, a former exotic car dealer, who believes certain items, need not be declared to his new country of fiscal residence.

"If only you had decided to relocate to Switzerland, Mr Van Bommel. We are somewhat more open to business-minded people than your current administration. But I think you know that, these days, all countries, large and small, are struggling to meet budgets. Tax offices are being directed as specific easy targets."

"Like wealthy foreigners," interjected Van Bommel.

"Well, yes, this is often the case. They have no mercy. Your accountant, whatever his level of competence, should have made it crystal clear that when you become a tax resident, all investments, property, bank accounts, whatever, should be declared."

Arno knew his avenue of options was limited, even though the meeting had only been going for twenty minutes. Even a high-flying Swiss tax lawyer could not simply hide his undeclared assets. He thought that the world is getting far too full of recorded transactions.

"Okay," he sighed, "plan B. I have only been in France for a few years, mostly to be close to the chateau project. It took a long time, with plenty of regular investment, to keep on top of the building details as proposed from the owners. I did my level best to keep paperwork, legal documents for my other interests out of the country. It's looked after and it's tidy. How could they know about anything else?"

"Like I said before, banks are being forced to declare where clients are located. A notary keeps detailed records of property transactions. For sure you use email, the internet. If hackers can break into the US defence system, maybe ... Well, you see my point."

"Sure I see your point, but I was hoping for some sort of angle. We all know the French are happy to take the usual ten percent deal, say nothing. And if not can I be an innocent tourist, who was not aware of the new system in my country of residence?"

Now Grass came back with a broad smile.

"Very sorry, Mr Van Bommel. This may have worked some years ago, I say may, but these days they have no sweet side. It's simply go for the maximum, and more if possible. If you end up on the street, they couldn't care less. The government is on their side. They can break the law and hide behind the system. You can break the law and end up in jail. It's as simple as that ..."

At this point, Arno had almost heard enough. His initial enthusiasm was waning; the old tricks didn't exist these days.

"Shall we stop here, Mr Grass? Sorry, but you do not seem to be in a reasonable position to help me. I have to hope that certain things will blow over. Maybe this bloody tax girl does not have all the information I fear about?"

Grass wanted to agree, but his legal training taught him to never take the client down the easy road, fees can grow dramatically if you play the time card, but he knew this would be difficult with a man like Arno Van Bommel. Over the last few days he had been in similar meetings with Jack Rafter, Henry Cameron and Dan Lancaster, all well balanced men who would not be fooled by lawyer's promises of a happy ending. These men would certainly talk together. Best to stop now and hear how they want to proceed.

Arno got up to leave with a final.

"I'll be in touch as things happen. Any more thoughts from your side would be appreciated."

Grass was sure such types would either leave the country or strike a deal. They always did. But even with his extensive experience he felt uneasy; this was an unusual case, even by modern day standards. Something did not feel right. Never before had he experienced such a concentrated tax inspection over one residence; such a diverse group of people with very different backgrounds. He considered making a few phone calls, search out old contacts. Perhaps this situation required a different approach. Something felt odd, making him genuinely interested in the Chateau Montjan dossier.

"Of course, Mr Van Bommel, I will give it some serious thought, discuss it with my partners and perhaps revisit some old files. I'll be in touch if and when I have anything worthwhile."

Grass watched Arno Van Bommel drive away from the client parking. Unknown to the male clients from the chateau, Grass had already made checks on the Chateau Montjan project. According to property agent contacts, he was surprised to learn that the owners had spent close to twenty million euros on their dream residence.

Two extremely clear avenues of thought came to him. This could be a large fish for the partnership with fees to support his firm for years to come, or, as he suspected, the tax office was a mere puppet. Would he be playing with a fire he could never put out?

6

Returning from a business trip to Brussels on Swiss Air gave Jack time to reflect on the current business climate and enjoy reading the *Financial Times* on paper as opposed to his screen. His seven meetings had all resulted with the same familiar vague promise of, "further investment, as and when the markets stabilised." Try as he might, clients were not convinced about the current trends and economic woes.

The over-friendly steward filled his coffee cup, smiled coyly as if he had just poured vintage wine and minced away, clearing his throat ready to announce the descent towards Geneva. Jack was glad he'd risen early to catch the first flight back, knowing more traffic would be flowing into Geneva than out at this time of the morning. He almost jogged through the airport towards the long-term parking, cursed a Munich-plated Golf for parking so close to his door and quickly tapped his speaker icon to let the family know he would make it home in time to collect his sons from their weekly swim.

"Hey Dad, it's no problem. We'll leave the pool at eleven and walk straight home, promise. No drugs, no girls... well, and no conversation with strange men on the street. We promise."

"Okay, trust you. Call me if you need to. Have a great swim."

Normally Jack would have joined the boys, but events at the chateau clouded his mind. Work had to come first. Somehow he had to extract the family out of the current nightmare.

As his boys began their regular swimming workout, at least 50 laps each week, two unlikely spectators filed into the pool's seating area.

The other spectators could not help but stare occasionally: the two men had never been seen at the pool before, probably not even in the town. Dressed in suits they appeared uncomfortable and out of place and their sole interest was in watching Jack Rafter's sons, whispering together suspiciously.

Back in his office, Jack made calls to clients around Europe and got updates from brokers. "How are the current trends looking? Can these funds make some decent money in the difficult trading conditions?"

He was trying his best to focus on business and move forward when a rapid knock at his office door halted his concentration.

"Hey Jack, Carly, let me in. Hope I'm not disturbing you. Are you in the middle of something maybe?"

"Always welcome, Dan. Nick and Simon felt sorry you could not make the swim today."

"Yea, I feel I should have gone. Don't know why, but... gut feeling,"

"What do you mean, gut feeling? Is there something they're not telling me?"

"No, nothing like that. Your sons are solid Jack, we both know that. I can't put my finger on it. I just feel something today; maybe it's the whole bloody atmosphere around us, like they need protecting..."

"You're making me uncomfortable Dan. You know what a close family we are, and you ... well, we look upon you as family also. What the hell is it?"

"Don't know why I came up to you. Kinda feel something's about to happen, got a knot in my stomach."

Jack patted the car keys in his pocket. "You coming? My concentration is shot. I need to check on the boys."

Jack and Dan took less than a minute to get to the garage.

All calls were missed by Nick and Simon, their mobiles buried deep in the sport bags, vibrator mode not helping.

"Did you see those ugly creeps watching us in the stand?"

"No, bro, but I did see that blond who followed us out of the pool. She was not at all ugly."

"For a guy who plays Call of Duty, you miss a lot. Focus Nick, like dad told us..."

The walk home from the pool usually took thirty minutes, but this day Nick and Simon decided on a short cut, through a small tree-lined park leading into a narrow passage, small enough for one car to pass through at a time. The area was void of shoppers, it being Monday morning, Banks, shops and restaurants were closed.

"Fancy playing GTA5 at home? Dad always agrees and Mum's gone shopping?"

"You bet. I'll give Dad a call to tell him we'll be back in fifteen minutes."

Before Nick could reach into his training bag, the Mercedes bonnet was barely two meters away from the boys' backs. As they turned in surprise, the two front doors were smashed open against the narrow alley walls. They froze. The large ugly men from the pool moved quickly for such heavyweights, the dark sunglasses adding to their menacing presence. They were both sweating like pigs. Within seconds, Nick and Simon were grabbed with hands around their necks, their breathing increased rapidly; mouths open to gain maximum oxygen. Their heads were pushed hard against the jaggid brick walls.

Nick the elder brother fell into roll. "Don't worry, Simon. Give them whatever they ask for. No resistance, bro."

The open-hand slap to Nick's face caused him to scream; the gorilla's other hand was now tighter around his neck.

"Funny boy, hey, telling your brother what to do? It's me who tells you what to do. Okay? Listen to this. You're living in a dangerous place. A chateau, they have a serious history of accidents happening in them. Maybe you should tell your Dad to move home. I don't like looking at your pretty faces."

Simon let out a screech. "HELP US !"

This caused the monster to bring his massive fat hand backwards and forwards across the boy's face, as Nick shouted, "No, leave my brother alone, you bastards."

He too received more smashes to his face. Both boys were now loosing their balance, falling in the continued neck hold towards the cobbled street.

Jack and Dan almost parked inside the pool entrance, making it hard for swimmers to leave. They couldn't care less.

The lady at the reception looked anxious.

"Two boys, tall, fourteen and sixteen, red bags. Have they left?"

"Yes, about fifteen minutes ago. Why? Some problem? "

Turning on the spot Jack and Dan ran back towards their badly parked vehicle.

"I'm running the route home through the streets. Can you park the car?"

Jack was already across the road. Dan did his best to catch up.

Nick and Simon were crouched on the ground on opposite sides of the small alley. As they simultaneously touched their mouths, blood dripped off their hands. Even with the fear factor high in their bodies, they could both not resist watching the Mercedes reverse out of the tight space. One cold face with sunglasses was fixed on them; the other turned controlling the car's direction. Then a third person appeared in the back seat, sitting up with neck stretched to obtain a better view of the damaged metered out. Nick blinked. There was something familiar about the third passenger.

Jack could hear Dan shouting behind him as he crossed the empty square. He considered the three possible choices: the main road, the river walk or the smaller back streets.

"Young men never do the obvious thing," he said to himself. "Dumb, but I bet they took the quiet route."

Dan was now closing in on Jack. "So sorry about this, Jack, all this shit around us and I do this to you. They're safe, they must be. Most likely home by now."

Half way across the small square Jack's head shook, then froze as he focused on two old ladies; arms raised high in the air, the conversation far too loud for a calm Monday morning in the old part of town. As the men's pace slowed, two familiar forms appeared to be consoling one another at the far end of a narrow alleyway. The old ladies began babbling, unsure if the new male arrivals were also part of the attack that they had just witnessed. They swiftly moved to one side as Jack and Dan rushed to the boys.

"What happened guys? So sorry I didn't come with you, what the hell happened here?"

As Nick began a stuttering explanation, the old ladies arrived behind them.

"We saw it, taking coffee together in our apartment. Here, just above. There was a large black car, and then two horrible big men jumped out and started hitting these nice young boys. Are they your sons? Terrible, this never happens here. Why, they seem so sweet, why?"

Jack held his boys close whilst wiping the blood from their mouths. He was shaking, but unsure whether this was for his loved ones, or pure uncontrolled anger.

Dan moved from Simon to Nick like a pacing lion determined to show they were now safe, back in the pride.

The car now pulling into the alley caused even more interest from the gathering crowd. Two serious-looking gendarmes in their mid-thirties approached the four still crouched on the ground, keeping a hand on their pistols as if the two large guys could give problems. They quickly understood from the old ladies about the determined efforts of the *horrible* men responsible. A volley of questions directed towards Jack's boys produced a simple confirmation that a mugging had taken place, but no valuables were stolen. However, both Nick and Simon knew the details could only be discussed with close family. The gendarmes took one full page of notes, contact details from Jack and Dan, also promising to check out the ladies vague description of seeing a large black French car pulling away. Fortunately Jack's boys were able to confirm the vehicle: a Mercedes with Geneva number plates.

Carly Rafter almost fell down the chateau stairs when she saw her boys walking through the open doors.

"No, my babies... What happened to your faces? You went swimming ..."

"They were attacked, in the old part of town. Two gorillas got out of a car and hit them, but it's only bruising. Their eyes, teeth are all ok," confirmed Jack. The anger in his eyes showed he could explode at any second.

During the afternoon, the same two Gendarmes made a visit to the chateau. No further information had been collected from their enquiries. Jack had the impression that protecting the local image and the quaint old part of town was more of a priority than getting to the bottom of the attack.

Dan came and went throughout the day, offering basically, "anything he could do to help the boys get over this."

Promising more strength training, defence techniques when they felt ready. Jack wished, if only he could have been with his boys this morning...

Later, as the Rafter family watched television that evening, Jack wanted to ask the boys more about what the attackers had said. But he felt for his sons. They needed more time before talking.

By 10 p.m. both boys had decided they needed sleep. Jack turned to Carly, determined that she heard the full story, leaving no loose ends.

Later he checked on them. Simon was fast asleep. Jack hoped like hell he would not dream that night. Nick also appeared to be calm and relaxed.

"Dad, can we talk?" Jack spun round, disappointed that he had woken his son.

"Are you sure? Of course if you want to..."

"They said we live in a dangerous place, a chateau where bad things can happen..."

"How could they know where you live?"

"Because..., maybe I should not say this, but... Simon and I are sure we saw someone we know in the back of that car. We're not completely sure but..."

"Please tell me."

"I don't know, it was so quick. He was wearing sunglasses, but something was familiar. Maybe someone we know from here?"

Jack held his son very tight. Had he decided to leave the room and follow his initial impulse, the gendarmes would again be at the chateau this evening to arrest Jack Rafter.

7

Henry Cameron retrieved the second recorded delivery notice from his post box.

After the many shared conversations with other residents – some positive, most negative – lawyer meetings, and knowing in their own minds some wrongs had been committed, surprises were hard to come by. And Henry knew as soon as he saw the envelope addressed to:

Henry James Cameron
GER SARL Property Consultant
Chateau Montjan

That it could only emanate from one source: her again. Even he was beginning to feel a large amount of negativity.

"The mean bastards," he said to himself out loud. Keep up the pressure, abuse your advantage, he thought.

As he entered the chateau, Gerard Crappy was walking out of the lift. Both men looked uncomfortable. At two metres apart, the normal handshake routine could not be avoided.

"Morning, Mr Crappy, how's life?"

"Oh, you know. Too much paperwork, too much tax. The pleasure of living in modern times."

Henry was about to make one of his off-the-cuff remarks, "Come on, you know we foreign types pay the most..." but it would have been lost. Crappy was through the large doors and a weak *"bonne journée"* was all that Henry heard.

His mobile rang with a high pitched piano tune as Jack's name flashed on the screen.

"Henry, sorry to bother you so early. Where are you?"

"I would guess about fifteen, twenty meters from you if you measure in a direct line, assuming you're at home."

"I am. Can you come up?"

"Sure, with my level of fitness and the stairs, I should arrive in half an hour."

Henry, always the clown, thought Jack.

"A large fresh orange juice is waiting."

Henry licked and stuck the registered letter notice to his forehead just as Jack opened the door. He lost a little of his usual control.

"Ha... Best looking lady I have ever seen from the tax office. Come in, darling."

The men exchanged a solid handshake.

"This is why I was calling Henry. I picked up the second letter myself this morning. Spoke with Arno, he has one. The way this thing moves, for sure the others will have them as well ... but now we are going up a gear. This letter is from the Director, Madame Fouchard. Our celebrity status is improving."

Henry downed the orange juice quickly.

"So they are going for max damage, bloody typical administrators. What else do they say – your French is far better than mine?"

"Well, this is what worries me most. Our new contact, Madame Fouchard, the chief, invites us to a personal meeting in March in Annecy, along with her colleague Sylvie Boustain. If I've got it right, she is demanding that I show a list of all the assets that I own on that day, followed by the usual legal paragraphs of failure to do so could bring the risk of legal action, confiscated assets, under the law act no. 2584128. Why, oh why, are they now going down this route? They couldn't possibly know about anything I own outside of France, or could they...?"

Henry took a deep breath. "Not being smart here, old chap. But can you imagine how many assets I have outside this country? To make matters worse, if, as Annabel is proposing, we consider a move to another land, it's certain these low lives will pass on information to our next fiscal authorities. We have nowhere to hide...simply buggered in all directions."

Jack's mind was in another place. Try as he might, he could never understand how such information could have been obtained. This caused the constant thumping inside his head. What do they really know? This was turning into a sink-or-swim situation. Jack felt a slight sensation of drowning.

"Sorry, Henry, something is just not right here. If, and with a very big if, they had our foreign asset information available, why would the simple girl Boustain pretend this was all about TVA and set up issues here in France? If they had access to this we would have seen cops at the door, computers being taken away, probably in jail by now. Something stinks, it's not logical, and I'm beginning to choke from the smell."

The owners had become untrusting towards their surroundings. Instead of using their mobiles, personal face-to-face get-togethers were the norm, with the exception of Valerie and Nina Osperen who couldn't seem to care less.

Strangely, Eva Critin became closer to her chateau neighbours. Initially a somewhat cold woman, aloof as if her natural beauty protected her from life's mishaps, she was now often seen in serious conversation with the others, happy to share, "why us" type exchanges with anyone she bumped into.

The owners were rarely seen before 8 a.m. most mornings, unless a family ski trip was planned or Dan was jogging in the park, Jack doing the school run. So the large black Citroen taxi arriving at the main gate went unnoticed. As the large metal gates opened, the taxi came in slowly, very slowly for a local Savoie taxi, almost as if in stealth mode.

The car stopped a few metres from the chateau's main entrance, behind a large dark green wall designed to protect the ground floor residents from wind and the prying eyes of the chateau workers. It was almost invisible. Only one apartment could possibly view the imminent departure.

Sophie and Bernard Mardan slipped out through the chateau doors, their six silver suitcases lined up on the chateau steps. The driver eased out of his car and quietly placed the suitcases in the ample boot space.

Sophie moved quickly into the back seat with Bernard. As the car slowly pulled away, Eva stared down from her bedroom, realising that the man had been telling her the truth. Things were that bad. His poor wife...

Eva was tough, Paris tough. She had dealt with more sewer creatures than she could ever remember, but this early morning departure came as a shock. These people were good. They'd made a bad choice in life maybe, but it was sad to leave everything behind. Maybe she should have helped, made a call or two at least. But it was too late now.

Before the Mardan's bags were checked in at Geneva airport, Eva had informed both Jack and Arno.

Gerard Crappy smirked from his apartment window, immersed in a very long mobile phone call.

8

"Over eight hundred kilometres so far this morning and it's only 7:30. What a great cock-up that place is."

Arno was lying in bed, watching his massive HD screen, listening to the Dutch news updating him on his homeland's current traffic problems.

"Okay, so here they drive with two possible options: old and dead at the wheel, or so crazy fast an imminent accident is guaranteed. Chambery's got to be my favourite. But the congestion that Holland suffers is something I don't miss. What da hell. Any more coffee, Stephanie?" demanded a yawning Arno.

The Van Bommels were planning a day in Megève catching up with old friends, mostly car buyers from Arno's previous business in Amsterdam. They were second-home owners who always loved to meet up again, talk about cars and new driver technology, while the wives gossiped about the latest Dutch celebrity divorce.

"How many times will this guy get married, now number five?"

The drive to Megève would take a little over an hour; maybe less if Arno became agitated by the local driving expertise. His snow tyres were still new so grip was at its best in the dark blue Porsche Panamera, his car racing experience unchallenged on the mountain roads.

Knowing the lunch would be long and lazy, Stephanie made a quick visit to the gym for some toning then twenty minutes on the treadmill. The gym was empty, the way she liked it, with no men to stare at her excellent cosmetic surgery.

Arno thought the gym a nice idea, but only at the weekend. His weeks were too full of watching stock markets, making business calls, staying in touch with his vast network of contacts. No time to train, sweat, and then blow the workout with a good bottle from the Burgundy. Training plus wine at the weekend made Arno happy.

Jack and Carly Rafter were also invited, but they passed this time. Jack was well versed in the Dutch male attitude towards cars and modern tech advances. Being a fan, he could also spend hours swapping stories, and was always ready for Arno's jibes about, "the Brit in the chateau who drives an Indian Range Rover." Both men had developed a great respect for one another, drawn closer by the developing tax inspection.

As Stephanie walked into the bedroom, Arno stood up, sharp, almost standing to attention.

"How long will you be, my Cardio Princess? Did you have time to run a marathon?"

"Arno... replied Stephanie, too quickly for his comfort. "Do you prefer a classy well-dressed woman by your side or a sort of gym teacher, fresh from a sweaty workout ... Well, Arno?"

He knew when to hit reverse gear, and this was such a moment.

"No problem. I shall take a slow walk to the post box and check if the evil administrators have come up with more ideas for stealing our money."

As he pulled the heavy chateau door open, leading onto the tiled approach, Arno froze. He blinked and refocused at least three times. About a hundred metres away in the park, he saw a small party of darkly dressed individuals, standing at the edge of a small clump of trees. How strange to see such a group in their park. Too many for a local property agent, plus no one has plans to sell, as far as he knew. Anything official would have to be discussed and arranged by agreement with the owners. This land is protected under French law and can't be sold. His mind shot back to a conversation with Eva, she talked about something unusual going on a couple of weeks previously.

Arno hit Jack's number on his Samsung. Jack, seeing who was calling, picked up after one ring.

"Hey, Arno thought you would be on the way to Megève by now. All okay?"

"All okay, planning to leave soon, but do something for me. Walk onto your balcony and look towards the main gate."

"Okay, what's up? Has Henry taken up jogging again?"

"Just look. Tell me what you see."

"Who the hell are they? Eva mentioned this type of intrusion a few weeks back."

Arno cut Jack short.

"As you and I are large part-owners of this place, do you mind if I go and ask this bunch what the devil they are doing here?"

"No problem Arno be my guest. Give me five minutes to put some clothes on and I'll join you."

"Okay but quick."

The site of such a large forbidding man standing in front of the dark wooden chateau doors was quickly spotted by one of the party. Heads turned, but only from those standing in the open. The rest of the group in the trees had not noticed the man from Amsterdam.

Arno knew his time was limited. His pulse began to increase; no time to wait for Jack. He launched his one hundred and twenty kilos towards the open park. He was never a great short-distance runner, just happy with his recognition as a Dutch heavyweight judo champion. But today would be one of his greatest efforts. After fifty metres though, the forest group had also been alerted to his pending arrival.

Arno heard panic in the voices, only male voices, a mix of French and the heavy Swiss-German accent he found rather cosy from his many ski trips to Klosters and Davos.

Now at least eight faces, eyes wide, were focused on the imminent arrival of something too large to ignore. Now with fifteen metres to go, Arno decided to jump into the forest. The only person who had not been alerted to his arrival was happily crouched in the centre, transfixed on the laptop balanced across his knees, headphones attached.

Arno was never accused of being a ballet dancer, two sharp branches scraped his chest, his jacket tore immediately, but the laptop operator was no more than two metres away. The stress and babble from the man's associates now alerted him to Arno's presence behind his left shoulder. The machine was smashed flat. The panic made the small forest sound more akin to a frantic dealing room. The laptop man stood quickly, his headphones falling around his shoulders. As he stepped out of the forest, the rest of his party were at least twenty metres away on a rapid march to the small side gate next to the main entrance.

Arno, in shock and short of breath, called out, "Hey, I want to talk to you… I don't think you have business here. What the hell are you doing in our park?"

Not one head turned. Within seconds the side gate was slammed shut. Arno turned, still breathing heavily to see Jack running towards him.

"Did you see that? Those ill-mannered bastards, walk around our property with a tech guy, then leave when I come over."

Jack only witnessed the final moments of the brief encounter. He felt that, even with a far superior level of fitness to Arno, chasing after them would achieve nothing, but thought that other residents must know more. These people did not want to talk.

As Arno extracted himself from the forest, Jack was aware and focused on the sound of two maybe three large V-8 engines coming to life. He moved quickly to gain the advantage of the view down a small hill, the only approach to the chateau. The engines were revving hard, the small convoy gone in no time. Jack was sure the last Mercedes displayed a Swiss number plate.

Arno, now capable of normal conversation again, joined Jack and asked, "So did they leave a calling card, wave goodbye?"

"Afraid not, but I would bet a lot of money that the last car was Swiss-plated, Geneva maybe. So why should we have Swiss visitors in our park?"

"Absolutely no idea. The longer I live here, the more confused I get. First the French tax office is after us. Now it looks like the Swiss are close behind. Do you have any assets in La Suisse, Jack?"

"Nothing at all, not even a bank account. The Swiss have messed all that up by passing out client lists. Do you?"

"No, never did, but we know one neighbour who does. Dan. Remember his confession on boys ski day? Do you think this could be connected to him?"

"Unless we have a pending drug deal going on in the forest, no. Why?"

"That's a bit unfair. He did say that part of his life was well behind him. Maybe paranoia is setting in. Who or what comes here next?"

As the men walked back towards the chateau, Gerard Crappy drove through the main gates. He rarely gave gestures of recognition to his neighbours, pretending to concentrate on his bonnet instead. Today was typical, followed by the slow descent to the underground parking.

Arno excused himself.

"Stephanie must be ready by now. Better move."

Jack took the stairs to the underground garage, time to pick his boys up from school.

The automatic lights were still on as Jack entered via the fire door. At the far end he saw the small figure of Crappy walking up the garage entry lane. Unless Jack was going senile, Crappy was wearing a very similar long winter coat to the Swiss visitors who'd just left in such panic. After the attack on his boys, Jack suffered from a constant urge to smash Crappy whenever he saw him, convinced on no evidence at all that he was responsible. All of the owners treated Crappy as a very suspicious character, but advice and pressure from Carly, Henry, Dan and Eva had persuaded Jack to back down, just in case it hadn't been Crappy. They needed proof, but Jack convinced himself that the Frenchman would pay dearly one day. He had not the slightest doubt he was to blame.

As Jack drove slowly out of the parking, Crappy was walking back from the main gate, the mail under his arm, his stare fixed on the small forest. His concentration was so great that Jack's presence was barely noticed until the last second. Crappy raised a hand acknowledging his neighbour.

Jack stared coldly at him, if looks could kill, the man would die on the spot.

"Revenge for my boys will taste good, you sneaky little bastard," said Jack under his breath, but Crappy was once again only focused on the trees, not the beautiful chateau.

"Calm it, Arno." Stephanie demanded. "I would like to arrive with air in my lungs. This is not a race circuit..."

"Sorry, any decent driver knows that a large 4x4 doesn't take bends like this baby."

"Yes, darling, but these guys don't care, they're simple mountain boys. You measure your turns, you're a racer. They live in hope. Let me drive on the way home. I promise I'll only drink the odd glass."

Arno eased back. The Land Cruiser stayed close behind: the mountain boy had no choice but to enjoy the German design from behind.

Megève was busy at 12:30, the time for late-season skiers and workers to consider where to take lunch. The sun was strong, but with a decent sweater or jacket a terrace would be a good option. Arno pulled slowly into the parking of Le Fermes de Marie. He spotted Henk's black Q7 and three cars away Wouter's Hummer, both deals arranged by Arno for a decent price.

"Great, they're all here. Come on, Steph."

From the reception area, Arno could here the loud voices. His Dutch friends sounded full of late winter spirit.

"Hey, hey, hey, ladies, men. Great to see you here again."

Four other tables, already half way through lunch looked a little concerned. Was this a small Dutch invasion? Would the volume continue at this level?

After the customary three kisses and compliments on how healthy they all looked, drinks were ordered. Arno requested the latest snow report and Henk confirmed the current conditions were still excellent.

"Wonderful conditions up top. Pity we had to break off for lunch..."

The girlfriends, Lucy and Margot, were already forming a small circle with Stephanie. So much Dutch gossip to catch up on, could it all be covered over lunch?

The large G & T hit Arno's dry throat, one of his favourite all time drinks. Wouter stuck with Perrier, no doubt planning at least one run later that afternoon, Henk took a large glass of Pinot Noir and the girls shared a bottle of Rosé from the Provence. Stephanie could not resist telling the exact location of the wine producer, "this comes from a small vineyard just behind Saint-Tropez, Ramatuelle, we buy cases every year."

The Italian waiter proposed the large round corner table, most likely to keep the enthusiastic loud voices away from regular guests. Six menus were placed neatly on the large red napkins and the waiter stood by the table for a good twenty seconds more but nobody noticed him. The volume was increasing.

As glasses were emptied quickly, conversation was rapid; the wonderful aroma from the kitchen tempted an early move to their corner to make a selection from the menu. Some heavy mountain food perhaps, maybe tartiflette or cheese fondues? Arno insisted on Foie Gras, "the only starter possible today."

Stephanie knew her man as well as any woman. She was not concerned, but Arno was suspiciously subdued this day. His was normally the first voice to be heard in the room: a quick wit with character that appealed equally to men and women. Today he listened more than he talked.

Eventually after several attempts their eyes met. Stephanie nodded a silent *okay* with her lips. Arno stared as if he was not entirely sure who she was then immediately snapped out of his trance.

"Fine, fine," he said so that the whole table heard. After a second the moment was forgotten, but not by Stephanie.

Something was on his mind. He had been the normal Arno when they got up, but a different Arno by the time he returned from the park. Fine company excepted, this could be a day to return home early. Something was bothering her husband.

By the time coffee was served it was 3:30. Stephanie had already whispered to Arno, "Let's make sure we leave before the rush, skiers going down the mountain."

Out of character for Arno, he did not resist. His reply was a simple, "Okay, darling, if you're happy to drive. Whenever."

Outside, there were kisses and long embraces in the car park, then into the cold cars, the sun having left the area at least an hour before.

Stephanie led the cars out, knowing Arno would have it no other way. Within seconds they were alone, their friends making their way towards a log fire at their mountain homes. Stephanie concentrated on the long winding descent towards the autoroute; Arno closed his eyes whilst thinking of the day's events.

Back at the chateau, Stephanie took a long lazy bath while Arno prepared a light salad. He warmed a flute in the oven and poured two large glasses of Chablis. As they sat close together at the kitchen bar, Arno again displayed the same lost look.

Stephanie could not hold back any longer.

"Talk to me. What's on your mind? This is not you. What happened today?"

Arno knew it was time to come clean, but what could he say?

"Look Steph, this morning things happened so fast. I'm not the fittest, but those guys in the garden gave me the creeps. We're all in possible deep you-know-what with the tax here. Now these people show up. Could this place be, I don't know, a new site for a hotel? Are they planners?"

"Arno Van Bommel, big Dutch business man, have you lost it? You know how the French love their history. We live here in an historic monument. They would never destroy this place, no way. So many rules to protect it, it's really not possible. Anything else on your mind?"

Stephanie was even considering the fact that Arno could be interested in Eva. She was a true beauty, a few years older than herself, but who knows, men living in France have been known to act out of character.

"To tell the truth, I'm confused."

"Oh no," said Stephanie softly, "here it comes."

"My mind keeps trying to show something, like a picture, a graphic, but the view is just not clear. When you looked at me over lunch, I thought I had it, but nothing came. It's like a need to understand something, but it won't come out."

Stephanie looked relieved. Maybe the stress of the recent problems was weighing on her man. Best not to push more today.

"Let's have an early night, a swim tomorrow, time to relax a little. Things have been heavy lately."

They left the bar cluttered, maybe for Stephanie to clear the next morning, maybe the maid. Today's problems needed closure.

After fifteen minutes they were warm, close and almost asleep.

"Yes, that's it..."

Arno's voice almost made Stephanie scream in panic. She rose quickly from the soft pillow.

"That's what?" her reply tense almost angry. "What's happening, tell me?"

"I did see something on that laptop before he closed it."

"So please, tell me what?"

"Well it looked like mountains with lines moving below them, strange colours."

"Arno, darling... France is famous for its level of medical care. I am so happy we live in this country. Tomorrow, I promise, we'll visit the doctor; get something to help calm you down. This was the big headache today?"

"Sorry Steph, it comes and goes."

"Sleep honey, please sleep."

Within five minutes Stephanie was deep asleep, but Arno laid awake seeing mountains with coloured lines moving below them.

9

"Can we slow down a little, please Dan? My legs are starting to burn."

Louise, a rather sexy advertising executive from a premier London ad agency was aching. Her friends, Sandy and Brenda, were determined to show that they could keep up. But Dan knew they were all showing signs of spring snow fatique. The tight parallel style from earlier morning was less tidy now, plus the late season snow-cover had lost its morning texture, the afternoon sun had made it soupy and hard on the knees, even for the pros.

"Okay ladies, let's take a break. There's a nice sunny terrace about half a kilometre from here.

Give some time for the legs to recover, also my dry throat ..."

"No problem, Dan. I could carry on all day," said Sandy, trying to impress the man, whilst at the same time skiing past her friends.

Dan knew the type well. He could guarantee that she would try her utmost to seat herself next to him on the terrace then probably ask, "If my friends are tired later, maybe we could make a couple of runs together?"

A couple of years ago, maybe, he thought, but his life had changed so much recently. He was sure more grey hairs were showing. The once eager, quick-response-Dan of old was gone. Now a more reluctant half smile replaced the one-time eager beaming ladies man. The people from the *fisc* were taking their toll.

The wooden terrace was close to full. Afternoon sun worshippers and relaxed lunchers meant that tables were moved from inside to out to accommodate the extra late guests. Sun-beds were turned to follow the afternoon tanning lines. Waiters stretched to clear the empty glasses.

As they removed helmets and adjusted sunglasses, Dan spotted a small table with four chairs close to being vacated on the edge of the terrace. He upped his pace; he could easily run in ski boots, stop, turn, slide, the benefit of years on the mountain. The departing family seemed almost pleased to see such a handsome man with his entourage taking their sunspot, the mother with a warm smile and raised eyebrows seemed tempted to wish him, "a nice afternoon." But her husband's hand behind her back persuasively suggested maybe not.

As Dan suspected, Sandy almost knocked the tray from a waiter's hand and managed to place herself next to him, edging her chair closer as she sat.

Louise and Brenda were more relaxed, surveying the bronzed male population and watching any new arrivals from behind their designer shades.

Dan detected at least five different languages. In honesty he preferred this time of the season; more relaxed. The January crowd always appeared to be more on the move, possibly due to the cold.

These days for him were more about getting the job done: keeping the clients so-so happy, then going home to the chateau, checking the mailbox and catching up with Jack, Arno and Henry. Following his heavy confession during the boys ski day out, he was relieved, even comforted by the reaction of his close neighbours. They understood his position as he understood theirs. This was an attack to fight together: guys all in the same corner.

Sandy now rubbing knees with her ski teacher thought it best to turn up the tempo.

"Dan darling, an old flame is in town tonight. He's pestering me about dinner, but ... he can be a pain, never knows when to stop talking shop. Okay, he has worked on some serious campaigns, for sure, and a great deal less vodka would have been consumed without his copy writing skills but I prefer talking about sport, mountains. Are you free?"

Even for a man as chat-up-line-experienced as Dan Lancaster, this was direct. His mobile suddenly came to life. He swiftly turned his head away from Sandy.

"Hi this is Dan."

"Dan, kick whichever girl is sitting on your lap off now. Jack here."

"Hi Jack, what's happening?"

"Kind of strange visitors here, at the chateau. Where are you, far away?"

"Megève, small party with me, but if you need I can get down the mountain fast. Car's close, guess back in around an hour."

"Do it, please. A van, no markings just arrived, three local-looking guys. Seen them carrying weird rods and things towards the cellar, but I have a client here. Arno is in Holland, Henry still not back from Geneva, Eva, the others ... well, rather you checked it out. Sorry."

Dan drew a crafty smile across his tanned face, pushing his glasses higher with his index finger. This was exactly what he needed to escape the advances of Sandy.

"Uh, ladies, so very sorry, but something has just came up. Kind of emergency where I live. A neighbour needs my help so would you mind if I leave quickly? One more easy run to the base station. You're all on good smooth snow here."

Sandy's knee moved like a karate champion. Suddenly the handsome ski teacher was not the dinner date. Better to relax with her own kind.

Copy writers can be so very entertaining...

Louise, the most mature by far handed Dan his helmet. "Go darling, the drinks are on us. We'll give you a call for the next day together. It was truly super. Thanks again."

Sandy was already focused on a French ski teacher two tables away. After polite kisses on the ladies cheeks, Dan moved off the terrace like the pro he was, sticks in the left hand, skis thrown into parallel position, boots clicked into bindings, sliding from left to right through the new arrivals, bending to click the upper boot fasteners. The three girls could not resist watching him leave, even Sandy. This was a cool man in action. In no time he was over the crest, out of sight and moving at a pace few of his clients could ever dream of matching.

Within ten minutes his Jeep was winding its way out of Megève.

As he took the many sharp bends, tyres screeching under pressure towards the Autoroute, he began to feel good. He was experiencing a feeling that had been missing for so many years: the empty life of a different girl, different bed every night held little value for him now, despite the misery of the tax inspection and the undeclared Swiss bank account. Dan had good friends in his life; guys who would go the extra mile for him. He felt like part of a team again like the old days; much better than the bimbo lifestyle he had become so accustomed to.

His mobile announced a text from Jack:

Locked into this meeting for some time yet, are you close?

Dan left a voice message: "Say another half an hour. I'll go straight to the cellar, pretend I'm busy with skis whatever, see what they're up to."

Jack was in full swing. His British client was enjoying the presentation and asking only the standard questions.

"You know well, Jack, that the returns on cash are awful these days, not even protecting me from inflation. Even if you get 5, maybe 6% a year, I'm happy."

Jack was doing what he did best, selling investment ideas to private clients. This was a clear buying sign from the man. Jack offered him another coffee, which was really an excuse to check if the white van was still in place. It was. Jack itched to leave the meeting and visit the cellar, but business was slow with Europe in crisis. He needed every deal that came his way. This client should sign the investment forms before leaving, but only then could Jack feel relaxed, when the job was done.

Henry happily closed his empty mailbox door, got back into the car and guided the vehicle with one hand slowly towards the underground parking. As the automatic lights flicked on he spotted the half-open door to the cellar.

"Sloppy bastards," he said angrily. "Just close the bloody door. It's not summer yet."

Pulling his small briefcase from the passenger seat he turned, focused on the door, strode towards it, ready to kick it shut. Voices from inside the cellar caused him to curl his head around the partially-open metal door. The voices were louder now. As Henry eased his large frame around the door he saw three men, close together bending down in the middle of the cellar. Instinctively he felt compelled to say something. "Bonjour, you guys sorting out the heating system? It's a pain..."

The two larger men stood rapidly, looking nervous and uneasy. Henry gazed at what appeared to be a long black rod driven deep into the cellar floor; the screens of two small laptops flashed with what he quickly judged to be some sort of mountain view with many lines around it. He was so focused, so determined to mentally register a clear picture that he missed the large metal hammer launched in his direction. The blow on his forehead was direct and stunning. His back smashed against the cellar door, his briefcase burst open and papers fell out, scattering between his shaking legs. Instinct caused him to close his eyes tightly. His breathing immediately reached a panic level; he began to choke, the oxygen he so desperately needed was not available. His lips whispered his wife's name, as if she could help him ... "Annabel."

"*Allez vite, prenez l'ordinateur, allez, allez*"

The cellar door smashing into his bleeding head.

"That's a little urgent. Not much respect for the nature in this beautiful park."

Jack's client was easing a rather dated green ski jacket on whilst gazing out of the office window. Jack turned his head quickly away from the signed contract on the table.

"Sorry, someone was doing something daft in the park?"

"Yes. Look at that white van, almost flew out of the garage, nearly hit the beautiful palm. Now it seems he's trying to push the gates open with his bonnet."

Jack quickly decided something was wrong, maybe more than wrong. Even if this had been the biggest deal in the world, it was not, he had to get to the garage. The overpowering need to visit the cellar made Jack's speech rapid and stressed.

"Well, thanks for coming today. I will look after everything as we agreed. Look forward to a long and profitable relationship together. Can I show you down?"

"Thanks again to you. Left my car at the front. Sorry, have a history of getting lost in garages."

Jack's mind was elsewhere. "Oh what a shame."

As he opened his client's car door, followed by a final handshake, his body language was obvious: he had to be somewhere else. As the client manoeuvred his Toyota slowly towards the main gate, Jack was already half-way down the slope into the garage, he could smell the burnt rubber and exhaust fumes. He took in large gulps of air. Something had happened. He took every corner wide, just in case. The cellar door was closed, but before his hand touched the door Jack saw a trail of red footsteps. He shook his head in confusion.

The door could only open a quarter of its normal movement.

Jack focused on the open briefcase and strewn papers then coiled his head around the door.

"Henry, what the hell happened, man? Henry... Henry..."

Blood covered the whole of Henry's face, and was still pouring from a large wound above his right eye. It dripped down his neck and disappeared into his once blue shirt. The body was motionless. Jack bent over trying to detect breathing and the weak, short puffs caused Jack to jolt back, shoving his hand into his suit pocket. He hit 18 on his mobile, the French fire emergency accident service.

Within two rings his call was answered, "Bad accident at the Chateau Montjan. Need your help very quickly. One man, severe head trauma, he looks bad."

"Okay, we are on the way. Do not move him. Keep him warm, a blanket maybe, but leave his head alone. We know what to do."

Jack was torn between the best way to aid his friend and the advice just given. As he tried to collect his thoughts, the automatic lights went out. He turned to push the small round plastic button behind him, and pressed it twice, which illuminated the whole cave instead of just the first section. Turning back towards the long cellar's centre aisle, Jack saw a large pool of water forming, now only two metres away from Henry's body. Once again Jack experienced the feeling of needing to help his friend, at least to make him more comfortable. Fortunately, the the sound of the approaching sirens, the *pompier-SAMU* stopped Jack from making things worse.

He ran across the garage and as he neared the end of the parking bays, he saw that the now-dusty uncared for Audi of Pico Latouch had received a hit to the front. A large white scrape ran along the bumper, the number plate hanging by one screw.

"The bastards," said Jack angrily, "if Crappy is behind this again ... Where the hell is Dan?"

The *pompier-SAMU* vehicle arrived at the chateau gates at the same time as Jack. The large red vehicle came in rapidly, followed by Dan's Jeep. Jack waved his arms indicating they should follow him and ran back into the parking.

"He's in here. Be careful with the door, he's behind it."

The four men in sombre black uniforms were calm. They had experienced everything in their chosen profession from autoroute crashes to shocking ski deaths. They moved swiftly towards the cellar, arms already loaded with familiar-looking equipment to assist the motionless Henry.

Jack knew the questions were imminent, questions he didn't particularly care to answer, but which the *pompier* in charge had to ask.

"Do you know this man? What exactly happened to him? This doesn't look like an accident."

Behind the cellar door a flurry of noise and activity was taking place. The chief stared towards the ground, holding silence for what seemed to be many minutes.

Jack and Dan felt powerless as as they heard one of the *pompier* start talking to the control centre. The urge to look behind the door was strong, but equally strong was the need to let the professionals do what they did best. Time did not exist for this period. Henry must come through ...

The chief was now behind the cellar door talking softly on his mobile. Suddenly an eyrie silence filled the garage. Then Jack and

Dan watched as the pompier team placed the emergency equipment back inside their vehicle. As the chief came across to Jack and Dan he then looked towards his sombre looking colleagues their heads bowed, slowly moving from side to side.

"*Je suis désolé, mais il est mort.*"

Dan placed his hand on Jack's shoulder. Both men took a very deep breath.

Their faces telling all. He cannot be ... No, not Henry, not dead.

Jack glanced at the chief *pompier*: Henry had been murdered.

Jack turned to Dan thinking: how the hell can they break the news to Annabel. Jack returned his gaze to the *pompier*.

"This man is a close friend of ours. He came back from a meeting and ..."

"Let's wait for the Gendarmes, Monsieur," advised the *pompier* chief.

But Jack needed to talk ... he just needed to. "Three guys arrived here earlier this afternoon in a white van. We're normally informed of any work that needs to be carried out – we all jointly own this place. I thought it strange so called my neighbour, Dan, to check what work was being done, but Henry arrived first. I can only guess he disturbed them, but what ...?"

Jack tailed off staring at Henry's motionless body, now half exposed behind the cellar door, the blood congealing around the wound. Jack desperately wanted this to be a dream, but it was not. And Annabel would be expecting Henry home soon.

Two vehicles entered the garage: the blue Peugeot of the *Gendarmes* followed by a long black van.

The *gendarmes* spoke rapidly to the pompier chief, and then approached the cellar talking quietly to each other. Leaving his partner to start the scene-of-crime process, the senior *gendarme* approached Jack, doubt all over his face.

"Bonjour, monsieur, were you the first person to discover the situation?" The *pompier* chief showed relief knowing he was no longer alone with a potential hammer attacker.

"Yes. He's a neighbour of mine. Henry Cameron. We all own apartments here. I was having a meeting in my place. I asked Dan here to check out three guys who arrived in a white van but they left in a massive panic before he arrived, so I came to see why and found Henry Cameron like this."

"Why would he be attacked by workers? From the amount of blood it looks like a severe attack. Can you describe the workers?"

Jack hesitated. "Three local-looking guys. Saw them from my window, you know typical ... maybe plumbers, carpenters ... I don't know."

The senior policeman instructed one of his colleagues to make an urgent call.

Photographs were being taken of Henry, the constant clicking sound and flashing light confirmed he was never coming back. More police personnel arrived with large metal boxes. Protective clothes were pulled on, glasses and mouth covers with a high degree of urgency. Now at least six men and women surrounded the one-time chateau comedy guy.

The third gendarme, who'd been continuously busy on his mobile since arriving, now turned to Jack.

"You can imagine, Mr ..."

"Oh, Jack Rafter."

"We have to treat this situation as suspicious. It's a possible murder, until someone can identify the workers. I need both of you to come to the police station. It will take some time."

The voice of the senior policeman came across as calm and collected. This was certainly not his first encounter with a murder scene.

He continued, unimpressed with the emotion shown by Henry's friends. "This area will be closed off for some time. A forensic team will arrive to search the area. We need to know exactly what happened here, and why. Anybody who cares not to comply will immediately be arrested. Do you understand?"

Both Jack and Dan took a step back. "No problem, of course. We also want to know why our friend has been ... well taken today." This was the best Jack could manage.

Yet another police car descended into the parking. A short exchange took place between the chief and the new arrivals, two women and one man, all casually dressed. They immediately took tape from the boot and began to seal off a large part of the parking area around the cellar. White plastic suits were opened from a sealed bag and pulled up from foot to shoulder; two large black cases were placed by the cellar door.

"I think it best if you go back to your apartments now, but give me your contact numbers. I will be in touch soon, at the latest tomorrow. Could you show me this man's apartment? It's now my unpleasant task to inform his wife."

Both Jack and Dan knew by exchanging glances that the next few minutes would be a dramatic moment they would never forget.

Annabel opened the door smiling, the smell of freshly baked cakes wafting through the air. Her smile fell away as she locked eyes with the sombre-looking gendarme. Her head began to shake, her beautiful green eyes immediately filled with water. Moving her head from Jack to Dan, her legs began to give way. Jack thrust the gendarme sideways as he reached out to catch Annabel.

"No, Jack, he can't be. Please tell me, no, this is not real."

Jack held Annabel as tight as he could; Dan put his arms around both of them. The gendarme stared calmly at the floor. Again, not his first time.

In a small bar close to the lake of Aix les Bains, unknown to the tourists because of its backstreet location, three local workmen were enjoying their third glass of wine, sharing jokes in a heavy Savoyard accent about a man badly damaged by a hammer blow to the head.

"Bet the bruise will last at least six months ..."

The three men could not resist constantly checking the tight brown envelope in each of their back pockets.

10

Geneva was beginning to show signs of winter's end. Tourists were arriving in the customary large tour buses, cases blocking the entrances to the best hotels. The visitors seemed to be mostly from China on a punishing see-Europe-in-ten-days schedule.

The occasional cabriolet braved the city centre, the locals again taking interest in the lake, as opposed to rushing past the large expanse of cold grey icy water.

Didier Grass made an early start. Living along the lake in a suburb of Lausanne he hated the traffic queues which seemed to form earlier and longer every year. He sometimes chose the boat if his day was office-bound, but this particular day he was expecting an important call from an old university friend in Zurich, so the late winter chill on the lake was no match for his plush Bentley Azure.

He placed his two mobile phones neatly on the desk in front of his large HP computer screen, prepared a clean sheet of writing paper and hoped that his secretary, Celine, would bring coffee before his Blackberry rang.

Celine always preferred the early routine at the firm's office. Living in Annecy, a twenty to twenty-five minute drive away, this was not such a hardship, although today she was intrigued. Grass greatly appreciated Celine's incredible research work – many compliments came her way, making her feel special in her boss's eyes.

On this Wednesday morning she recalled the short conversation from earlier in the week.

"Join me early on Wednesday, please Celine. Depending on a call I receive, it may be necessary to delve into a couple of large corporations. I need to know a lot about these players. The accounts are important, but certain areas of their activity may be of real interest for me. I'll tell you more on the day."

Both smiled warmly at the same time. Didier Grass had seen more than his fair share of treasure hunters file through the firm: from the body beautiful to the aspiring legal top gun, they never survived. This firm was too serious for most, old Swiss money and contacts. Image seekers were not welcome or tolerated.

Celine was confident and happy working for Bayer, Merlot & Grass. She was somewhat plain but as reliable as they come, never failing to fulfil her tasks to the bosses satisfaction.

"Good morning Mr Grass, I do hope everything is ok today. Coffee is a maximum of two minutes away. Breakfast? Or maybe it's a little too early."

"Yes, let me get this call taken care of first, and then depending on the content of the information, breakfast may or may not be welcome."

The Blackberry began to turn slowly on the table.

"Coffee's on the way, Mr Grass."

"Carl, good to hear you again. Life good in Zurich?"

"All fine here. The snow has left the city, but it's still great in the mountains. I spent last weekend at my Dad's place in Davos. Super conditions."

"Lucky for you. My skiing times are shrinking, the work increasing. I think I need to increase my hourly fee..."

"Not sure which is the worst, Zurich or Geneva? We are both getting a well deserved reputation for charging some of the highest fees in Europe."

Both men were slightly uncomfortable now, feeling that the opening chit-chat routine had gone on long enough.

Didier threw the business opener, thinking it best to recap.

"Well anyway, I guess your brother passed on all the information I gave him. Don't think I missed anything. A strange situation. A group of fairly wealthy, interesting clients, living in a beautiful chateau an hour south of here, being seriously pestered by the local tax office. And now it seems, and this is a surprise to me, they are being investigated for non-declaration of assets, which, if this goes to the wire, are far more substantial than the recorded values listed in France. This is why they're so worried and talking to me. It's like the administration has been gifted a list. I've never come across such a focus in this way before, especially as most are recent fiscal residents."

Celine brought in the coffee on a small silver tray, two brown sugar cubes as always, but never making eye contact when her boss was under such high concentration. The pending answer from Carl was far too important to allow a short thank you.

"Yes, the best person I know in these matters is my father. You remember he spent years in Paris, involved in some incredible situations. The politics that played out sometimes blew me away. I could not get my mind around some of the stories shared over dinner. He prepared me for this business, but I barely remember getting the university degree"

"Yes Carl, George is an impressive man. If I live to one hundred I doubt I would ever manage to accumulate such a network as his."

Carl continued, but said little of value.

"His contacts were made before technology screwed up our lives, clandestine meetings in old bars and coffee houses in the old parts of the city. These days you can bet he will soon be the victim of a long-range listening device. I hope he retires before that happens."

Didier was getting anxious. He recalled Carl being a popular student in Lausanne, guaranteed a good career because of his family and his father's contacts, but this made him lazy, and struggle to get to the point. Time to go up a gear.

"Look Carl, I see something strange going on here. I feel the tax authorities are trying to conceal their real motives. It could be that people are hiding behind one another. Okay, they often try that tactic, but what does your father know about this? Is this the same old, or is it something to dig deeper into?"

"My father tells me the tax officers are far more aggressive than ever before. Doing their research, they are well prepared before they even contact the possible evader. Certainly they are under pressure from the government to collect the maximum."

"Think we all know that, Carl ..."

"He also confirmed how they are using far more dubious tactics."

"Sorry, Carl, but I'm not exactly getting electrified here. It's the tax not the local boy scouts..."

"Okay, Didier. I well remember you are not a man to linger in a conversation when you are on a trail. My father is rather sure that this is not about the tax inspection, not about the amounts involved, although they certainly need the money. Unemployment going up around one thousand per day."

"Keep it boiling, Carl, please. I know all this..."

"My father could not get to the final hurdle. It appears even he cannot get total disclosure, but from his extensive experience he, well, he feels sure the tax office is being used as a front. They have the perfect excuse to enter anybody's life, delve into it. However the lives of your clients are not so exotic. He thinks that this is some way of getting back at, say, business tricks, someone paying off an old debt."

Carl said that George had checked out the chateau location and found that the local mayor was an old lunch buddy from his Paris days. The chateau's a wonderful monument, with rich grounds worth a lot of money, so a possible developer crossed his mind. But with the French administration they would never get planning permission; all protected ground; the old guard would come down like a ton of bricks. That part of France doesn't have any worthwhile mineral deposits underground. It could be the site of a battle, some value there, but why involve the tax office?

Didier was getting fed up. He scribbled some brief notes on his pad and finished his coffee. Carl was being the old friend he remembered from university days, taking the easy route. His bills will get paid anyway; he thought to himself, but Carl, for Christ's sake, man up and say something concrete for once.

"Okay, Carl, what I get from this is the following. Your father thinks a tax inspection is a cover-up for some other plot or plan from another party, I'd already thought the same. Maybe someone sees another plot here, but the total sum of ruin for the owners still leaves me wanting. Sure the tax office gets a big pay day, assuming they find all of the undisclosed assets and can get them sold in the current financial climate, but I still have a massive *why* going around my head. This is priority number one for me."

Carl breathed in. "Sorry Didier. My father could come up with little more at this stage. Of course I will let you know if I get any more information. Strange for him. I got the impression he was holding back, but from me, his son...?"

"Thanks, Carl. Next time you find yourself in Geneva, lunch is on me."

"That's a date. Have a good day my friend."

Didier felt compelled to throw his Blackberry across the table. The expectation of a breathtaking here's-the-little-key-that-opens-the-dirty-deed had not materialised. Only what he suspected: that the tax office could be a cover for something. But what the hell could it be? His well-fed lawyer's ego was not accustomed to telling clients still-not-there-yet stories. He needed more, but from where? The last moments from the conversation played over in his mind: "holding back, but from me, his son?"

Celine arrived at the office door, looking eager to start on the promised research, but her female intuition told her to tone it down. Her boss looked pensive.

"Where shall I start, Geneva, Zurich, maybe Paris?"

"Hum, let's hold off on that for the moment. I need to look up some other contacts. Give it a couple more days, and then I promise you'll wish you'd never asked."

Celine took the coffee cup, smiled a knowing smile that showed she knew her boss was on the case and closed the door quietly behind her.

Didier weighed up who best to call first. From the four chateau residents he had met, not one deserved to get this breaking news before another. He was aware of the death of Henry Cameron. If only he could obtain more background on the remaining residents. He was sure they were all hiding a lot from the tax system, but that was not his first task.

His goal was finding the party who were perhaps co-operating with the tax office.

Arno Van Bommel's card came up first; he came across as a straight Dutchman who would appreciate the latest information.

Within three buzzes Arno picked up.

"Good morning, Mr Grass, this could be good timing. I'm taking coffee with Jack Rafter. I'll put you on speaker. Over to you."

Arno had never been good with the chatty opening lines so many like to use when starting a telephone conversation. He'd been brought up to be direct and get to the point.

"Are we doing a deal or not? Sweet talk me at your peril ..."

"Yes, good morning to you, Mr Van Bommel."

Feeling urged to move on Grass began.

"This morning I spoke with one of my old contacts."

Arno was already making yawning signs towards Jack.

"It's looking as I suspected. My contact's father by the way is a well respected lawyer. He knows Switzerland as well as he knows France, certainly Paris. Without, as I believe you say, beating around the bush, he is fairly convinced that the tax office is, well maybe, a cover for something more sinister. Sadly he does not at this stage know more, but I will be working on this."

In a smug manor trying to give the maximum confidence, Grass explained, "I have many contacts that could help with this but, as you can imagine, anybody with specific information will not be ready to impart this over the telephone. It may take a little more time, but I am confident with my firm's resources that we can dig far deeper into this."

Jack lifted his index finger towards Arno, raising his head ready to speak.

"Good morning, Mr Grass, Jack Rafter."

"Mr Rafter, good morning to you."

"Tell me; tell us, if this could be some greedy developer who managed to manipulate someone senior in the tax office? Of course, this chateau cannot be taken down, but if we panic and move out with the vast park around us, only five minutes to the city centre, a clever architect could develop a dream site here. At least thirty large homes could be built, say one million a piece, easily enough money to pay a hand-some bribe."

"Even for a large well connected developer this would be difficult. France has many old rules they cling to and they would rather die than give in to yet another housing development, especially around a beloved chateau. I feel some deeper digging is required."

Now Arno chipped in.

"Come up with something soon. This is really not pleasant waiting for the next recorded delivery letter to arrive, each time a little more pressure applied. Now they talk about the potential consequences if you have not declared all your assets ..."

Grass closed the call by confirming that he was seriously well aware of the urgency involved and promised an update in the shortest possible time.

Arno walked towards the kitchen mumbling something about "Big invoice, low work-rate bloody lawyers."

Jack asked for a coffee refill, but Arno was not listening. Instead he was staring out of his kitchen window. On the edge of the driveway, close to the chateau's main doors, a tall elegant woman was immersed in a telephone conversation, making gestures, up and down with her left hand, as she talked. She appeared agitated.

"Hey, do you recognise this woman?"

Jack stretched forward narrowing his eyes.

"Unfortunately not," said Jack,

"But I do remember Dan telling a story about a woman who looked rather like this one, who made a visit to Gerard Crappy some time back. Could be the same."

To the amazement of the men, a large black Mercedes then reversed alongside the elegant woman; the rear door was opened by a passenger allowing her to slide inside. Clunk and the chateau gates were already opening. Arno opened his mouth but no words came out. Jack provided the confirmation that they both knew.

"Like the other day. Geneva-plated Mercedes. You remember, Arno? The crowd in the forest? Just pissed off that Dan is not here. With his female radar he could have confirmed if this was the same woman."

"How can we check who's here at the moment? She didn't simply appear here. Somebody let her in, same for the Mercedes. Check the garage maybe?" Suggested Arno.

Jack and Arno moved together, both trying to get through the apartment door at the same time. This became messy and nature took over: fittest first. Jack, then Arno raced down the stairs. Jack had his key ready to open the large grey garage door. As it swung open, crashing against the wall behind, the automatic lights flicked on and both men surveyed the parked cars.

The Audi of the late Pico Latouch, untouched since his suicide, was gathering dust. Next the two Peugeots of Bernard and Sophie Mardan, the Dutch-plated Mercedes and Porsche of Valerie and Nina Osperen, the men's own cars and the badly parked Volkswagen Touareg belonging to Gerard Crappy. All the other spaces were empty.

Arno was still breathing heavily from the rapid stair descent. He normally preferred the lift. Jack was focused on the Volkswagen.

"We're no doubt thinking the same. Who has been so lost regarding neighbourly manners during the last months? Suspicious, almost avoiding contact yet strangely around at times like this."

Arno took a deep breath.

"Let's go to his place now, put some pressure on, tell us what you know or else. He's up to his French fucking neck in it."

"No can do Arno. I promised Carly I would not put the family in jeopardy because of him, even if he was behind the attack on my boys. If we're wrong, things could get even worse, and he could simply deny all knowledge. He could be too slippery to catch. We need some solid proof."

"You're right Jack, that's the only safe way."

That evening Jack checked the availability of rental villas in Sainte-Maxime, a four-hour drive to the south. With school holidays and the bridged weekends of late April and early May coming up, he knew a break was needed. The constant pressure of someone breathing down his neck was now showing in his tired face. What with a tax attack, his business under constant pressure from the negative market sentiment, Italy in February, Cyprus in March, Portugal in

April, the bad news never ending, a relaxed time on the beach with his family must be the answer. Carly would agree in a heartbeat.

Unknown to Jack, Arno was also planning a trip, but north to Amsterdam and not at all like Jack's relaxing trip with the family in the sun. This was based on Arno's growing hatred for Crappy. Since the attack on Jack's sons, all the remaining residents saw Crappy as the hate character they unfortunately lived close to. They were simply waiting for a chance to make him pay. Arno was fired up, whatever the cost. Some serious action needed to be taken.

Arno scrolled down his mobile phone contact list:

Boris Von Phren
Company Security Specialist
Amsterdam based, but available anytime, anywhere.

The trip was planned within half an hour. The collective noose around the owner's necks was tightening and urgent action was the only possible remedy.

Arno suddenly began to look forward to time in his homeland.

Jack only wanted to leave the chateau, look at his boys every day, relax with Carly and convince himself that all would be back to normal sometime soon.

The police came and went, they quickly realised that the chateau residents could never carry out such a despicable act towards Henry Cameron. Regular requests were made to the police as regards their search for the three workers in the cellar, but a Gallic shrug and lost shakes of their heads were their only answers.

Jack and Dan regularly trained together, their conversation so often drifting towards Henry and his special sense of humour. Annabel had decided to stay living in the chateau.

"How could I replace a family like the one I have around me here."

Dan wished the Rafter family a wonderful holiday, promising to look after everything whilst they were away. He assured Carly that Annabel would be his priority.

"I'll look after her like she's my sister."

As Dan closed his door, Jack and Carly climbed the stairs to their apartment. Something must break soon. Jack's stomach was too tight for comfort.

11

The route du Soleil is always busy from Easter to the end of September, especially the section from Valence-Avignon to Aix en Provence, the autoroute splitting, Barcelone to the right, Nice to the left. Cars from Switzerland and Germany filter together with the Parisians, Brits and Scandinavians coming from the North.

Jack was concentrating hard. After many years of living and working in France, he still had serious concerns for the French attitude to the automobile: too fast, too slow, or too busy, on the phone, eating, smoking, discussing the divorce, all whilst driving. It all happened on the autoroute. His sole intention was to get the family to Sainte- Maxime safely, and on time for lunch at La Voile on Nartelle beach.

Carly had observed a typical successful man-mood-swing of late and it bothered her.

"Do you really think you can switch off this week and forget about taxes and business problems?"

"This was my idea, so I should make it work," grunted Jack.

"But you have changed, darling. I've known you for so many years. At the moment you are often so deep in thought..."

"Sorry," was the best Jack could manage, his mind split between road safety and the last conversation with Arno.

If the Dutchman could really come up with the old contact that protected his car business security so well, would this man be prepared to come to the chateau and employ his technology to the owner's possible advantage? It would certainly uncover any deviations regarding the more reserved neighbours. Knowing Arno, Jack allowed himself a quick grin, yes. If anybody could do it, Arno would be the man.

Ninety-five kilometres to Nice. All going to plan. Jack could already taste his favourite starter: chicken nems.

"Hey guys, will you be joining me in our favourite dish?"

The boys answer came immediately although they were still focused on their mobile phone screens. "What do you think, Dad?"

"Could we maybe start with a large glass of rosé, full of ice," demanded Carly.

"By way of a change..." added Jack.

Early May and the temperature was almost twenty-six degrees. Soon the sign for Sainte- Maxime would show. One more toll, then the slow winding road to the town. After a long lunch on the beach, there was just the supermarket shopping to do, and then they'd move into the Villa Ste Rose, high in the Domaine du Golf.

Jack was certainly beginning to relax. He truly loved this part of the world: the air, a positive family atmosphere and the distance from the chateau all combined to help put things into perspective.

A good move, thought Jack. Pity he had to bring the laptop.

Jean Mark was already well tanned. He beamed at the car he knew so well, the usual Range Rover of the Rafter family. His parking area was only half full; his season still had far to go.

"*Comment allez-vous, mes amis? Bienvenue.*"

"*Salut, Jean Mark, trés bronzé déjà...*"

"*Oui, vous aussi dans quelques jours.*"

He received a mix of hugs and handshakes from the family and slipped into their car to park it, aiming for a place in the front row next to the beach road. Jack could never work out how Jean Mark fitted all the comings and goings into a rather small parking area.

Bernard smiled as his saw his regular clients walking towards the beach bar. The owner had reserved a table by the side of the sand, soft Latin music played; the Mediterranean was early summer blue. Jack surveyed the relaxed bodies on the beach and felt at home.

Again hugs and kisses.

"Vous restez ici tout l'été si possible?"

Jack gave a tight smile. If only that were possible. The pressure back home would not allow more than one week; he'd better start enjoying it.

"Malheureusement une semaine mais sûrement de retour cete été."

"Bon appétit, relaxez bien et profitez."

Bernard knew just how much time was required to welcome his clients whilst giving them space. The boys were already on the beach. Jack and Carly eased onto bar stools.

Two larges glasses of rosé with ice were served by a young French girl who believed in serious dental hygiene. Her smile was a wonderful welcome to the beach.

"In around one minute we will be starting our descent to Schiphol Airport. Please make sure your seat belts are fastened and trays stowed away."

Arno touched Stephanie's hand. For all his macho ways, flying still made him anxious. A stiff G & T helped but the concern was always just below the surface.

"Wow, Steph. Heaven forbid we hit an air pocket, or a strong cross-wind makes for a difficult landing." This wasn't the first time Arno experienced this. It was a common occurrence with the mix of the often stormy and volatile North Sea being beside the flat land of Europe, Holland.

All passed without incident. Then the long walk through the airport went on forever. The usual mix of travellers, every size, shape and nationality, from football fans to business groups passed on the moving walkways, at least ten different languages every hundred meters. A five-minute wait for the cases, then they were welcomed by the brotherly smile of Frank, Arno's big brother as the exit doors slid open.

"Hey, my French relations are here at last. Long time no see..."

"We were having so much fun living in a chateau, we forgot all about this crowded place..."

"From our conversations of late, the word *fun* seems to be a little misplaced. Now we're together I'm interested to hear what's really happening down there. The tax authorities here are also more of a pain than ever before. I closed my Belgian account just in time, the Luxembourg one is about to be cleared out and transferred to ... well, maybe it's better we talk about this in private. The car's across the road."

Arno agreed with the concerned look of a man who had been living under some pressure of late.

The black Mercedes gleamed as if it had hit the road only a few hours before. Frank loved cars and had worked with them his whole business life, like his brother. Stephanie took the back seat. She knew the brothers needed to catch up on so much so why not start now. The journey to Wassenaar would take at least forty-five minutes, and with the build-up of traffic leaving Amsterdam for the suburbs maybe longer.

"So now, tell me what those creeps are trying to do. Of course I'm also worried. A lot of this we planned together. I signed as much as you did. I never declared our restaurant in Marbella so if they investigate you it will eventually lead to me."

Frank was obviously more worried than was first evident at the airport.

"I really don't know," shrugged Arno. "From conversations with my close friends, you know the names, Jack and Dan at the chateau; we believe this is more of a focused attack. Even the lawyers in Geneva find it hard to swallow. They think it goes deeper than just a tax inspection, but even the best of their contacts cannot put a finger on it. Bloody bizarre and a pain for all of us. This was supposed to be a lazy retirement."

Arno's mobile halted the conversation. Jack had found time in his busy Ste-Maxime schedule to catch up with his friend.

"Bet you're thinking I should have gone South with the Rafter's... It's as good as ever here. What are you up to?"

"Well my chateau neighbour, just getting into the details with my brother in the car en route to his place. Frank and Steph say hi. Steph says don't get too brown ..."

"No time for that. May figure in my tax bill."

"Well, we're relaxing tonight and tomorrow I will try to get in touch with Boris Von Phren, the security guy. See what he thinks about getting involved in our situation. He usually has good ideas that normal people can't get their heads around. Don't worry, Jack, soon as I get something concrete you will be the first to know. Best we let Dan know at the chateau but the phones and email may be tapped. Come to think of it, what are we doing talking like this?"

"Arno, we're learning every day. That's why I'm calling you from my UK mobile on your Dutch mobile. Can't imagine they can get into these. The local French technology we leave alone for such conversations. Okay, gotta get back to the beach. Hugs all around. See you in one week, and don't forget only call if you have to, Dutch mobile to UK mobile."

"Got it. Get brown, drink a pile of Rosé for me. Over and out."

Frank smiled confidently towards his brother.

"Looks like you have a real friend in Jack."

"Yea, he's a good guy, solid, like Dan, but I feel for him. He's the only one with a family – teenage boys. If we had decided on kids, those two would be the perfect sons for me. Doing his best to keep all of this shit away from them, but I think he is ... well ... very exposed. If this goes wrong their life is blasted, and that's not on. Christ he hasn't killed anybody. Families like this should be supported, not destroyed."

"Maybe not, but these days if you kill somebody, you had a screwed up childhood. Mom never supported you; you get ten years, out in five. But hide some money, lie on the tax form, man you're a mega criminal. They do their best to take all you have and a jail term on top." Frank tailed off whilst easing back on the speed.

Arno shook his head. Above the car, a 747 was on its final approach to Schiphol. He let himself drift away for a few seconds.

Maybe the romance of a French chateau had clouded his judgment. A beach apartment in Florida or somewhere close to LA would have been far less complicated. Perhaps that's the next move. No, the biggest property investment he had ever made needed to be sorted out whatever it took.

Stephanie had closed her eyes. Frank, the superb driver he had always been, just cruised on. Now ten minutes away from the peace of a Wassenaar villa.

Jack updated Carly on his brief chat with Arno.

"Nothing special yet. He speaks with his contacts tomorrow, although I do feel a bit guilty. We're lying on the beach while Arno is doing his best to sort out the problems ..."

"Shut up and enjoy the holiday, darling. This was your idea, we all agreed, you have a family, so get into it. Your health may benefit from this, OK?"

Jack held Carly's hand, the other attracting the attention of the beach bar girl. She already had the bottle in her hand.

Boris Von Phren lived in central Amsterdam, close to the Vondel Park. He had loved the place since his parents moved there when he was five: from the easy bike commute to his office plus the great variety of restaurants. Every day he passed and greeted long-term friends and clients, lawyers, florists, bar tenders, designers, though most knew little about their friend's work.

"Some sort of heavy tech guy ..."

"Seems to be a security advisor."

"Bit of a smartass. Acts like he's the local Bill Gates ..."

This was the way he wanted it, a mystery profession. Secrecy rules. His style still retained a hippy look: faded jeans, bright shirts, the same style since he graduated from Rotterdam University, the best technology student the Profs had ever seen, if a little weird. No one could really figure him out or get close.

As he passed over the third canal of the morning commute, a call to his mobile made him bring the bike to a halt. The number looked familiar, but he was not so sure.

"Hi, Von Prehn."

"Is this Boris, the same Boris who protected Van Bommel Motors some years ago?"

"Yes, it's me."

Boris stared down the long straight canal. That had been one of his biggest jobs. He rocked from foot to foot smiling. Today could be a big day.

"Do you remember me, my brother? We remember you with a very positive influence on our business, especially those very tiny cameras."

"Same Boris, but now more experienced. Getting asked to travel out of Holland more and more these days. I have developed some killer set-ups. Really updated since my days at your showroom. I don't have competition, only serious solutions."

Arno nodded to Frank with his right thumb up.

"How quickly can we meet up, Boris? You're the specialist I need with some urgency."

"If you can make it, I'll be in Amsterdam all day. Is lunch possible?"

"Perfect. How about Café Zwart on the Dam, twelve-ish?"

"See you there."

Jack woke early, determined to keep the problems at the chateau, five hundred kilometres to the North. The recent letter from the tax office confirming he would now be investigated as a private person, on top of the continuing process against his French limited company, Rafter Investments, was on his mind daily. He kept this turn of events away from Carly. Maybe a smart decision, maybe a dumb one, but this holiday had to work for the family.

As he lay by the pool overlooking the golf course, which was busy for 7 a.m., his French mobile came to life. The screen announced Dan Lancaster.

"Morning, Dan, how are you today? More importantly, how's the situation there?"

"Jack, knowing you're an early riser, I knew you'd be up."

"No worries, Dan, family still sleeping. I'm just gazing at paradise and doing my best to forget where I live."

"Where we live is why I'm calling. I know we agreed to keep mobile calls discreet, but as this is really happening to all of us, I wanted to let you know that I've also received the letter confirming that a personal investigation will follow on top of the company investigation. So most likely they will speak with the IRS. Do these bastards ever stop?"

"Seems not. No time to catch our breath. Any idea if more letters have arrived at the chateau?"

"Passed Eva in the garage yesterday. Man, she's getting wild. You know how she can be, half French, half English in one sentence when she's pissed. She told me someone has to pay for this, slammed her car door and raced out of the garage."

"That may be a good thing. Eva seems one well-connected lady, but look, I have to keep this short. I can hear the boys are up. Arno is busy in Amsterdam, you know with what. Let's catch up next week together."

"Have a great break, Jack, you need it. Cheers."

Jack barely managed to slide his mobile into his shorts before the water hit him. His boys were up and in swimming mood.

"Still the same awful shirts. He must have made enough money now to buy some decent gear."

Arno and Frank spotted Boris Von Phren from fifty meters as they walked towards the café. Boris was already seated at a corner table, just as you would expect from a security specialist. An old Dutch couple were his only neighbours and they were more focused on the menu prices than the three serious Dutchmen about to commence a rather important meeting.

"Hello, Boris." Arno offered his massive hand.

"Surprised we could arrive at the table without you seeing us coming. Security business slow these days?"

"Excuse me, but you look like the same two guys who almost got neck cramp one hundred meters in that direction. But she was in very good shape ..."

Arno looked sheepish. "Okay, point taken. You appear relaxed but still see everything"

"Don't think two tough business guys would catch up with me after all these years and expect any less?"

Same smartass techie, thought Frank.

Now seated, the three men locked eyes and there was a let-battle-commence feeling at the table. Frank spoke first.

"Let me be clear, Boris. I loved your work for our business here, but today is all about my brother. Sounds like he needs your specialist skills and he needs them quickly."

Boris looked at Arno, raising his eyebrows, ready for the pressing news.

Arno cleared his throat and took a sip of cold Heineken.

"Since we last did business together, I moved out of the Holland for France. After the sale of the business I fancied a new life. Still love cars of course, but wanted more time to live, less time pushing paperwork."

"The sale of your business was certainly a big deal. I read the stories about the German buyers. They loved the security set-up."

"Well, Boris, even that complicated deal was a pleasure compared to what I find myself embroiled in these days."

Boris flashed a quick glance at the next table. The prices were still being discussed, but now with the waiter.

"We bought a large apartment in a restored chateau. It's a spectacular place; huge park surrounds us, very private as you can imagine, owner's gym, indoor pool. We have it all. But when we first moved in there were ten apartments, all occupied. In the last months two have become empty. One single guy committed suicide before Christmas, and a couple just disappeared never to return. And a close friend was murdered in the chateau cellar."

Boris tilted his head to one side. "Suicide, murder, living in such a cool place. What brought this situation along?"

"That's exactly why we need you my friend. Since early this year, several owners have become involved in a French tax inspection, a dirty one. In fact we suspect every owner has but a couple of them are ... well ... say acting as if life is a dream."

"Are they also Dutch or Brits?"

"No, French, and this is where things become strange. We have approached top-of-their-reputation lawyers, a Geneva law firm, and thrown money at them. Our accountants know nothing. These are the old business elite, very well connected men, but all we get back is, It's not normal to be targeted in one place, one chateau like this. Could be another source at work here.

And that's where the trail goes dead. We have our suspicions, but short of putting a gun to someone's head, we need to find solid proof."

Boris was feeling glad he got up this day. There was a trip to France in the offing, a chateau full, well, almost, of wealthy types. He could tap phones, utilise the latest camera technology, and hack any system he came up against. He was feeling confident the Van Bommel brothers had come to the right place.

"Tell me Arno, it's maybe a stupid question, but do the tax authorities have real reason to come after the owners?"

"That's a good question actually. Sad to admit but it seems we are all guilty of hiding money outside of the French system. Not only money but property, investments, you name it. We did our utmost to keep everything low key – you know mail kept away, secure computers, regularly change pass codes – but they appear to know things about us."

"Why are you smiling, shaking your head?" Enquired Frank.

Boris displayed a geeky show of confidence. "Sorry but computers are not that secure. Do you know how long it would take me to hack into your *secure* system at the chateau?"

"Probably by the time I down this beer?"

"At least before you put the glass back on the table."

Frank reminded Arno to mention the group seen in the chateau grounds.

"Yea, another weird thing, Boris. We've seen, and I almost caught up with them, a group of well-dressed business-looking types checking things in the chateau park. They followed a man with a laptop."

"Really?" Boomed Boris. "This just gets better. Did you see the screen?"

"No, not really. The bastard closed it just as I arrived. He was panic struck. However I did recall a misty picture later, maybe mountains, with lines underneath. But the place is surrounded by mountains. I think they could be engineers checking building possibilities, maybe."

"I could see that screen from a hundred meters away. Record it if you want. We can see exactly what they see, but they won't know I'm there."

"Great, Boris, but you'll have to be very careful. These guys are on another agenda, creepy." Arno now looked more concerned than at any time in the morning. "We assumed that the neighbours all being, say, semi-retired, with enough money, that the last thing we would need would be computer security. Why the hell would someone be interested enough in our background to organise a laptop party in the park?"

Boris had heard enough. He could never comprehend how street-smart business men always, but always, believed their computers were a closed entity. What they gained in deal-making expertise they lacked in tech knowledge.

"When would you like me to start? I'll come by car. Some of my equipment is not so airport-check friendly."

Arno suddenly felt a twinge of relief. Not only could he give his good friends at the chateau some positive news for a change, but Boris could shed light on what was really going on. This could be the best news for many months.

"We're back over the weekend. Can you make it next week?"

"Old clients deserve the best service. Is Tuesday ok?"

"Perfect. Let me know when you want to arrive. You'll have a large bedroom overlooking the park, desk, en suite. Tell me whatever you need."

"That's an important part of what I do. If I arrive looking like a consultant full of high tech boxes, any possible traitor in the building would be on guard. I'll place my gear into wine boxes and sports bags. Normal old buddy from Amsterdam hanging out with the guys for a week or two in a top luxury French chateau, a party every night."

"I think we can pull that one off."

Arno was improving by the minute. Where's the Dutch mobile? Jack needs to hear some good news ASAP.

Jack missed Arno's good news call. He was bouncing over the sea on a Jet Ski with the boys. Carly was reading on the beach.

Jack, call me back soon as you can, our guy is coming next week. He's the best.

Midway between Sainte- Maxime and St-Raphael, a party was being hosted onboard a luxurious Benetti Vision yacht, the lower rear deck full of well-dressed men in expensive Italian jackets, ladies in bikinis and shoulderless tops. The sparkle from the sun hitting the jewellery could be seen from a long way off. Jack's boys spotted the yacht, blinking from the surf and the reflections on the rear deck.

"Hey Dad, let's make a close pass by that craft. That's one cool yacht."

"How can I refuse? Maybe we'll get invited."

As the Jet Ski neared the Benetti, several heads turned, more in distaste than anything else.

Bums on jet skis, stay away, was the message of the body language.

Jack was covered in a mix of sun cream and sea water. That and his large sunglasses made any possible chance of recognition unlikely.

Suddenly a face in the party stood out. He stared at Jack; Jack stared back, his eyes narrowing. The face was standing next to a tall tanned man, most likely the Benetti owner.

Girls were laughing loudly, waiters jostled between them. This was a serious party. As Jack powered the Jet Ski away from the yacht, he allowed himself another glance back. The face was now leaning on the yacht rail, side by side with the best dressed man, still staring in his direction.

"Hold on tight, guys. I need to get back to the beach, make an urgent phone call."

"Yea, Dad go for it"

The Jet Ski bounced over wave after wave, the boys screeching in pure pleasure, Jack preparing the call in his mind.

As they slid onto the beach, Jack gave his boys their instructions.

"Tell them we will take the Jet Ski again later, but I need to make an urgent call."

"You got it, Dad. We're just behind you."

Jack ran along the beach towards Carly. It was obvious to those on the beach that this man knew how to run but his large frame caused concern.

"An accident? The sea looked calm. Maybe call the Pompier?" Could be heard as he ran past concerned-looking families.

"Hey, honey, give me my phone quick, please, the UK one."

"Where are the boys? What's up?"

"Nothing wrong with us, but I need to speak with Dan urgently."

Dan, even after years in Europe, retained his Californian accent. "Hi, Dan Lancaster."

"It's Jack."

"How's the break, Jack?"

"We have to keep this short, you know why. But I have a very important question for you. Is Gerard Crappy in the chateau at the moment?"

"No, think not, Eva told me he's been away this week. You know him. Dodge any contact, always keep it vague."

"Thanks, Dan. Then I'm right, he's here. It must be him. Bet my car I just saw him on a large yacht with some very wealthy-looking friends. But it's possible he also saw me ..."

"Not good, Jack, he's a sneaky little bastard."

"I know, but it's hard to hide on a Jet Ski. Look, thanks Dan. We're back at the weekend. Catch up then."

"Look after yourself, Jack. Kiss for the family."

Jack told his boys to stay on the beach, clearly to their disappointment. He ran back to the blue Jet Ski.

"Need it for, say, half an hour."

"Sure sir, long as you like. Enjoy."

At full power back towards St-Raphael, the boys watched their father pass two hundred meters from the beach.

"He really acts strange these days," Nick frowned.

Carly shook her head. "He's a guy like you two. Tell me, please."

The Benetti was moored in the same place, but the party was over. Jack allowed himself a disappointed, "fuck no." He so wanted to be 100% sure.

Making a pass close to the yacht, he could only observe crew members cleaning up after the party, and they had seen so many Jet Ski riders. Not even a disinterested glance came his way. He cruised slowly away from the craft. Time for a late lunch, but his appetite was missing.

"This is the Brit who owns the penthouse, Harvey. I give him maybe another two, three months max, probably less. He's in deep trouble, just like the others. It's all going to plan."

"So glad we never lost contact, Gerard."

The two men smiled politely at one another from behind the tinted glass on the upper deck.

12

During the business week, Harvey Lasalle resided in a glass tower on Quai du Mont Blanc overlooking Lac Léman, the old city of Geneva to the south, the lake stretching towards Evian les Bains on the south shore and Lausanne on the north. He was the CEO, COO and President of Best Global Investment Brands.

On the eight floors below his office, a five-and-a-half-day week of frenzied activity takes place from early morning to late in the evening. Directors, lawyers and accountants on the higher floors; marketing and design below; then administrators; and finally the reception, managed by two beautiful immaculately dressed Swiss girls. By force of habit, Mr Lasalle walked through the reception area every day. There was no real need as he had a personal lift from the garage to his top-floor suite, but in La Suisse, regular checks need to be made and this was one of his more pleasant daily duties.

Linguistically trained the Swiss way, should a German sales manager arrive, an Italian designer or a British product manager, all were made welcome immediately in their mother tongue, without a flicker of hesitation. Then, for the male arrivals at least, the treat of following one of the girls to the plush meeting rooms, one floor above the reception.

The rooms were spacious, well-designed, with subtle colours, facing the lake and filled with expensive furniture, mainly of Italian/Swiss manufacture; modern paintings covered the walls, mostly of the Alps by young modern creative artists. Large tinted windows kept the visitors cool, and below, a passing motor show: Ferraris, Aston Martins,

Mercedes and an occasional Bentley. For first-timers in Geneva, this was an impressive lakeside experience.

On this particular Wednesday morning, Lasalle displayed a look of worry across his tanned face. A man who always looked after his appearance, profiting from his remote alpine chalet in Megève to keep up a good winter tan and a mega yacht for other times, today his face was showing the years of business strain, meetings, battles with government administration, accountants promising an advantageous tax avenue that often became too narrow to escape from, clashes with competitors, and always the complications lawyers enjoyed bringing to the table, with yet another clause in the contract to make him feel, *protected*.

"We may be over exposed here. The competition will slaughter us if this is not covered."

They never believed in the straight and clear route to a deal.

"Get what you want whatever the cost," was his preferred way of doing business.

He stared at the dossier on his oval Italian glass desk. The latest monthly figures from his global empire had been delivered by his long serving chief accountant; Jean-Marie Pac. Jean-Marie knew the protocol well. If the figures were looking impressive, hang around, illustrate the better performing parts of the group, highlight the positive – a sort of invisible pat on the boss's back. Lasalle would then offer a coffee, or if the meeting occurred later in the day, something stronger may be proposed. Today the protocol required exiting the office as soon as physically possible. Leave the man ample time to reflect on the figures.

Lasalle knew this latest dossier would be difficult reading. The business world was in a slowdown, Chinese productivity showing signs of easing back, few figures from Europe looked promising and unlikely to improve anytime soon, the USA struggling to gain momentum. People were cutting back on everything, from cars to cosmetics. On top of this the media was doing its usual best to paint the picture darker, highlight the negative GDP and PMI figures. To heap further worry on his shoulders, the partners were pushing on new projects, proposing a move away from the old lines, luxury goods, chemicals, designer clothes and accessories, mountain water, Swiss food products, renting out office space in buildings acquired around Geneva over the years, mainly to financial operations. All were currently struggling. Banks were cutting back on staff numbers, regulation making business expensive. He detested the constant flow of letters from human resource departments apologising for the urgent need to, reduce their operation.

The pressure was now on to get out of the trough; find the growth sectors in any market. After all, this firm had a fifty-year history; Harvey's father having built the original blocks of the now global empire. But he felt vulnerable. So many of his old business friends had either retired or moved new blood into the firing line, fed up with the daily pressure. Harvey was not a quitter, but like his father before him, he would be happy to use any method, trick or contact to get his way.

It was 11:30. He tried hard to divert his attention away from the dark red dossier. Right now, another issue was more pressing and to move this along he needed to leave his office, take some fresh air, walk along Quai du Mont Blanc, through the Jardin Anglais for an appointment at the Hotel Métropole.

As he walked through the reception area, both girls gave the more radiant smile reserved for the top man, looking over the shoulders of a Spanish product manager who blamed his late arrival on the lack of parking in the area. The girls were having none of this, ushering him towards the smallest of the meeting rooms, knowing he would have a long wait for his Swiss director to descend from the seventh floor. Lia left him with a smirk on her face.

As he neared the hotel entrance, Lasalle saw a taxi pull up. A tall, dark-haired woman stepped out onto the pavement. He recognised Anna Tina Geisinger. Considering her chosen profession, she could not have looked more inappropriate, at one meter eighty-five, beautiful, olive-skinned, an almost model-like creature, dressed like a designer's dream. Her Victoria Beckham coat made her look even taller.

She walked into the hotel not looking left or right. He quickened his step. As Lasalle pushed through the revolving door, she looked down at him. He looked up the reception staircase to her; they exchanged a firm handshake and polite smiles, their formal Swiss German upbringing showing through.

"Good to see you again, Anna Tina."

"Nice to be in Geneva, Mr Lasalle."

The waiter showed them to the reserved table, Lasalle's favourite in a quiet corner with views towards the lake. Once seated, he could not hide his impatience.

"It's been a few weeks now. I hope you have some good news for me?"

Anna Tina knew how to handle demanding business types. Her father was one, her two brothers maybe even worse. In fact, much of her world these days revolved around such characters.

"Your contact would be more respectable to work with if he kept to the game plan instead of hitting on me. My work is very intense, exact. Small stressed Frenchmen do little for me, especially when they invade my personal space. Maybe you should buy him a toothbrush ..."

Lasalle smiled. "Come on, you can't blame him for that. You're not exactly everybody's typical geek. He feels somewhat favoured that you were chosen to do this job with him, he speaks very highly of you."

The reaction from Anna Tina was embarrassing for Lasalle. He was a well-known man in the Geneva business community and no one looked at him without speaking, most people babbled anything just to hold his attention, he was currently being stared at like an irritating schoolboy.

Now it was his turn to squirm.

"So... do you think we have extracted all the available information? Must be more ugly background in their computers. Are they feeling the pain, looking wrecked? Any more screws we could turn? I do need results very soon now."

Anna Tina preferred this more business-like approach. Business time was just like that, and downtime was spent with her endurance sport boyfriend. When working her current profession, that of highly qualified computer hacker, nothing could get in the way. There were too many stories these days of hackers ending up in jail. This was not a route Anna Tina even considered.

"You know, I only obtain the information. What your contacts manage to do with it has nothing to do with me. But from what I see, initially these folks are in deep trouble. They have really screwed up. The current fiscal witch hunt is, if anything, going up a notch. They thought they were too smart for the system: declare the minimum, hide the maximum. Now the system has them in a corner with the noose firmly around their necks. You remember the suicide before Christmas?

He panicked because of so many enemies in the French administration system. They were after him before we were, but it did unsettle the others. Another couple have already gone, hiding in an apartment in Thailand. Not a problem for us. The place is empty – had a panic attack and left overnight. The Brit, Rafter, acts like he's tough, always training with his friend Lancaster, but he'll get the worst news, under suspicion of hiding money for his client bank, in a matter of weeks. The rest, who knows when. Guess it's up to you as to how and when your old lady friend applies the final twist. But like I told you before, keep a close eye on the French woman, Eve Critin. She's classical old contacts. Could be a phoney but, and I can't put my finger on it, some of her mails are a little worrying ..."

Anna Tina's gaze became suspicious. "And the owner who was murdered in the cellar... I hope you had nothing to do with that?"

Lasalle cocked his head and sat back feigning insult. "Heard about it, but ... no terrible situation, poor man, how awful."

He then allowed himself a tense smile. "So, generally good news. Thanks. When can you be sure all their evil hidden secrets are extracted?"

"That will need another visit. I got close last time but the real dirt was hard to reach. Ran out of time. I've seen better, but their security is rather up to date. They constantly panic and change pass codes. The best situation would be when they are all away, then there's no chance of us bumping into one another on the same computer."

"You know I need these documents, real evidence. What we have so far is just not powerful enough."

"I'm doing my best. If I go too often they could become suspicious, I hardly look like I enjoy Crappy's company..."

"Okay, when you deliver this my contacts can proceed with the necessary pressure to achieve my goals. And from the way the global crisis is looking, sooner rather than later. Now I need to show my partners what a big fish I just hooked."

The coffee was quickly finished. Anna Tina almost jumped into the waiting taxi. Lasalle could not understand her urgency.

"Bank Larue, the main office."

Anna Tina needed to confirm that the latest fees had been transferred to her account, and then discuss a new apartment with her manager.

Back in his plush office, Lasalle bit the bullet. The latest figures were still sitting on the table – dare his secretary move them. He selected the Chemical Section reports first in the hope that this would make some cheerful reading, leaving Luxury goods for later, the firm being weak in China; this was one of the few places luxury was still selling.

Lasalle quickly became depressed with page after page of negative data. His only remedy was to make a call to a lady who could cheer up his day.

"Good afternoon, Madame Fouchard. How do I find you this afternoon? Positive I hope."

"Mr Lasalle, I was expecting a call around this time, but I do hope you are not expecting me to go into much detail, specific names, etc. This is not the first time I have asked you to refrain from calling me. Meeting in private is always my preferred choice."

Harvey Lasalle was feeling insulted, the second time in a matter of hours that a woman had put him down. Most women gazed at him in admiration. Two in one day had put him on the back foot.

"Sorry, very sorry. I am under some serious pressure. Just a general update is really all I need. Matters do seem to be taking a long time."

"Unlike your business methods, I must follow the law. I have to. This process will take time but the wheels are turning. I cannot disrespect the law. If I make that mistake, the high-fee lawyers whom these people use could tear me apart. One small error in the process and they will find it. Do you understand that?"

"I guess I have to, but tell me, do you have enough information available to increase the pressure? More is coming but when, I'm not sure."

"Your information source is impressive. Even after so many years of chasing tax evaders, being the director of operations in this area, I have rarely received such comprehensive information."

Lasalle allowed himself a confident smile. This was the best news of late. Anna Tina Geisinger had done a good job. Soon he could update his board, a day he was very much looking forward to: the main man back in full control.

"Thank you Madame Fouchard. Let's plan a quiet meeting soon. I will come to Annecy and invite you to lunch at the Imperial Palace. They know me well. I can promise a secluded table. Maybe plan a small celebration for late summer."

Madame Fouchard shook her head, nose in the air and teeth tightly clenched. She did not like the man, his tactics even less, but the promised use of his villa overlooking Tahiti beach close to Saint-Tropez, a fully cared-for week on his luxury yacht, and the envelopes full of fifty euro bills passed discretely every time they met up, made her tolerate even a deviant of this stature.

"Looking forward to it, Mr Lasalle, very much ...."

Before Lasalle left his office, he made a quick check on the cash balance in his wall safe. Because of the multitude of liquid handouts made lately, the code flashed through his fingers within seconds. Staring at the piles of crisp fifty euro bills he cursed his poor judgment for paying such a handsome sum to three dumb gardeners from Aix les Bains. Because of their panic reaction to what could have been a simple confused situation, that avenue was now closed for good. The chateau's cellar still had to be fully checked but it was imperative not to involve the police again.

13

HAVING RETURNED TO the chateau from some well needed down-time in the south, Jack and his family found getting back into the old routine hard. They were regularly the early risers in the building, preparing the boys for school. Jack felt positive, despite the dubious sighting of his questionable neighbour on the Benetti.

The boys dropped at school, he cruised into the underground parking, thinking how rarely neighbourly contact happened at 7:30 in the morning. He had the place to himself.

Striding towards the inner garage door leading to the gym, pool and stairs for the ground level floor, stretching his neck and yawning, he seriously wished the short holiday could have been longer. As he reached towards the handle, the door was rapidly opened in front of him. Two tanned faces stared uncomfortably at one another. Gerard Crappy had no idea what to say or do.

"Um, hello Jack. You look like you found some sun ..."

"You too Gerard, anywhere nice? You don't pick up a tan like that in this area."

Jack was struggling to keep the attack on his boys under the surface. He so wanted to put both hands around Crappy's throat and shake him.

"Oh, some business in Spain, Madrid. Um-huh well close to. An old contact needed some financial help. He's um selling a place, so yea."

Crappy was almost pushing his way through the door past Jack, his body language that of a very uncomfortable man.

"Really..." smiled Jack, his face showing the most disdain he could manage.

"Having spent a great deal of time and money on bronzing over the years, your tan looks the sort you pick up on the sea to me, deep brown…"

"Oh, oh if only. I would love to spend time on the sea again. Only a dream these days."

Jack noticed tiny beads of sweat on Crappy's forehead.

The two men stared intensely at each other; these were looks of insult and doubt.

"So to avoid us getting stuck in the door together, I think you need to pass." Jack looked down, shaking his head condescendingly at Crappy as he brushed past.

"Anyway, enjoy the day, Jack."

Crappy hurried towards his car, hitting the command at least three times. So Jack was right about the sighting in the south, and Crappy was as sure about it as him. No doubt possible.

Boris von Phren checked his GPS display. One hour remaining, ninety-five kilometres to the chateau. Time to call Arno.

"Hey, Arni. Boris on the road here. Should be with you in about an hour. Does that fit your plans?"

Arno was at first taken back. He shook his head at the casual voice, then quickly remembering, this was supposed to be an old mate from Amsterdam coming for fun. Of course he could not announce, *this is your tech consultant* on an open phone line.

"Sounds good, buddy. All looking forward to catching up. Did you bring enough wine?"

"All in the boxes. Will need your help to unload."

"Call me when you arrive at the gate. Jack and Dan will help us take it up from the garage. They look forward to meeting you."

"And when do I meet Eva?"

"When we allow it, and if we allow it… Ha"

"Okay, see you real soon."

Boris clicked his headset button to end the call whilst noticing motorways signs announcing places he dreamt of: Turin, Marseilles, and Lausanne.

Arno had given a detailed briefing to Jack and Dan, with the usual loud music playing in his lounge to drown any possibility of a secret device picking up their conversation. Now as they waited in serious anticipation for Boris to arrive, their exchanges took on a more positive tone after the recent events. Jack's sighting of Crappy in the south plus a top tech guy arriving this day, made for an atmosphere like the old days. A plan of sorts was more or less coming together.

Eva pushed Arno's doorbell twice in rapid succession, then again to emphasise her mood.

"Eva, what a pleasant surprise. Guess you're here to model your latest mini bikini for the guys. We're all here ..."

Eva rolled her eyes back, her large red lips pulled back tight over perfect teeth.

"Well, I could give a hundred smart answers to that question, dear Arno," his name pronounced with a slight Eastern European accent. "But the most appropriate is no. I'm here, as a person in exactly the same tax-attack mess as you all, and I get the impression that something is happening. Could you maybe let me in on whatever this may be?"

Eva gave an overpowering look which Arno found hard to handle.

"Well, of course, we're not trying to conceal anything, especially as you're getting hit like us so, please, come in."

Jack and Dan stood up in unison, half smiling and half focused on Arno, who stood behind Eva raising his eyebrows and shoulders whispering, "don't blame me, I'm not brave enough to stop her..."

Eva always appeared comfortable and relaxed in the presence of men, so chose the large red leather chair at the end of the lounge. As she sat, her short skirt became even shorter, her tight blouse, very tight. This gave the guys a brief where-to-focus problem. Dan pretended his shoes needed attention.

"So, as we're all in this focused chateau attack together, perhaps you could share the latest goings on, gentlemen."

The three looked at one another innocently for direction.

"Shall I make it easy for you?" Eva looked from left to right enjoying the moment.

"We all now know, from the recent letters, that they suspect us of not only transgressing French tax matters, but are now suggesting we all have money and assets undeclared outside this country. We've all been through the meetings. Even with my female brain I suspect someone or something has been sneaking into our very personal backgrounds. Am I getting warm here chaps?" The Eastern European accent became even more pronounced.

"Nothing wrong with your female brain, or the rest of you for that matter." Jack felt like a leader after the events on holiday. He continued. "You're right Eva, damn silly we didn't invite you here. Sorry."

The others nodded collectively.

Jack moved forward, determined to keep up the leader role.

"Over the last week, a lot has happened. Arno has a special business security contact from Amsterdam who he caught up with. This guy will arrive at the chateau today. We believe he can put equipment in place to well ... shall we say find out where our secrets are being exposed. The guy is at the top of his profession and one very impressive man."

Eva's large green eyes were only focused on Jack, an intense look that made him feel slightly uncomfortable.

"On top of this, I took the family for a break last week, to Sainte-Maxime. Playing around on a Jet Ski with my boys, we spotted a large yacht, a Benetti. As we got closer, I am now one hundred percent certain I saw Gerard Crappy on the deck. He was close to a very well-dressed man, who looked like the owner."

Eva nodded with an expression of agreement.

"This does not surprise me. If we have one doubtful character living with us it's him. If I ever hear it was him behind the attack on Nick and Simon, well, you know what I will do, Jack. But I heard he used to be in the yacht business. An accountant, so? But more importantly, what was the yacht called?"

The room stared at Jack. His roll as leader was heading slightly south.

"That's a darn good question. We um didn't get that."

"The flag maybe?"

"No. I was more focused on the people on the yacht. You know, my surprise at seeing him, but we can probably check these things somehow. Internet?"

Arno felt motivated, to add, "Boris arrives soon. He may know how to check this out. Jack, do you think you would remember the yacht from a picture? Maybe your boys have some?"

Dan now chipped in. "Not trying to be cool or anything, but I have, for my sins, spent some time in the South of France and on yachts. There are not so many large Benettis in that area this time of the year. Full summer, yea, sure, but this is early season."

Arno's mobile came to life.

"At the gate, Arni, and seriously impressed. You live here? Please let me in." Boris was in the area and on form.

"Head for the garage and park next to the Cayenne. We'll see you there."

Eva excused herself, the rising out of the red chair as interesting for the men as the earlier sitting. As she exaggerated her walk towards the door she felt good about living with such cool men, and nice guys to boot. Not a breed Eva had always been lucky enough to be associated with.

The men eyes were focused one meter above the ground. Eva gave a small wave with her left hand, sure that they would hardly notice it.

Boris opened his car door wide. He had never seen such a large parking space for so few cars. As he clicked his boot open, the three men appeared at the inner door.

"Hey guys, great to be here."

Introductions were quickly made. Even by Dutch standards, Boris felt challenged by the three large men, thinking to himself everything here was larger than life.

"The wine, the wine, show me the wine," sang Arno.

"It's all safe and ready to be appreciated. One box each, I'll bring my clothes. Please be careful, they are all *very* good years."

Boris was seriously impressed with his accommodation. In the distance he could see the Alps showing very little snow cover, but the afternoon sun gave a spectacular brightness, a sight Boris could never imagine from his cramped Amsterdam apartment.

The wine boxes were placed carefully on the large wooden dining table, everyone treating them as if the world's most expensive vintage lay inside.

"Join us when you're ready. Guess you need to freshen up after the journey."

"Thanks, Arno, or shall we stay with Arni?" Boris thought it maybe time to get back into respect-the-client mode.

"Whatever you like, as long as everybody sees you as an old Dutch buddy"

"A small point, Harvey. Maybe nothing, but could also be something."

Gerard Crappy sat by his second floor window, iPhone on speaker, careful to stay half behind the long green curtains. His head moved very slowly, following Dan Lancaster who was enjoying a mix of fast walking and slow jogging in the park.

"You remember the Californian ski teacher? He was very involved after that situation in the cellar."

"How could I forget, Gerard? An expensive mistake to believe they could simply check a few details for me ..."

"Maybe the pressure is mounting for me, but considering what is happening to this guy, his undisclosed Swiss account ... Of course, he knows the IRS will soon be on his trail, witness to a murder,... he's now taking a run."

"Yes, I know all this, Gerard. Where are you taking me? I have a directors meeting in ten minutes. So what, he's in the park!"

"He looks well..., rather happy, and that's not all. I was in the cellar earlier and heard a car arrive. I stayed there, behind the door. Some Dutch guy drove in. Within no time, Rafter, Van Bommel and Lancaster came into the garage, all real buddy-buddy with this guy. I could just see that they took several large wine boxes out of the boot. In no time they left for Van Bommel's apartment."

"So again, have I missed something here?"

"Simply, Harvey, would you be so happy in their situation, having friends arrive with oversize wine boxes? They should be packing moving boxes, not opening wine boxes. At least leave the boxes in the normal place, the cellar. This is not normal human behaviour."

"The pressure is getting to you. I'm also not immune. I had hoped this would be tied up by now. Just keep an eye on them. For sure, it's a last blast to pretend they didn't screw up. I hope to soon show them how much they did. The meeting's imminent. Goodbye."

As Lasalle entered the board room, two older Swiss directors were deep in a quiet conversation next to an original Kandinsky painting. The conversation halted immediately. The men took their seats. Harvey Lasalle was feeling more uncomfortable by the day.

"I can't believe this, it's so small. Is it a camera? Why did you not come up with this man before?"

Jack slid his knife around the edge, helping to open the wine boxes. Arno sat back, happy to wait for Boris's explanation, and Boris looked proud.

"I brought a lot with me. When Arno, sorry, Arni, mentioned this was a chateau, I guessed all sorts of wood, large dimensions and distance would need to be handled. This is one impressive beautiful building."

Arno looked serious. "What I hope will be a big advantage Boris, is that we live next to Crappy. Maybe even better, Jack lives above him. So depending on what you think, we must have generous options to see into his place. As you know, we all feel he's the rotten apple."

Boris had descended into geek mode, only focused on his toys being spread across the table.

"And this rings a bell from my military days, is it a ..." Dan was quickly silenced as Boris burst into conversation.

"Thermal image screen. This will tell us where his computer is, so I can place the camera in the best position."

"Can't we simply hack his computer? Did you see the Travolta film *Swordfish*? Must be easy for you Boris."

"Yes Dan, hacking into his computer would be easy for me."

Arno realised the smartass geek was back in town.

"First I want to check out his set-up, hence the camera. From Arni's briefing in Amsterdam we could be dealing with talents similar to my own. It would be a disaster if we alert him to my skills. He probably has all kinds of security, firewalls already in place, if he is the guy who's been stealing your data. So when shall we start?"

In her dark distant past, Eva often dreamt of meeting the perfect man. In reality she never came close, too possessive, too old, or just not a turn-on. She was rather attracted to Jack, and also Dan. Jack, happily married, put him on the back shelf. Dan? No, he would most likely get bored as she became older and revert to a firmer feeling bimbo.

After the hype of a man arriving from Amsterdam, Eva felt the need to check him out. After all, her past was virtually void of anyone resembling a geek.

Jack opened the door of Arno's apartment. Arno was busy wishing he knew more about the geek world. Even the best equipped cars he'd ever sold could not come close to the technology level inside Boris's wine boxes.

"And this gentlemen, is the quietist baby drill in the world. Similar noise level to a cat walking across a Persian rug. It's a ... wow."

Eva's long bronzed legs were the first thing Boris saw. He felt embarrassed sitting on his knees holding a tiny bright silver machine.

"You must be ..."

"Eva Critin and you must be the much awaited Boris Von Phren."

Arno and Jack exchanged broad smiles. Now their very own geek in a bright red shirt got the meeting he wanted. His mouth was open, eyes dodging between legs and face. Boris was stunned.

Eva felt pity.

"Only wanted to say hello. I guess you fellows are going to be far more familiar with the contents of these boxes than I will ever be. Please do a good job, Boris, this place needs to return to normality soon. I'm crazy about these guys and their families. Appreciate you coming to help us."

Eva gave a little wave with her left hand and turned, heading for the door.

"That was Eva?"

"No Boris, that was the cleaning lady. They're all like that in France. Come on man, she introduced herself. That really was Eva."

"Okay, ok, sorry Arni ... Did I explain about this small drill?"

Gerard Crappy seemed to spend more time in the chateau these days. He even made polite gestures, the occasional *"Bonjour"* to his fellow neighbours. Nobody fell for this. The people suffering managed to continue with day-to-day life as his mood appeared more positive. This was just not logical.

Within two days of his arrival, Boris had achieved high-quality thermal images of Crappy's apartment from the large wall in Arno's lounge, and even better ones from above using Jack's lounge and bedrooms. He decided that the best and probably only place to set up the camera would be next to a large marble fireplace in Jack's lounge. All of the apartments benefited from two rooms with fireplaces. Most residents opted for one in the main lounge and the other in the master bedroom. However Crappy chose to have a fireplace in his office. His office desk was measured at exactly 5.4 meters from the top of his fireplace, the exact position Boris intended to install the small camera. Crappy's large Apple screen sat in the middle of the desk, so focusing was going to be routine work.

"Arni, tell me, does this Crappy man have a cleaner?"

"Yes why?"

"Because there may be a small deposit of dust that falls from the hole I drill. The fire place is a good cover in winter, but at this time of the year I guess he's unlikely to use it."

"Everything is strange with him. Most of us use the same cleaning company, but he uses one woman. I think she's here on Friday mornings, but usually he's also there."

"Damn, the ideal situation would be Crappy out of the way and the cleaning woman busy. That would be about as close to perfect cover as we could hope for."

"Okay, I'm so dammed fed up with being under the spotlight, waiting for the next problem. Leave that to me. As soon as the woman arrives, I guarantee Crappy will have to leave his apartment."

Boris look bemused, but knowing Arno of old felt sure he'd sort something out.

Most evenings, Boris enjoyed the company of some of the friendliest people he'd ever had the pleasure to meet. There was a barbecue on Jack's balcony; his boys could not believe their luck: game talk.

"This guy knows everything."

Heavy wine consumption with Arno. Even visits to the health centre with Dan: swimming and light training followed by real American hamburgers. Sadly for Boris, Eva kept geeks at a distance, even if he did dress up in more subtle Ralph Lauren shirts these days.

"This is her now, always parks the car before the descent to the garage. Are you ready, Boris?"

"Never more so, but still not sure how you plan to get him out of the area?"

"Just leave it to me. Is this Crappy's apartment?"

"Yep, thermal image. I want to follow her work pattern. When she hits the office I'll start drilling."

The small silver drill was in position by Jack's fireplace, several drawings with measurements surrounding the tiny machine.

"She's in, he's taking her coat. What a mean bastard, straight to work, not even a coffee in sight."

The vacuum cleaner motor lit up bright red on Boris's screen.

Boris could see Crappy seated at his desk. This was far from perfect. His computer screen showed as a large red blob.

"You know Arni, she is close to the office, but what the hell is he doing? Can't he let the woman do her job? Arni ... Arni, are you there?"

Arno's face was tight as he touched the starter button, his Cayenne burst into life. He had never crashed a car deliberately. What a pity to do it this way. He quickly judged a smash at the back would be more advantageous than the front. The reversing camera gave a perfect image of Crappy's Volkswagen. Arno hit the accelerator hard. The Cayenne responded immediately, the smash pushing Arno's head too close to the steering wheel for comfort. The Volkswagon's alarm lit up the garage. The repair bills for both cars would cause pain at the insurers, but Arno was only focused on the fastest way to Crappy's apartment door. The lift would not create enough drama. Arno's legendary poor fitness would give a more convincing impression by using the stairs.

He pressed his thumb continuously on Gerard Crappy's door buzzer.

Boris observed the image of Crappy dashing from his office towards the door, almost knocking the cleaning lady to the floor.

"This is one rude git," sighed Boris.

"Good... morning.... Gerard." Arno was indeed well out of breath.

"I am so, so bloody sorry but just had an accident in the parking. My foot got stuck, blasted back into your car. It's a bit ... ah, smashed up."

Crappy did not know how to react: a massive Dutchman in his doorway looking humble, his car smashed up.

"Come on, down, I'll show you how it happened. Of course, one hundred percent my fault. I take full responsibility. What an idiot I am."

Crappy hesitated. The cleaning lady had never been alone in his apartment before, his car was smashed, and the man looking at him was under investigation due to his actions. His mind froze momentarily.

Slowly Crappy turned back towards his hallway.

"Martha, I'm going downstairs for a few minutes. No need to clean my office, I'll look after that."

Arno kept offering his apologies for being so stupid. Crappy appeared to be in a trance, following Arno into the garage.

"Oh no, that's terrible, I heard you were some sort of racing driver before. Is this normal driving for you?"

Arno stopped his rapid pace and stared at Crappy.

"Well, race drivers do tend to crash a lot, especially if you go for it." For a split second Arno almost blew the situation.

How could Crappy know about his racing past? That all happened a long time ago and was certainly only ever discussed with his closest friends at the chateau.

Boris was getting edgy. Crappy had been gone for two minutes now, but the cleaning lady stayed clear of the office.

He started the miniature silver drill, the extra long bit began to pierce the cement around the corner of the fireplace then into the heavy wood surround. Virtually no sound came from the device. Only a vibration in Boris's hand told him the instrument was making progress.

Boris had measured the thickness of the floor to be twenty centimetres. The drill would complete the small hole in thirty seconds. Crappy's office remained empty.

"My insurance will pay for a full repair, no problem. The dealer in Chambery can sort this out I'm sure. Do you have accident papers in your car?"

"Yes, but do we need to sort this out now? I was in the middle of something in my office."

Arno nodded and thought, I know you were. I saw you on a screen.

"Let's do it later, in the afternoon. This is a great pity, the car was nearly new."

"Again, my stupidity." Arno noticed an uneasy Crappy turning back towards the garage door.

"Can I offer you a glass of something at my place, I don't know, coffee?"

Arno was trying too hard and Crappy felt it.

"We can catch up later?" Crappy said, aiming for the garage door.

Boris the specialist slid the thin metal camera tube into the hole. As he focused the lens and checked his laptop screen, he shook his head. A small pile of wood dust had been deposited to the side of Crappy's fireplace. This was not good, though everything else had gone to plan. Boris knew the normal reaction would be, look at the dust pile, look up to the ceiling, the camera was tiny, very tiny, but the risk of it being seen was possible.

Crappy was hitting the first flight of stairs, sixteen more to the floor of his apartment. Boris was distracted by Martha the cleaner. Her image showed movement into the office, her outline closely followed by the vacuum cleaner glow. Her head moved left and right, making quick sweeping movements with the machine. She lunged the pipe towards the fireplace as Boris turned to the camera image. His broad smile told the story: a clean fireplace.

"What are you doing in here? I specifically said to leave my office to me. Well?"

Crappy held one hand on the office door, the other held open towards his cleaning lady.

Martha switched the cleaner off.

"Okay, just trying to do a good job for you, nothing more. Sorry, but men never clean like women. I could not believe the dust around your fireplace."

Crappy stared doubtfully shaking his head at Martha. What the hell was this woman talking about?

This was the last time she cleaned for him.

"At first we thought where were you? Then Crappy left his office. Guess you arranged that. We're all in place. Come and look at the image. It's perfect, but has something gone wrong?"

Jack and Boris faced the depressed-looking Dutchman.

Arno looked glum. "Yea, yea, all in place, fine. But my Cayenne looks sick. I used it to smash Crappy's car. It worked, but I hope the price was worth the result."

During the evening Jack and Carly invited their close friends in for drinks. All were seriously impressed with Boris's work. But Crappy's computer remained dark.

14

THE SWISS MANIPULATOR who had achieved so much during his business years was beginning to lose his magic touch. He desperately needed his contacts to revisit the Chateau Montjan. Urgent progress must be made. His position as the top man was currently fragile.

The old days of casual walks through his building reception were, for the time being, over. The beautiful girls who managed the stunning reception couldn't care less; they found his warm smiles more a business tool than a genuine greeting.

Lake Geneva was now full of activity, the tourist ferries in full early summer swing. Lasalle found himself spending far too much time staring at the activity on the lake, his gaze drifting onto the shining French Alps in the distance as if they were the key to his dilemma. His vast office had become a place to walk around. The man was pacing his days away, waiting for the regular updates he demanded from Madame Fouchard in Annecy which never came on time.

Why was this project taking so long? The chateau should be empty by now, the naive owners lost, in hiding, anywhere but out of *my* chateau.

Lasalle caved into the daily pressure circling around his head. He placed a call to a Geneva number; one more check in the chateau grounds must be made.

Boris felt confident that Crappy was unaware of his tiny camera, but after being in place for four days little interesting data had been seen. Regular images of yachts supported by financial breakdowns were viewed but as Boris had been made aware of Crappy's earlier career, nothing appeared strange, at least not until Jack flicked through the collection of images on Boris's laptop.

"This looks exactly like the Benetti I saw on holiday, the Vision 145, same colour. Boris, can we see more detail?"

Boris relished questions asking him to go up a gear.

"Of course, Jack. Best if we enlarge the financial sheet that came with it, like this. Here we go. No surprise, it sails under a Gibraltar flag, registered to a Swiss company, Manning Holdings. That's about as vague as you can get. Sorry not much more. Current place of mooring, Antibes."

Jack was already flicking through his mobile contacts. Bayer Merlot Grass, Geneva flashed up.

"Good afternoon, Jack Rafter. Didier Grass, please."

"Of course, Mr Rafter, one moment please."

"Mr Rafter, its Grass here. How are you?"

"That's a pretty good opener, feeling better by the day actually."

"Good to hear. Has something changed, because, I'm sorry to say, I have no further news."

"Could be. Small chain of events lately. How quickly can we meet up?"

"As you say quickly, shall I come to the chateau?"

"No, that's not a good idea. I'll come to you. Day after tomorrow possible? Anytime suits me."

"Okay yes, I can do that. Can I offer you lunch? The terraces are fine these days. Say 11:00 here then onto lunch?"

"Perfect. See you then."

Boris looked keen. "Jack sees yacht pictures and immediately calls his lawyer. What's the link, Jack?"

"I took a break with the family recently, Sainte-Maxime. One day, out on a Jet Ski with my boys, I came face to face with Crappy on the back of what seems to be this Benetti. Then we bumped into one another in the garage the following week. He was real embarrassed, pretending he of course was nowhere near the area. Used Madrid as an excuse. But actually I'm more interested in the yacht owner. Manning Holdings could lead us to him."

"Can't help you there, sorry. I'm just a techie; you know codes, screens, laptops, what connects the dots."

"For some time now we, that is the owners who are under this tax attack, suspect some other force is behind this. No news to you – that's why you're here. The simple question is, why would Crappy be on the Benetti and deny it? What's he got to hide? Is he protecting the owner? So I hope Didier Grass can turn up something. He has extensive contacts. Did you hear about the people in the garden?"

"Arno told me about them."

"Did he tell you they arrived in Swiss-plated cars?"

"He did."

"This is why we're talking to Swiss lawyers. They must be able to come up with something. It's not the French style to let the Swiss do their dirty work."

"Like your thinking, Jack, I'll check my recordings again. Maybe I can give you more for the lawyer."

Jack and Dan were sport lovers and a mutual respect had grown from their first meeting at the chateau. As the treadmills flashed a distance approaching ten kilometres, Jack sometimes took the lead, sometimes Dan, but very little separated the two men. It was still only 7:30 in the morning but they both agreed to turn off the air co in the gym. Building up a sweat felt more natural for these guys than a chilled workout.

As ten kilometres showed up on the digital display, the men simultaneously slapped each other on the back.

"Thought it best to go easy on you today. Guess your legs are shaky. Too little skiing these days?"

"You real sure, Jack? I was the one holding back. I want your boys to see their dad grow real old one day."

"Ha. What do you think? Quick circuit around the park? I need some fresh air."

"Fine, Jack. Let's go via the garage, the slope's good for my shaky legs..."

As the two men pushed their bodies hard up the garage entry lane, Jack suddenly reached out using all the energy he could muster towards the left shoulder of Dan. The expression from Dan was pure confusion. Jack was slowing down to an almost immediate stop, but why?

"Down, Dan, quick, here by the wall, quiet."

As the two men slowly raised their heads towards the garage entry, about a hundred meters away in the forest, a black Mercedes was being manoeuvred behind a dense conifer hedge. Within five seconds the car was invisible.

Jack pulled Dan aggressively backwards down the slope.

"Come on, we gotta find Boris. If he's in bed, this'll be the quickest wake-up call ever. Don't give a dam, but he has to see this."

"Jack, you must have eyes like a hawk. I didn't see a thing."

Arno opened his door still half asleep, his black dressing gown with the Ferrari motif offering some dignity. He was visibly not an early riser.

"Sorry Arno," jestured Jack, taking a deep breath, arms wide.

"Boris, we need him and quick."

"Come on in, I know he's up. Heard his weird music half an hour ago."

"Boris," yelled Arno, "are you decent?"

Boris appeared looking dishevelled, like he was guilty of something. Jack raised his voice.

"Boris, they're back. Big black Merc trying to hide in the forest. We need that what's-it-called, long-distance viewer thing. If they have the same guy with the laptop, you have to record this."

Boris was already unzipping a black leather case, the long lens showing first with a bizarre miniature laptop attached.

"My place is best. We can see most of the park from the balcony."

Jack, followed by Boris, Dan and Arno still in his black dressing gown, shot through the door taking the sixteen steps upstairs two at a time. Carly quickly hid behind the kitchen door. So many men racing through her apartment before she had time to shower made her feel a little awkward.

As Jack gently slid the balcony door open, the four men moved forward in a crouching position. Being the third floor, a perfect view lay before them. Boris decided to lie on his stomach, the lens perched on the edge of the balcony rail virtually invisible to all below. His friends took up the same pose.

Carly stared from the kitchen window trying to get her head around, just why would four men race through her apartment a little after seven thirty in the morning, and then lay side by side on the balcony staring at the park? Carly had a few questions for Jack later.

"Do you see anything Boris?" Whispered Jack.

"Not yet, but it's a big park. Doing a full sweep."

Dan smiled. Boris was doing his utmost to use military terminology.

"Thank god we don't have to engage the enemy," mused Dan.

"There they are... Four men, and yes, looks like one has a laptop."

Seeing vague shapes in the distance frustrated the other men but they certainly weren't going to ask for a quick glance. It was paramount Boris did what he did best: get some evidence.

"Zooming in. Nice gear for this time in the morning. They look more like bankers than anything else, except the laptop guy. He's in a leather jacket and bright shirt. Must be a geek like me."

"Can you see the laptop screen? I still have nightmares from the brief glimpse I got."

Arno edged closer to Boris, trying his best to see the image.

"I need him to turn. One clear shot, please. I'm focused and ready." Boris's index finger circled around the shutter button.

The main chateau gates began to open, the group were startled, they moved their position away from the entry doing their best to put trees between them and whoever was coming or going. The pool guy cruised through the gate, his white van moving as if he could have spent more time in bed.

"Got one..." yelled Boris.

"For Christ sake, turn it down Boris. This could be a life-changing moment." Jack was not amused.

"Stay there. Please stay there." Boris clicked several times, each time a soft, "yes, yes, yes." Jack gave a quick nod of approval.

The group in the garden were looking nervous, as if they needed one specific something before they could leave. The laptop was only half open now, a conversation taking place. It seemed they agreed on something; one gave a quick pat on the back to the laptop man. The group then moved quickly and cautiously towards the hidden Mercedes. In the distance, a deep hum could be heard as the engine came to life. Within twenty seconds the Swiss-plated car sped through the gates.

"Don't worry; I got the number plate. Two shots, just to be sure."

As the four men stood up, Boris felt like a professional, his status growing by the second.

Carly watched the four guys leave the apartment, she observed the mood now much more relaxed, something must have been achieved.

Boris connected his long-range camera and listening device to the TV screen in Arno's lounge. Anticipation filled the room. Could this be the moment life began to move forward again? Were the answers so close?

Boris flicked through the telecommand as if the apartment was his.

"Not great. This one, he was moving too much. Next should be better."

Jack was frowning. One shot had to be good.

"This is good. What do you think? Mountains, the lines underneath. Not so sure."

Arno sat legs crossed, Indian position, in front of the large screen. "This is exactly what I saw before, the mountains, lines underneath. It's exactly the bloody same, fuck me Boris you're good."

Stephanie picked her way in between the men, serving chilled orange juice and constantly watching her husband.

Boris was too focused to notice any activity around him. "Okay, now the sound."

"Man, you got the voices as well?" Dan sounded impressed.

The verbal exchange between the visitors in the garden was in heavy Swiss German. Even the Dutch linguists in the room found it impossible to get a word. For Jack and Dan it could have been Martian.

"You know I'm off to the lawyer this morning. Boris, can you put the shots and this conversation on my iPad. I hope the lawyer can make something of it..."

By 10:00, Jack was suited up, iPad loaded and taking the lift to the garage. In less than fifteen minutes he was accelerating hard up the long hill away from Chambéry. Within another hour he would be in Geneva.

Celine quickly descended to the reception, greeting Jack Rafter with a broad confident smile.

"Good to see you in Geneva again, Mr Rafter. I managed to book a wonderful table at Carvettis. Mr Grass is sure you will love the place, and the weather's beautiful."

Jack half smiled back, thinking he couldn't care less about a wonderful lunch. Results from the recent events were all that mattered to him.

Didier Grass waited at his office door; hands clenched together, his Valentino suit making the perfect presentation for a top Geneva lawyer. He always looked immaculate.

Celine offered tea or coffee, and politely closed the office door.

"So Mr Rafter, I do hope things are looking better for you and your neighbours these days."

"They could be, really. Let me explain what's happened. We believe there is a rotten egg in the chateau."

Grass initially looked confused, and then remembered how strange some foreign language sayings can be, "Yes, so you mean a bad person?"

"Exactly, a French chap, Gerard Crappy, retired. Since the whole thing started he's been acting so different to the rest of us. Impossible to get more than a surface conversation out of him."

'That's very French," confirmed Grass.

"I took the family for a break recently, Sainte-Maxime."

"Nice place, I often play golf there."

"Yes, well this holiday was a little unusual. Out on a Jet Ski one day with my boys, we came close to a beautiful Benetti yacht, the Vision 145. I was sure I saw the neighbour onboard. Back at the chateau I bumped into him. No real surprise, he denied he was close to the area, pretended he spent the last days in Madrid, but his suntan told a different story."

"Understand." Grass was being lawyer cautious, slowly nodding.

"Can you or your friends come up with any reasons why he should act this way? Maybe he is some sort of puppet working for whatever is really behind this."

Jack slid his iPad from his briefcase.

"This, I'm sure, is the same yacht. It sails under a Gibraltar flag and is owned by a Swiss company called Manning Holdings."

Grass pressed number one on his desk mobile system. Celine would arrive in seconds.

"May I ask how you obtained this information, Mr Rafter? Normally luxury yacht owners of this calibre do everything possible to hide the true ownership..."

Jack knew he should not disclose the presence of Boris in the chateau. Lawyers get edgy when clients appear better at fact finding. Stay elusive, he thought to himself.

"Let's just say for the moment, we have a source."

This was the best Jack could come up with. What the hell else could he say? We have our own security expert...

Grass shook his head.

"Okay, we all have our sources... Ah, Celine, check out Manning Holdings. It's Swiss. All you can find. Priority please. I'd like to know before Mr Rafter leaves us today."

Celine noted the name and left without saying a word.

"There's more. I'm sure you have heard the stories about people being seen in the chateau grounds. Well dressed, always one person carrying a laptop."

"Yes, Mr Van Bommel mentioned this. It seems they come and go, but rather quickly."

"They do, but this morning ..." Suddenly Jack knew he was heading for dangerous territory again. How could he explain obtaining this information? He had to go for it. Grass was working for him and that was that.

Grass was staring at Jack, waiting for the next instalment, a nervous expectant grin showing.

"This morning, and please don't ask, we obtained a picture of the laptop screen, plus this recording of their conversation. This is the number plate of the car they left in."

"My my, Mr Rafter. If we ever need surveillance specialists, I think I need to call the chateau. I am impressed. It will take a little time to check the number plate out. My old contact just passed away."

"How's your Swiss German? I didn't get a word," asked Jack doubtfully.

"Not great. I prefer English and the Latin languages. Let's try. Please play it."

As Jack touched the screen, Didier Grass turned his head; his eye's narrowed whilst trying hard to work out the image, like mountains with lines underneath. Many lines.

Grass relaxed his tie nott, as if serious work was imminent.

"Could you play it again please? These guys are from back-street Zurich, or a very small mountain village.

"Well, I get the word *water* several times, weird mentions of ground, terrain and a lot of measurements, constantly. How many meters back and forth ... Don't worry we have people who can clear this up. I'll get you a full and clear translation in the next days."

Jack shook his head, thinking not a dead end, please. He desperately wanted to return to the chateau with good news. So far all he had gleaned was that a group of heavy accented peasants were considering building a swimming pool in the chateau grounds.

Celine printed several pages covering the detail available on Manning Holdings, placed her work into a discreet green folder and returned to her boss's office.

Jack watched her place the folder carefully on the desk, just close enough to create attention, but not interrupt the ongoing meeting. Celine gave a confident nod to her boss and left with a look of achievement on her face.

"She's quick. Hope it's interesting." The tension showed on Jack's face, his suntan fading fast.

"A true professional. Not many around, I'm afraid."

Grass was studying the open folder intensely.

"Does the name Harvey Lasalle mean anything to you, Mr Rafter?"

"No nothing. Should it?"

"He controls Manning Holdings, which in turn owns a Benetti Vision. This is a rather famous Swiss business man. Old money, been around for a long time. One of our billionaires. He has business interests everywhere."

"Do you have a picture of this man?" Jack asked cautiously.

"Celine, could you come up with a recent picture of Harvey Lasalle? He's often in the newspapers, taking something over. There must be plenty available.

"So now, Mr Rafter. We have to form the link between your neighbour, Mr Crappy, and our own Harvey Lasalle. That may be difficult."

Celine slipped through the door with another green folder, making Jack ease himself closer to the desk.

"Here is our very own takeover king, looking a little tired these days. I heard his businesses are suffering. The crisis is hitting him hard."

"I don't believe this... I'm close to 100% sure this man was talking with our rotten egg neighbour on his yacht. This must be him."

Jack was now feeling good about his decision to meet up with the lawyer so quickly.

"Well, Mr Rafter, do you think your *sources* can make a link between these two men?" Grass gave a smirk of sarcasm.

"Thought we were paying you for that work?"

Grass controlled himself quickly. "Exactly. I will do some digging. I feel sure something will show up."

As the two men walked the short distance from Rue Francois Bellot to Carvettis restaurant, Jack felt confident that Boris would be the key to a link between Gerard Crappy and Harvey Lasalle. It had to go deeper than simply a party on a yacht.

Before Jack could open his car door, Boris, Dan and Arno were standing in line next to him, rallied up, the expression on their faces hoping for positive news. Boris felt like he almost lived in the chateau.

"What did he think of the conversation Jack? Did they say something special?"

"Let's go for a walk in the garden, guys. Geneva was bloody hot. Nice lunch, had to be polite, but yea, things to tell you."

"Okay, nobody can hear us here, unless Crappy has equipment like yours, Boris?"

Boris shook his head, smiling confidently.

"Not with his computer set-up, I've watched it a lot now. He's not a techie like me, more a basic accountant-type guy, piles of boring figures."

"You're not going to believe this. I was right, that yacht in the south. Crappy was with a big Swiss player. It's owned by Manning Holdings, which is controlled by a man called Harvey Lasalle. Seems this guy owns all sorts of businesses. An important man in Swiss business circles, a billionaire."

"The little bastard... Why would he pretend he was somewhere else?"

Arno never warmed to Crappy, a sort of pit bull-poodle relationship that could only end up in a bad place.

Jack had hoped to come home with news that would clear things up, but the garden visits tormented him. What could they be looking for? As he circled around his friends an idea came to him, a crazy one, but one that had to be discussed. He suggested they sit on the wooden garden seats hidden in one of the forests.

"This is the way I see it. We can threaten Crappy, but he will call the police. All we have are pictures of yachts from his computer. If we disclose how we got them, trouble. We know the garden visitors are looking for something here, but we only have shots of mountains with lines passing under them. Call me a lunatic – could be happening to me these days – but listen to this. I have some great contacts at ESA, the European Space Agency in Noordwijk, Holland. Everybody from scientists to managers, you name it. Many have been clients for years. How about I try to set up a satellite scan of this area? It may cost us some money, you know, satellite time, but afterwards we'll know as much as anybody. It's a long shot but a shot worth taking. Am I making sense here?"

The heads began nodding, Boris even more then the others.

"Can I get in on this? I've always wanted to visit that place. They must have some cool systems. Promise I'll wear a discreet shirt."

"You're part of the team these days, Boris. We'll probably need you to explain the whole thing to us." Jack gave Boris a reassuring punch to his upper arm.

Arno remained quiet.

"You with us, Arni?" asked Jack.

"You know me, chaps. Any excuse to visit Holland. Of course, yes. You know what they say; if you dig deep enough you'll always find shit, so let's go digging."

Jack started planning calls to his best contacts at ESA. He recalled a meeting with one of the senior managers, Roger Davies, during a portfolio review. Their conversation drifted away from the investment world towards the latest space technologies and their potential applications.

As he closed his office door he realised the importance of the call he was about to make. The more he played it over in his head, the more thought he gave to the reason behind it.

I'm asking someone I don't know so well to use a satellite, owned by several contributing governments, most likely worth many millions, for a scan of our chateau and surrounding park because we think something could be under the ground and, oh and by the way, we are all under threat of financial destruction from the tax office, so can we make it real quick ...

Jack allowed himself a short smile as he touched the direct line number for Roger Davies, Dario Mission Manager.

"Good afternoon Roger, Jack Rafter. Are you free to talk?"

"Yes, good afternoon Jack. Nice to hear from you. Don't tell me that fund's going down again?"

Not the start Jack wanted. "No, it's stabilised for the moment. No further losses since we last met."

"Good, well like I said, I don't have any more money to invest now. Just helped my daughter buy her first house."

"Actually today my call is for a very different reason. Sure you have a few minutes for me?"

"Of course, Jack."

Davies was concerned this was some ploy towards making further investment. He shook his head and stared at the one hundred or so space publications on the shelves around his office.

"Excuse me if I use wrong terminology, but my neighbours and I have a delicate situation affecting our lives at the moment."

Jack had always played down the chateau bit and the size of the park.

"We have a place in a nice old building, with nine other neighbours. We collectively pay for the garden upkeep, the surrounding area."

Roger Davies now complimented his judgement; this was an offer for property investment...

"Sorry Jack, property in France with the taxes trying to hit foreign owners. That's not for me."

"No, nothing like that I assure you." Best to get to the point, thought Jack.

"Basically we would like to buy some satellite time. We are being pestered by local developers, nasty people. We believe there could be something interesting under the ground here. Would you agree that a satellite scan would show it up?"

Davies immediately lost interest in his book collection. This type of request was on the increase, and his director recognised the financial potential of such cooperation.

"I understand Jack. Sorry, I was sure you were looking for more investment. Of course we can help, common occurrence these days. All sorts of companies are asking for terrain scans."

Jack looked out to the park. He could almost see the satellite going overhead.

"Let me check with my friends here. We are under pressure, so sooner rather than later. Maybe in the next week or two?"

"Should be possible. Depends of course on the satellite path, correct orbital position. I'll check with our Space Operations Centre ESOC in Frankfurt who control the satellites. Also I'll need the GPS coordinates for your home. Give me that so I can propose the best day and time to come here."

"I'll email this over today. We can fit days, dates, whatever suits you. And thanks for this Roger. Look forward to seeing you soon."

Jack updated his neighbours, and Carly received an unexpected hug and kiss.

"Off to Holland with the guys in a few days, darling. Could be a very interesting trip."

15

Boris left early for Holland, his Dutch business needing attention. Eva seemed keen to make the trip, the wives were not. So Eva did the politically correct thing and decided to stay at the chateau.

Annabel was making constant gestures about moving to another country. "One where you can live a life, not worry who's looking over your shoulder."

The Space Agency visit was left to Jack, Dan and Arno, who planned to catch up with Boris for the viewing of the satellite images.

Packing a simple bag for the two-night stay Jack reflected back to the recent lunch with Didier Grass in Geneva. Having a good selection of clients in the legal profession he knew their characters well. Never lecture about the law too much, keep asking a constant flow of questions, be a good listener. But Grass was different. He talked, actually talked a great deal. It seems Harvey Lasalle had a dirty reputation in the Geneva business community, same as his father before him. Grass described him as a vulture. This caused Jack to stop eating – the green salad dressing was one of the best he had tasted – but when a top lawyer calls someone a vulture, some history must have occurred. Jack thought it best to let the moment pass. With this, the link between Lasalle and Crappy became paramount, much more important than just a yacht party in the south of France.

"Where shall we stay? My brother said we're welcome."

Arno was showing off his driving skills, one hundred and fifty showing on the display as the sign for Annecy flashed past.

"If you don't mind, I've made reservations at the Kurhaus Scheveningen for the three of us. Call me a pain but I have to eat Indonesian in The Hague one night. You'll join me, I hope?" Jack was building up an appetite already.

Dan nodded a polite ok, whilst wondering what Indonesian's actually eat.

Boris had confirmed by text that he would meet up at the entry to the European Space Agency at 10:00 the following day, signing off with, *"can't wait, special day."*

Jack, Arno and Dan, dressed in casual summer shirts, took a cab into The Hague. Arno was just happy to speak his mother tongue again.

"Denneweg, ash to blieft." The driver immediately knew he was an Amsterdammer.

After beers in the early evening sun they took the short walk from the Denneweg to Nordeinde. Jack had good memories of the restaurant; so many client meetings had taken place there. The waiter gave a glance of faint recognition at Jack and promptly showed the men to a corner table, perfectly placed for views onto the exclusive shopping street.

"I am dam hungry. Good idea this Jack. Pity our part of France hasn't discovered this cuisine." Arno eagerly checked out the white wine list.

Dan looked confused. The menus were in Dutch and Indonesian food was not at all familiar to him, although Jack had promoted it well.

"Don't worry, Dan. We'll just order a lot of dishes, mix, reorder. It's easy eating. I promise this will be a special moment. The spice, oh ... you won't forget this food."

Jack's mobile vibrated in his pocket, announcing a text from Eva.

Thought it best to let you know Crappy has a visitor, the tall dark haired girl again. She's been in his place close to two hours. Can I do something?

Jack quickly explained the text to his friends.
Arno shook his head aggressively.

"The sneaky little bastard. Soon as we leave, he gets up to something."

"Can't Boris do something from here? We gotta know what she's doing there."

"Good point, Dan." Arno hit Boris's number.

"Don't tell me tomorrow's cancelled?"

"It's still on, but something's happening back at the chateau. Eva just texted Jack that the mysterious tall dark haired woman is with Crappy again, and for a long time. Can you do something from here?"

"Already putting the code in Arni. Waiting for Jack's system to talk to me, then I can access the camera."

The anticipation and immediate stress killed off the appetite for the three, being so far away, out of control. Was this a coincidence? The first bottle of wine arrived at the table.

"Here we go. Well, she's telling our man Crappy off. He looks like a pissed off little French man. She's in control and she looks good, very good. Hold on, what the hell's this? Ask Jack if knows the address 1230 Cumberland Terrace in London? Your name's on this, a Bank of America statement, Jack..."

Jack looked stunned. She'd got into his computer.

"She's finished with the frog now, back at the screen. I really don't believe what I'm seeing, guys. Eva's name, a Luxembourg bank, she's wealthy. Dan, you have a Swiss account I see. Arno, do you own a restaurant in Marbella?"

"I saw her arrive once. She looks anything but a geek."

Dan looked glum, his jaw dropped.

Arno was changing colour.

"So this sad little bastard gets her to break into our computers. I wanna go back and smash his fucking head in tonight."

"Too late now, Arno, they already have the information. I hope tomorrow will tell us why they need it this way..."

For the second time Jack delayed the waiter.

"Okay, Boris. Well, this is what we feared. This ugly puzzle is coming together. Keep looking for us, record everything. See you tomorrow at ESA. And we're supposed to be hungry now after that."

Arno put his hand over his mouth and stared at nothing in particular.

The dinner conversation between the three men fell between the serious and bitter. Fortunately they heard the news whilst in Holland. Had they been in the chateau, Crappy would have been the target of spontaneous violence. Jack, now more sure about Crappy's deviousness than ever before could repay on what happened to his sons. And that would have only made their predicament worse, if that was possible.

Jack was determined to enjoy the Indonesian rice table. He hoped his friends would as well, but their heads were spinning. If this information had been passed onto the tax office already, they were doomed. They had to move quickly, so he made a mental note to call Didier Grass early the next morning. Maybe he could put the pieces together.

"You like it, Dan?" asked Jack, doing his best to be upbeat the evening and lift the atmosphere around the table.

"Great food. You're right, first experience but not the last."

Arno was still looking mean and angry, staring deep into his plate. The men were drinking wine like shots, their faces showing a mix of worry and confusion.

"Nice, Jack. Know you're doing your best to cheer us up, but this dirty little crumb has almost screwed up our lives, and we don't know why, do we... We never did anything against him?" Arno's volume increasing. The waiters looking uncomfortable.

Jack and Dan gave a lost shake of the head.

"Hope if I bump into him when we get back I can control myself. That won't be easy. Five minutes in the gym and I could change his life forever." Dan wanted to say more, but no one was listening.

The cab ride back to the hotel was silent. No one mentioned the customary boys-away-from-home nightcap. Within fifteen minutes, all three were in bed, staring at the ceiling. Sleep would be difficult this night.

Jack and Dan met in the reception at seven sharp, for a thirty-minute run along Scheveningen beach, then a shower and breakfast with Arno at eight. Jack allowed a ten-minute window beforehand to call Didier Grass. Their lawyer was fired up over the recent lunch so the latest news must be good ammunition.

"Good morning, Mr Rafter. Sorry I'm not in the office yet, still thirty minutes away, but I guess a call this early means that something has happened..."

"You could well say that. I'm in Holland with Arno Van Bommel and Dan Lancaster. Please don't ask how, but last night we discovered the neighbour you know about, Gerard Crappy and some ... how can I say this, beautiful geek appear to be stealing very personal information from our computers at the chateau. A whole slew of our most private details are showing up on his computer."

"Understand. As you request, I won't ask how you are aware of this information. Please realise it may come up later, but this is very worrying. I presume we're talking about the sort of things the tax office are making threats about?"

"Exactly that."

"Again the same question, why? What would he/she gain from this?"

"Either one massive pay day from the tax office, or someone else."

"Let's think the latter, Mr Rafter. The tax office are irritating but not so stupid as to take this route."

"Look, sorry Mr Grass, I have to leave soon, a very important meeting which may give the vital clue we're looking for. You'll hear from me as soon as we get back. That should be tomorrow morning."

"Listen, Mr Rafter, I will talk to someone I had hoped to avoid. From what you have told me this is something I must now do. This pressure will not go away. Indeed, we may discover vital information."

Grass clicked his car phone off whilst shaking his head in doubt.

The taxi pulled alongside the ESA security gatehouse. Boris was already waiting inside looking cocky, like this was his kind of world. Solid hugs and warm greetings were made by the four men.

Jack stepped confidently towards the reception.

"Good morning. We're here for a meeting with Roger Davies."

"I already have your badges. Just need a copy of your passports. Please be sure to wear these at all times. Do you know the way to his office?"

"No problem. Been there many times."

Jack led the way towards the main building.

Eva was doing her cautious best to bump into Crappy. She knew a call from Jack to update her on last night's action could be risky, so she was only expecting the full news when the men returned. She'd seen the tall dark-haired woman leave Crappy's apartment late in the evening, counting her blessings that the woman was not a permanent resident. The competition would be tiring.

Crappy never used the pool or the gym so her best chance to meet him would be the garage. Eva felt like a nosey old woman, starring out of the office window for hours at a time, but her persistence was about to pay off. The large black chateau gates opened for the arrival of Gerard Crappy's car. She threw her hair into a quick pony tail, undid a button on her blouse and headed to the garage. As Eva pushed the heavy door open she focused on Crappy, still sitting in his car, appearing to be on his mobile. Okay, let's play the waiting game, she thought, dropping to her knees searching the surrounding concrete floor as if diamonds were about to be recovered.

Crappy could not miss the spectacle. Eva, a few meters from his car, large breasts easing from side to side, her blouse loose, offering little protection for the wonderful pose. His conversation became awkward, he promised the caller, "more news soon."

"Eva, hello, have you lost something?"

The search immediately stopped. Eva stood up, much to Crappy's disappointment.

"Nothing special, a small earring, but I must say you look like a happy man. New girlfriend I see. She's beautiful ..."

Crappy frowned suspiciously, and then the frown turned to anger.

"Don't have a girlfriend. What are you talking about?"

Crappy began moving around Eva towards the garage door.

"Sorry, I could not help noticing that tall, elegant, dark-haired woman here last night. She came out of your place so I guessed ..."

"No, an old friend, quick drink."

Eva watched Crappy stumble through the garage door. Now another person in the chateau hated the lying Crappy as much as the guys in Holland.

Roger Davies greeted the small party at his office, his appearance making Boris look rather cool and coordinated. Broad bushy beard, open-toe sandals, black socks. A true rocket scientist.

"Hello Jack, nice to see you again."

"You too. And a big thank you from all of us for arranging things so quickly."

"Pleasure. My director will be joining us. He's keen to push a more open, commercial side to our business."

"Fine. I know Geoff well. Played eighteen holes with him last summer."

"Follow me then. We have a viewing room organised. I would say the satellite should be over your place in around half an hour."

The darkened room provided seating for at least fifty. Roger showed his guests to the fourth row, explaining that the view from there would be the most advantageous.

Boris felt compelled to share some techie moments with his new hero.

"Guess we can get the CD of this. Maybe needed as evidence. Here's my card."

"Boris Von Phren, Security Consultant, Amsterdam," mouthed Davies.

"It's all in the price, Boris. Always been interested in your line of work. You must have some incredible equipment these days."

The two men chatted comfortably at the end of the row.

Jack reflected on the Harrison Ford film, *Patriot Games*, where the SAS take out suspected terrorists in the North African desert, all watched via satellite from the comfort of an office in Langley. "Maybe the SAS can take Crappy out," he mused.

Geoff Beck gave Jack a small pat on the back. Jack introduced the director to his friends.

"How's the portfolio doing? That trend-following fund getting better?" whispered Geoff.

"Stable to climbing now. Trends are looking better. The current easing has to stop soon, from then the markets should see trends again."

"Good news. My wife was about to kill me. Anyway hope you enjoy the show today."

As the large screen flickered into life, three serious-looking young men started work at the control consul towards the back of the room.

Silence took over all in the room as a misty coloured image of south-east France showed up on the large screen some eight meters away, the Alps still showing patches of snow cover. Fortunately the sky was clear.

"How long?" asked Davies.

"Should be over the site in three minutes."

The men at the back of the room were making nervous conversation.

"That must be the lake of Aix les Bains," observed Arno under heavy concentration.

"That's right," a young voice confirmed.

"Very close now," said Davies tapping his fingers together nervously.

Gradually the image zoomed in, the satellite camera drilling deep into the Savoyard countryside.

Jack looked at Arno, but Arno was totally absorbed, trying to make out the images, like mountains with lines underneath. Many lines. A second image appeared to the right showing a beautiful ivory-coloured chateau surrounded by a forest.

"That your place?" asked Geoff.

"Um, a small part of it. Many owners."

Jack hoped this moment would go away quickly.

Again and again the men saw the same image, so many contour lines massing together, lines appearing to move in the direction of the chateau, sometimes the image clear, sometimes too vague for clarity. As the satellite camera zoomed towards a wider view, Jack's eyes followed the lines from what seemed to be the mountains, passing near the chateau, and finally disappearing towards the West.

"This is what several million gallons of water looks like from a satellite, gentlemen, and it appears to be flowing right under your home. Mountain water, simple as that."

Roger Davies waved his arms like a dramatic actor in a small budget play, whilst his director calmly smiled at the efficiency of his team.

"Now we have this cleared up, how about some lunch? It's Italian day in the restaurant, and at least you know what's under the ground now, nothing special, just nature..."

"If only they knew what we're going through," Jack whispered to Arno, "if only they knew..."

Boris was itching to talk, but he knew the protocol: keep it sweet and on the surface until they were alone. Jack, Arno and Dan could only consider the consequences of last night's discovery. If that information was now in the wrong hands, life would change for all of them.

Boris eagerly accepted the invitation to stay at the hotel that night, needing just a couple of hours to pick up some clothes from his Amsterdam apartment. Arno insisted he was needed back at the chateau.

"I'll get you on the flight with us. Things are changing by the hour now."

Three large G&Ts and an apple juice were served by an Indian waiter on the Kurhaus terrace. Arno placed a ten euro tip on his tray.

"Same again when you're ready, because we will be."

"Boris, we're really glad you're coming back with us. I imagine that case contains something special." Jack pointed to the silver metal Samsonite case clenched firmly between Boris's legs.

"Correct me if I'm wrong, but I imagine from what I saw and recorded last night that my first job is to get that information back to a safe place. If it's not too late this little beauty will help me do that."

"And if is too late, the beautiful bitch has passed it on." Jack could see demons everywhere.

"Sorry, if that's the case your lawyer has to step in. Out of my hands."

As the waiter placed the second round on the table, Arno put another note on the tray and winked at the waiter.

By 9:15 the following morning, Arno was doing what he did best, his religion: driving cars fast. Chambéry was fifty clicks away. As the previous night had turned into a haze of alcohol and apprehension. Even Boris managing a half bottle of Rosé, the four men were calm. Words were in short supply.

Crappy's car was missing as they entered the garage. Bags were quickly thrown in the lift with an agreement to meet up in Arno's place in fifteen minutes. Jack asked Carly to make sure Eva was also present.

Eva's customary confidence was lacking as she walked into the room. Although, *the team*, as Dan referred to the specific group, were happy to be together again, all the faces showed a deep concern.

"Hope I did the right thing letting you know, Crappy had the girl in his place for some time?" Eva looked doubtful.

"Boris, it's maybe best you explain this." Jack flashed a worried glance in his direction.

"First, you all need to know I'm solid, totally on your side. You brought me in here to do a job, but for me it's more. You're all one hell of a special family to me; my blood will spill before I let you down ..."

Mutterings of "same here, Boris, with you too" came under the usual background music.

"Now there's no doubt. I linked up via Jack's system, the camera, from my office in Amsterdam. The dark-haired girl is for sure a geek, like me. Crappy is only the puppet because of the location of his place. What I saw her access is, well..., your very personal data. All of the names came up. Eva your Luxembourg account, Jack's property in London, Arno's accounts in Gibraltar, Dan banking in Zurich. I recorded all I could see, not pleasant. She has got into all of your computers. She even had documents on that guy, what was his name, Latouch, the one who killed himself here."

Eva suddenly began talking to herself, but not in a language anyone in the room could understand, hands clasped tight just below her chin. Her presence was always powerful but on this occasion she had moved into new territory.

Jack made a polite gesture of "Okay Eva?" but it went unnoticed.

"This is enough for me, I'm going to Paris. I don't know how long for, but I need to get away from this chateau ..."

With that, Eva paced towards Arno's main door, and closed it sending vibrations through the apartment.

"What do you think? "Arno spread his arms out wide shaking his head in disbelief.

"Could be one of two things. Either she's so pissed off that she's trying to arrange something, or so fed up with living here with all this shit it's her goodbye. She's a no-nonsense woman. No real surprise."

Jack, trying as always to bring order to the meeting, asked Boris.

"Please can you check? See if this information has left the building. This is a priority. I can check with the lawyer but if our information is by now in the wrong hands, what can he do?"

Boris was tapping away wildly, his eyes showing full concentration.

"Even if you have to hack his computer, go for it. It could be the only chance we have." Jack exercised his hands like he was beginning a long climb.

Boris was in his own world,

"Give me five minutes, ten max."

Coffee was served, with offers of biscuits from Stephanie. All declined. Since Eva had left the room little conversation flowed.

Jack stood alone, close by the floor-length window, coffee in hand. As he stared towards the park, Eva's car exited the garage. Jack turned to the team.

"Eva just left the chateau ..."

No one said a word. At least five minutes passed, and then Boris looked up. His eyes were cold and frozen for his normally cheerful, upbeat character.

"I don't know how to tell you all this. She transferred the information from Crappy's computer to another, I guess hers. It's gone from here..."

16

ANNA TINA GEISINGER felt good about herself. The full-length mirrors in every room of her apartment complimented her height and beauty at every turn. On top of this, her technology skills were beginning to increase bank account and investment portfolios enormously. Her secretive business contact in Geneva was now putting more and more hacking jobs her way. Then there would be the constructor in Vevey the following week, who was about to lose control of his largest project. Soon after, a judge, who seemed to enjoy ruling against her new boss. His wife will immediately file for divorce when she hears about the parties in Lyon. Anna Tina could only see a wonderful future for herself.

As she eased into the tight office chair, reaching to open the sliding window, the sound of Evian morning traffic grew louder, distracting her. There were now more tourists than locals and this bored her. Concentration was required in her business. Soon her expanding finances would allow the purchase of a penthouse high above the sightseers.

The last file of detailed information required by her Swiss pay master was almost ready to send. Just one last check was needed.

Dan Lancaster, full Swiss account details, cash transfers in via an Italian business which abruptly halted, but were substantial.

Jack Rafter, property in London, sub accounts in various investment houses, London, Amsterdam, Frankfurt, offshore accounts.

Eva Critin, Luxembourg account, transfers from various Parisian based banks, also Morocco, Oman, a substantial trail between Monaco and Luxembourg.

Arno Van Bommel, restaurant property in Marbella, Gibraltar accounts, Dutch accounts, Munich accounts.

Valerie and Nina Asperen, accounts linked to their father in Holland, with substantial sums involved.

Harvey Lasalle was making new enemies by the day, even in his own office building. Today it was the turn of a Swiss products marketing manager.

"Why the hell did you ask me to sign the contract if you were worried about whether we could deliver product or not?"

"Being cautious, Mr Las..."

"You think I give a damn about your cautious tendencies... The contract's screwed, simple as that. We will be sued, and you could be job hunting. Get out before I have to hear more of your sad stories."

Lasalle turned to his daily comfort zone, the view towards the French Alps. As he flicked from screen to screen on his iPhone, the ping of a new mail was announced, his bad mood turning positive as he read the message.

> Here is the information you required. I cannot get more, for the many reasons we have discussed, not least your contact Mr C. I will not make further visits to the place. I look forward to you finalising our agreement.

As Lasalle scrolled down the list of chateau residents he even managed a sick chuckle. Just what he wanted. Now the real proof could be passed on to Madame Fouchard in Annecy, then she could put the final nail in the coffin. Soon the chateau would be his ...

"Madame Fouchard, Harvey Lasalle, how quickly can I see you?"

"Well, what do you mean by quickly?"

Madame Fouchard struggled to conceal her contempt for the man.

"I'm prepared to come today, tomorrow. You tell me."

"Okay, tomorrow morning. Come to my home in Annecy le Vieux. Shall we say 10:00?"

Lasalle agreed immediatly, wished Madame Fouchard a pleasant day before moving back towards his favourite window.

The thirty-minute drive from Geneva passed more quickly than normal. Lasalle only focused on the documents in his briefcase, pondering on which tactic he could use to persuade Madame Fouchard to act swiftly. Surely the bulging brown envelope, if offered early in the meeting, would help.

Parking behind an old blue Citroen. He never understood the French minimalist attitude to cars. Why were they so happy to drive old sad-looking-dented vehicles? This woman could afford something far more respectable with her salary, not to mention the new cash stream flowing into her life.

The red roses left and right of the large wooden door were well cared for. Several garden tools propped against the walls. Obviously she enjoyed her garden. Lasalle hit his knuckles twice against the dark oak door.

Nathalie Fouchard had been standing behind the door since his car turned in.

"Mr Lasalle, what a pleasure."

A brief, weak handshake took place then Madame Fouchard turned, taking a deep breath. Unfortunately she had to go through with this. Sadly her husband was a serious gambler, spending cash more quickly than the envelopes arrived.

"You have a beautiful home. The lake views are impressive, far more calm here than Geneva."

"We like it. We were born only two kilometres away."

Lasalle wanted to show her the latest information, but he also wanted to keep the most important woman in his life for this moment calm, collected and focused.

"Sorry to say, I have to be back in Geneva for a late lunch meeting so ..."

Nathalie Fouchard was pleased to hear this. Minimum time with the monster helped her humour.

"Let's sit here. Please show me the latest information."

The corner dining table was small. Lasalle struggled to fit his knees under. He could not help staring at the many family photos covering the walls, a large family showing at least twenty younger faces.

"You're welcome to take the family to Saint-Tropez, my villa, if you wish?"

"Thank you, but my new found wealth may not sit comfortably with my relations. Probably better alone with my husband."

Lasalle had already taken the file from his case, carefully sliding it slowly across the wooden table towards the sober-looking lady. She stared, a face of worry, knowing what she was doing to be a road of desperation. Her face took on a look of pity showing her age when Lasalle placed the thick brown envelope on top of the file. She clasped her hands tightly together showing the white of her knuckles. Words were not available.

"I hope you find this useful, Madame? "A quick nod accepted the gift.

As if awoken by a small electric shock, Madame Fouchard opened her hands, placed the envelope to one side and reviewed the file, her small round glasses moving up and down quickly.

"I don't know how you arrange these things, I really don't, but you do realise this information will destroy these people. It's my job, I know, but not yours. I sincerely hope no one ever connects us."

"You have nothing to worry about. I have all the angles covered. Nobody, and I mean nobody, knows about our relationship."

Lasalle wanted to push so hard, but ...

"Then I suppose I have to go to work, but remember we have to follow the law. I cannot make them pay up in days. Maybe the demand will panic them into submission, sometimes they disappear overnight. We can certainly attach a large security on their homes, pending a final court decision."

"Just do what ever you can to inflict maximum pain."

As she edged her chair sideways away from Lasalle, doubt again scrambled her mind. Even the tax office was unaccustomed to characters of this intimidating calibre.

"I believe this concludes our business for today. You did say you have a pressing meeting."

"Yes I have. I look forward to your updates."

Madame Fouchard stared directly at Lasalle, her unease showing.

"One small thing I should mention. Paris, which controls everything we do, is suddenly making changes. A new man, very senior, called me recently asking ... well, random questions about any new methods we were using. I can't think why. He also said I may have a new boss soon. I'm only telling you this in case our plans are moved around ... changed."

Lasalle drove back to Geneva in a trance. Everything was going to plan, but the last moments of the meeting made him uncomfortable. Why did she mention this? Paris changes, not now, not at this stage. For once in his life, Harvey Lasalle could not think of a single person to call. The situation he'd orchestrated was possibly spiralling out of his control.

Madame Fouchard, with the aid of Sylvie Boustain, her right hand, and her secretary, placed the copies of the chateau owner's accounts and asset lists neatly on the long mahogany meeting table. Three separate dossier for the three senior members of her team who were due to arrive any moment.

As they filed into the room, Madame Fouchard greeted them one by one with a brief shallow smile, followed by an even briefer nod. Personality and a good personal presentation were worthless in their chosen careers. The three were as dull as one another. Spontaneity did not exist in this profession.

"The files in front of you concern the Chateau Montjan owners. We have discussed this before. You know how they have all abused our rules and laws. This information relates to a series of accounts, property, possible other investments held outside France. In the briefest possible time I want you to calculate the maximum amount of taxes they owe from trying to hide these matters, plus the maximum penalties. I authorise you all to apply the largest fines possible. If, for example, a property was bought ten years ago in the UK, use any currency calculation to our advantage. I don't care if you use the rate of today or ten years ago, whichever makes the sum grow bigger. Am I being clear?"

The three ladies seated opposite Madame Fouchard were accustomed to being under pressure: apply penalties, pay in the time allowed, no more flexibility-type pressure. But this focus on one chateau caused them to stare in disbelief at the copied pages in front of them. As a result of their work, bar owners, bankers, restaurants, car dealers had all been ruined over the years, but this was just different. They knew parts of this inspection would remain a mystery.

The eldest of the three senior inspectors seated at the end of the table cleared her smoker's throat.

"Madame, I fully understand what we have to do. But you know they could challenge us with a lawyer, and then we have to follow the law. I'm only saying we have little control over the speed they may eventually pay."

Nathalie Fouchard's mind was elsewhere, considering how long the latest Lasalle envelope would last her husband. She snapped back.

"They are wrong, we are right. Let me worry about time scales. Just do what I ask you to do, no more. You're now wasting time."

As the three left the room, Madame Fouchard's secretary finished her notes, her boss now shuffling papers back into a large grey file. This was not the same person she had started working for seven years ago. Something had changed. The regular meetings at home, a mystery caller from Geneva, office rumours about her husband's gambling addiction and now Paris checking on the running of the office. Events of late had dramatically changed this balanced woman. Why?

17

Jack was determined to get on with life; he owed it to his family. It was too late to erase the past. He and his two friends had become closer, bonding like a team competing for a once-in-a-lifetime challenge on the other side of the world. Somehow the good guys had to win.

As Jack took the stairs to the garage, Arno caught him up.

"How are the markets looking, Jack? See gold is taking a hammering, Dow all over the place. What do you think should I go for? Sub-Sahara sand producers or Amazon basin GPS providers?"

"Pretty good question, Arno. Let me think about that one. In the meantime, fancy a trip into town? I have to pick up a few things."

"Love to. Of course. Give us time to catch up."

As they approached the main gate, Boris was seen walking through the grounds, headphones attached, staring at a tablet screen.

"He's still around. A good man, but what more can he do?"

"That's another good question, Arno. Heard he feels a little guilty, like he should have moved more quickly to get into Crappy's computer."

"Well, all the hindsight in the world cannot change things. Frankly, we are in deep poop and unless Boris can erase everything the tax office has, we're way upstream without a paddle."

"By the way, any news from Eva? She always looks at you with a misty look in her eyes."

"She did, but sadly no, not even a quick email. Hate to say it, but I believe she'd had enough, maybe gone into hiding. Probably Paris is her new home ..."

"So now we have three empty apartments. Feels like this is sort of the direction we are going in. The tide's against us. How long will you stay around?" said Arno, looking hollow and concerned.

"Impossible question. The boys love their school, Carly loves our place, but I fear a pending tax bill will close me down. Business is not that hot. Just don't know."

As the two men descended down the hill away from the chateau, the postman passed by on his scooter. Both shook their heads but said nothing.

Eva closed the heavy green door to the penthouse as silently as possible. The Minister inside would most likely awake with a bad hangover. This, combined with his generous belly and bad breath, ensured that Eva awoke early, showered, dressed and promised herself a large coffee at the first terrace she came across on Avenue Foch.

Jack and Arno searched the newspaper stands outside the local station, hoping for uplifting news from anywhere else in Europe, anything to take their minds away from daily living at the chateau.

Simultaneously their mobiles announced a text from Dan.

Guess you're in town. If close come back quick. Something to discuss.

Jack, already hand in pocket, grabbed his car keys.

"Come on, Arno. What do you think, good news, bad news?"

"You know me well, Jack, I'm an optimist, but ..."

Jack powered the 4x4 through the back streets, narrowly missing head-on collisions twice. He was more focused on Dan's news, than local driver courtesy.

When they got back to the chateau's garage parking, the places of Pico Latouch and Bernard and Sophie Mardan were now empty. It seemed the cars had been collected to pay off accruing debts.

"The bastards have done it now. We knew this would happen, they know everything. Bumped into Annabel. She wants to leave tonight ..."

Dan was shaking as he spoke, a recorded delivery letter in his right hand. As Jack stared motionless towards the large Californian, Stephanie could be heard in the background.

"Come on, we know this is some kind of stitch-up. We have to keep on fighting. Someone is playing dirty. We have to do the same."

Arno just sagged, his large shoulders hung low. Between a mean smile and a pained look, he said, "Really Dan, this is veering out of control. They know what we hid. That little bastard Crappy set us up. We can't deny this anymore, they have the whole list."

"Calm it, Arno, please?" Jack put his arm on Arno's shoulder to steady him, saying softly, "I know the same letter is waiting for me."

Carly gave a sarcastic smile of agreement.

As Jack arrived back from the post office, he stopped the car on the drive and gazed towards the chateau. Still the same beautiful residence, the summer sun, perfect lawns, trees in full bloom, but he could not resist a long deep breath. It should never have turned out like this. Why did it have to go so wrong? He knew the opening of this letter would be one of life's painful moments. How could he break the news to Carly and the boys? Arriving at his apartment, he opened the door as quietly as possible so as not to alert his family and headed straight for his office.

He slid the letter open with crude chopping movement as if he wished Madame Boustain was the recipient. His eyes were drawn towards the middle of the letter. This was ruination, no more, no less. One month to pay, or else. Suddenly the magnificent view from his office window became blurred. He no longer lived in a beautiful place.

Arno switched on the treadmill at the back of the chateau gym. He was really not sure why he came to the gym or why he found himself standing on the machine. It was certainly not his favourite piece of training equipment. He was more a free weights man. As the belt began sliding backwards he walked, a slow motion walk, his eyes staring at the digital display, but his mind recording nothing. The last conversation with Stephanie being the only thing on his mind.

"Why the hell did we move to this place, why were you so stupid about where our money was placed, why are they after us?"

Too many "whys" for Arno.

Dan was now half-way through a bottle of Jack Daniel's, with no intention of stopping. He very much wanted to be alone, at the same time desperately needing company. Soon he would be numb. Any company would not understand him, his natural panache failing miserably.

Later, Jack and Arno walked side by side in the garden, conversation coming in short bursts.

"Have you seen that piece of work Crappy in the last few days?"

"No, Jack. Guess now he's done his deed he's gone. Too bloody dangerous to stay around, probably never see him again. Cruising the med with his Swiss friend I guess"

"Anything from Eva?"

"Again no. I think she's out of our life. Great pity, but we all have our limits and I guess she reached hers."

"Your plans?"

"It's summer time. Supposed to be having fun with the family. Tonight I have to break the news. No idea how to handle this. You?"

"Steph is pretty level-headed, but think I pushed it this time. She won't give me much space. Females never see these things the same way we do."

"You can say that again..."

Boris stared at the two men from the shadowy safety of a large conifer tree, some one hundred meters away. He desperately wanted to ease their pain. Unknown to his chateau friends he had been trying to access a variety of computers to trace the lost documents. He knew where the mail had been sent, and he had viewed other information on a variety of names – Lasalle, Geisinger, and Fouchard – but the trail went cold. Even with his skills he could not repair the immense damage done to his friends.

18

"No, it's not a favour I'm looking for, it's information about someone, very delicate information, and I can say no more over the telephone." Didier Grass felt very uneasy.

The man with the heavy Swiss Italian accent paused for thought.

"Okay, we can meet, but you come alone. Understand?"

"No question about that."

"And don't bring any smart devices. If I hear anything from my friends about our conversation... well, you know, don't you."

"Tell me the time and place that suits you. I will do exactly as you say."

"You'll hear from me later. I want to check some things first."

As the line went dead, Didier Grass stood up and took a very long breath. He stretched his shoulders back as if a good workout had been completed. The voice on the end of his office telephone had made him uncomfortable. Only one meeting had taken place with the man before. He had hoped another would never be necessary, but the only way he could dig deeper into the Chateau Montjan file was via such an unpleasant contact. He reflected on the usual lawyer-sewer creature-type jokes.

Celine's name lit up on Grass's desk phone.

"I did as you said, no disturbance during your last call, but Jack Rafter called. He told me he was speaking on behalf of himself, Dan Lancaster and Arno Van Bommel."

"Interesting, Celine. What now?"

"They have all received massive, *pay immediately or else* tax demands, with a one-month deadline. He said none of them can pay the amount, it's impossible."

"I was expecting this news. I can probably delay things for them, but no more. Please call him back, Celine. Tell him I am very concerned about this. It's possible that I may be able to find something more out. I have a meeting in the next day or two, but the outcome is impossible for me to predict. I will update him after this."

Celine touched her screen on Jack Rafter's number.

The bulging jackets of Carlo Frascati's two bodyguards almost blocked any possible view through the front windscreen of the BMW. Their necks were thick, head movement slow, large wrap-around Italian sunglasses hiding their narrow aggressive eyes. The small and cobbled old city street made walkers scramble onto the uneven pavement out of the way. The driver's stare was hollow, showing he could care less. The car stopped outside a darkly painted café. The front seat passenger used his massive hand to push his door open, pulled himself up and out of the car, and quickly gazed up and down the tiny street before opening the rear door for his boss.

Carlo Frascati said nothing, appearing disinterested in everything around him. The bodyguard pushed the café door open as if swatting a mosquito. Two old men were taking coffee next to the window and a waiter hovering in long white serving apron acknowledged the menacing presence in the doorway. One more person was seated at the back of the room, his expensive dark grey suit and perfect colour coordination almost announcing his profession.

The bodyguard rocked his head slowly up and down like a large predator preparing to destroy his prey. Carlo Frascati nodded towards the two old men. Didier Grass stood, wanting to show ultimate respect for the second meeting with the man.

Frascati gave an instruction in Italian to the bodyguard, who seemed keen to stay by the door. The BMW pulled slowly away.

"Been a long time, Mr Grass. I hear business is very good for your types these days in Geneva ..."

"Well, Geneva has grown a great deal in the last years. I guess we all profit."

Grass immediately wished he had skipped the last words of his sentence.

The waiter arrived with two coffees. No further words were spoken until he was back behind the bar.

"You told me you needed information on somebody. Give me a name."

"Harvey Lasalle."

"That dirty little half-German bastard. What's he trying to do, mess with your law firm?"

"No, not my firm, but possibly a group of clients. It seems he could be behind some kind of attack on these people. They own a chateau in France. He wants the place, the ground, or something these people have. I believe he is using the tax office to push them out of the place."

"When you mention tax you don't please me, and Harvey Lasalle... I don't like two disgusting parasites working together. He's never done a clean deal in his life. I took his father to one side years ago. He understood me, real well. That's why he stopped and his boy took over."

Grass looked over Frascati's shoulder to see the bodyguard push a fat American tourist back through the door. Clearly this would remain a very private meeting.

"So if I can help you and your clients, what do I get in return?"

Grass knew this would come up. Swimming with sharks gave a good chance of becoming their prey.

"I would like to help my clients. What's happening to them is bad. They are basically good people in the wrong place at the wrong time. But the way in which these families could be destroyed, even for a lawyer, is evil in my eyes.

Frascati cocked his head to one side with a very faint smile, mouthing, "Yea, lawyers ..." under his breath. "Let me tell you, Mr Grass, this person has no code of conduct. I know he is into a lot of bad things. Seems to be using some Swiss girl these days to obtain computer information for his advantage. There's a lot more but you will get this one day in an envelope. Don't whatever you do contact me about it. I have no knowledge. You do understand, I hope."

"I understand, very clearly.... but, of course, I wonder how I can help you in return? You know the possibilities are limited." Grass tried to choose his words carefully. The man opposite him had a reputation where life or death often mattered little.

"I hear rumours that you, your firm, are well connected with the Swiss banks. This interests me. My friends and I have some issues. Say some money needs to be protected. If you can help me, I will remember you as a good man."

Grass suddenly saw his legal world changing. One of his favourite films, *The Firm*, shot through his mind. Was he turning his practice into Bendini Lambert and Locke?

Carlo Frascati lifted his head towards the bodyguard, who immediately took out his mobile, grunting a short burst of incomprehensible Italian. The two old men were allowed to leave the café and within twenty seconds the BMW stopped at the door.

"You gonna hear from me, Mr Grass. Stay healthy."

With this, the two men shook hands and Frascati turned towards the door. Grass waited politely, watching the car pull away before heading back to his office.

Celine caught the mood of her boss as he walked past her glass door. He was normally a proud man but this afternoon his head was held low. He said little about this meeting. This normally meant he was treading on ice, maybe very thin ice. Celine became more interested by the moment.

"All ok I hope, Mr Grass. Was it a good meeting?"

Grass looked tired, as though he had worked all through the night.

"Fine, thanks Celine. Tell me, have you found any more background information on Harvey Lasalle?"

Celine gave herself silent praise. She knew it.

"Some bits and pieces. His property business is very erratic. He also lost a large deal recently in Vevey, but now it seems he has it back. Strange."

"Not so strange, Celine, he works in dark places."

"Also his mountain water business is under serious pressure, close to collapse."

Grass suddenly lost his worn look. His back straightened, staring at Celine with an intensity that made her uncomfortable. "Say that again."

"Well we saw reports that he's being sued by various suppliers. He can't deliver enough of his famous Alpine water due to several broken contracts."

"Celine, get Jack Rafter for me, it's urgent. I don't care where he is or what he's doing, I need to speak to him now..."

The car phone announced Grass's call. Jack was in the mountains, working hard on a fun day out with the family.

"Morning, Mr Grass."

"Mr Rafter, I have a question for you."

Jack felt uneasy. Carly and the boys were listening, plus Grass was dispensing with the usual pleasantries. Could this be good or bad to hear?

Reluctantly Jack said, "Fire away, Mr Grass."

"I seem to remember you arranging a satellite viewing, images of your home and the surrounding area."

"You're right; I have contacts with the European Space Agency in Holland."

"Would you mind telling me if anything specific came out of this?"

"Well, maybe we wasted our time and money."

Carly raised her eyebrows.

"Seems the only thing unusual thing the satellite picked up was a great deal of water flowing under the ground, literally passing under us, millions of gallons coming direct from the mountains, pure mountain water. Like I said, nothing earth shattering."

"Mr Rafter, this could be the most important discovery since we first shook hands, really."

"Could you elaborate?"

"Sorry, not now. I need to go deeper into something, but you have made things a great deal clearer. I assure you something could break in the near future. You will hear from me."

As Jack tapped the phone symbol button on his steering wheel, he had no idea how to feel. Positive, negative, what did this mean?

"Bloody over complex lawyers," he shouted.

Carly sensed his mood and quickly suggested lunch at McDonald's. Nick and Simon suddenly became very hungry.

Carlo Frascati immediately arranged a meeting with his two brothers. He saw a chance to get even with an old adversary, as well as tidy up his current family banking problems. Grass would do this; he would not be offered a choice.

On the outskirts of Annamasse, close to Geneva, the Frascati family had been active in the scrap business for many years. Competitors had come and gone, most never to return, leaving for new ground far away. As the bodyguards pulled up by the side of the prefabricated building, Donno Frascati looked down at his brother's arrival. The office three floors up gave a secure view over the yard, where everything from old cars to small boats, even military vehicles came to be broken down, crushed and recycled.

The lift opened directly into the office of Donno and Freddy Frascati. Carlo gave his brothers a solid hug, took off his jacket and sat at the end of the cluttered meeting table.

"So, seen with Geneva's lawyers, my brother that bothers me ..."

Donno frequently challenged his elder brother at the beginning of family discussions.

"This one should not bother you. He can help us in a couple of important ways."

Freddy took on the same doubtful demeanour as Donno. Lawyers could be bad news for people in their business, and they already had enough on their payroll.

"If I say the name Harvey Lasalle ..."

Donno and Freddy simultaneously hit the table with their fists, softly swearing in Italian.

Carlo turned his massive shoulders to face his brothers, head in hand.

"Okay, we all hate this man, but if we touch him, you know who gets the blame first. Our history goes way back. Now we can use this lawyer to take him off the street, send him all the evidence we have. He's gotta go down this time."

Now the brothers were making faint nodding gestures in approval. This could remove one of their old enemies for good.

Carlo added.

"You know we have problems coming up. So many Swiss banks are talking. They're talking to anybody who asks. We need a man who knows the inside story, who can protect our money. I guarantee he will do this the right way."

Carlo's bodyguard placed a bottle of Chianti on the table with three glasses, grunted "Saluté" and returned to read his newspaper in the far corner of the room.

Carlo expressed himself to his brothers, eyes wide open, hands in the air, asking for their agreement. They both gave the customary double nod.

"Let's make him hurt."

Carlo got up, pointing an open left hand to his guard heading for the lift. The brothers finished the wine whilst watching him leave.

Didier Grass called a meeting with his partners, Jason Bayer and Riener Merlot, to explain his recent rendezvous and more importantly the position he may have put the firm into. The meeting went well, especially when the senior partner, Bayer, who quickly realised the potential PR angles, putting one of Geneva's business monsters behind bars and the possibility of saving the owners of a beautiful chateau, gave his full agreement. This could shoot the firm into the top league; ensure constant fees for years to come. However the pending tax demand for the owners was something Grass worried about. How could he defend them? After all, the tax office now had the proof of their deception. Even with his extensive contacts this mountain looked too hard to climb.

Celine almost burst into Grass's office. He was rather unaccustomed to such impolite entry to his personal comfort zone.

"Mr Grass, you told me to look out for a delivery from an unusual source. I think this could be it."

Grass gave an intent look at the thick brown envelope under Celine's right arm.

"You could be right. How did it arrive?"

"A young Italian man, very well dressed, handsome, suddenly arrived at the reception and asked for me. He said in a very serious tone, "give this to Didier Grass, no one else, you understand?" He smiled and left immediately. I saw him jump into a black BMW. That's it."

"Good work, Celine. I need some time to check the contents. Don't let me be disturbed. I'll take lunch here today. Usual light salad, Perrier please."

Celine so desperately wanted to ask what could be so valuable in the envelope, but she valued her career too much for such an intrusion.

As Grass picked into his salad, gradually spreading the documents over his meeting desk, he could not believe the envelope's contents. Lasalle had indeed been busy, very busy. The package contained many photographs of Lasalle on his yacht, courting a variety of known business faces, politicians, one of a lady or Madame famous for running a prostitution ring specialising in rich clients needing *special favours*.

There were many copies of documents covering business transactions in Switzerland, France and Italy, probably obtained from a Notaire. Grass immediately recalled several of the deals turning dirty with suspected pay-offs involved, and a bank that Grass knew well, one known for its quirky client list. There were pictures of a beautiful Swiss, maybe German-looking woman, coming and going from hotel meetings with Lasalle, making visits to the bank. She always wore large sunglasses, her address in Evian Les Bains, copy documents seemingly from her computer. An unknown lady who met Lasalle at her home in Annecy les Vieux, listed as a senior figure at the local French tax office. And a man called Gerard Crappy listed as a director for one of Lasalle's shell companies.

Celine was called in. Grass needed to verify certain documents before moving forward. Once this was done a close prosecutor friend could be approached. Didier Grass was about to take the chance of his life. If this backfired, his situation could make the chateau owners appear safe and secure compared to his future ...

19

JACK AND HIS friends had been made aware of the new discoveries by Grass. Now the groups seen in the chateau grounds, the death of Henry in the cave and the satellite data became more understandable. They were sitting on a very valuable commodity that held no personal value for them, but could be a possible billion euro business for the right company.

Knowing this was fine, but they still lived daily with the pending threat of personal ruin orchestrated by yet another person who had apparently also left the chateau. His clear link to Lasalle now answered the owner's tide of doubts about his character. Grass had promised to get the legal process delayed, but more depressingly mentioned in the same breath that he was sure the tax authorities would make attachments on their assets in France any day: bank accounts blocked, property seized, cars, anything else the bailiff could get his grubby hands on. Most likely they would then move on with the assets held outside of France.

By this stage, the wives had become bitchy together. The men were drinking heavily and referring to the chateau as the new prison Montjan; the post-box became a pending time bomb. Poor Boris came and went, always offering to do anything his friends demanded.

"How can I help? Tell me, please."

He never received a positive response.

Jack was still active in the investment world. The trend followers had improved, but only slightly. There was still a long way to go.

Dan threatened to make this his final ski season. A trip to California was mentioned, back to his roots on the beach in Carmel. He was missing the Pacific.

Arno and Jack pretended to visit the gym regularly. Everyone in the chateau knew this was an excuse to drink expensive wine in an air-conditioned environment away from the constant flow of questions.

Eva's name came up at times in conversation. Her apartment was still being regularly cleaned, but it was obvious the lady had chosen new pastures. Not even the courtesy of an update phone call or email. This hurt the guys. She had panache; Dan described her as *hot*.

The mid-summer heat caused the remaining owners to spend more time in the comfort of the air-conditioned apartments. Large red umbrellas and sun blinds showed up on the south side of the chateau. Jack spent hours on his balcony, focused on his family, playing poker, chess, even monopoly with his boys. Later in the afternoon, just as he became the proud owner of all four London stations, the sound of a distant engine disturbed his concentration. He missed catching a clear sight of the vehicle but was mildly hopeful that this could be Eva's return. He shook his head and threw the dice again after being pestered by Simon.

"Shall we barbecue, Carly? Carly?"

"She's gone to the garage," joked Jack's eldest son.

"Why?"

"Forgot a bag or something, girls"

As Carly walked back onto the balcony she looked puzzled.

"Jack, do we have a new neighbour? There's a green Peugeot parked strangely close to the door in the garage, it's full of boxes."

"Not that I know of, although the gossip circuit has dried up recently."

Jack went ahead and cleaned the electric barbeque. Now, early evening, his appetite was growing in line with his white wine consumption.

As the evening light gave into a covering of cloud, Jack rested on his balcony rail, his family behind him discussing tomorrow's plans.

"You won't believe this but I'm sure I saw a light in Crappy's place."

"Don't be ridiculous, darling, he's long gone, and why would he come back after what he's been up to? You and the other guys got worryingly serious after that day the boys were attacked. Have another glass. It may improve your vision."

"Yea, maybe. I wanted to see him, simple as that."

The evening on the balcony ended with the family deciding to watch *Point Break* ... again. Jack took an early night in preparation for a Geneva meeting at 8.30 the next morning.

The iPhone alarm was not necessary. Jack was long awake since 5:30, switching the vibrating device off quickly so as not to wake Carly. He took a shower, enjoyed a small bowl of cereal, a large orange juice and put his suit on. Collecting the prepared dossier from his office table, a quick kiss on his wife's forehead, within seconds he was halfway down the chateau stairs. He stopped abruptly, hand in pocket. Had he taken Carly's car keys by mistake?

As he fumbled pulling the keys out, the door a few meters in front of him opened slowly, very slowly. Gerard Crappy had his back towards Jack and was doing his best to pull a large wheeled suitcase through the door, but so silently.

"Crappy, you're back!" Jack shouted with all the available air in his lungs, intending to wake the whole chateau.

Crappy turned like a cat awoken by a gun shot.

"Um ... Er... briefly."

He pulled the case violently, smashing it against the door.

"Think we all need to talk with you. Appears you've done a lot of harm in this place."

Jack's volume was now even more impressive.

As Jack moved quickly down the next flight of stairs, Crappy almost threw his case towards the garage door. But Jack was too quick. Now he could repay Crappy for what had happened to his boys. With a short controlled jump from three steps higher his right foot connected with Crappy's upper back, a perfect side kick. Crappy hit the wall immediately bouncing off, another sidekick to his left ear followed with even more aggresion. Crappy hit the floor like a drunk in a bar fight.

Arno was now in his doorway.

"So the little bastard came back. Let me get my baseball bat.

Hold him Jack."

As Jack turned towards Arno, Crappy pulled out a mobile from inside his jacket pocket, hitting the redial button, covering the phone with his left hand as blood began to trickle from the swelling around his ear.

"Try moving ... please. First I'll break your left hand, then your right. That last kick was a warm-up. Can you imagine how much I would like to kick the life out of you? You little bastard."

Arno was now close behind Jack. Dan slammed his door open, Valerie and Nina Asperen peeping through a small slit in their door at the mounting testosterone in the hallway.

Arno did indeed bring his baseball bat, now gesturing for Jack to move aside so that he could take a clean shot.

"This little piece of scum. Let me do it, Jack, can't stop myself. I'll feel so good afterwards."

Dan put his hand on the bat.

"We all owe you one for what your friends did to Henry Cameron. Remember the cave attack, your dumb bastard friends?"

Crappy was cowering like a bock about to be devoured by three hungry lions.

"You're wrong, I did nothing. It's not me you want, it's someone else. I just did what they told me. I had no choice."

"Lying sad shit," said Jack lining up another side kick.

As the three men vied for the next shot at Crappy, they failed to hear the hum of a car engine outside.

"You're coming to our lawyer, today, to confess over a lot of things. You have no choice. Let's lock him in the cellar."

Jack bent forward to pull Crappy up by his jacket. As he lifted the small man from the ground he noticed the mobile in his shaking hand.

The Magnum was only ten centimetres from the back of Arno's head. A strong smell of sweat and cheap deodorant alerted Dan.

"You take your hands off him. I'd hate to put a hole in your smart suit."

Two large men in dark suits, sunglasses, stood uncomfortably close to Crappy's worst enemies. Their calm demeanor gave an eerie feeling.

"We're gonna take him with us. You try anything, you die. Call the police, you die. Got it?"

The situation called for common sense. The Magnum was being pointed from Jack to Dan, then to Arno. One man took Crappy's arm, the other his case, always keeping the right arm free for any possible challenge. They moved backwards out of the main chateau door, bundled Crappy into the back seat and sped away shooting loose gravel over the trimmed gardens.

"Tell me this moment did not happen," said Jack, craning his neck towards the chateau driveway.

"I considered making a move on those goons, but the danger of you guys getting hit, was high. So sorry," added Dan.

"Thank god my kids didn't see this. Like a bloody scene from *Taken*." Jack picked up his file.

"Think I'll cancel my Geneva appointment. Give the lawyer a call."

Arno put his hands on the shoulders of Jack and Dan. "No surprise that car had a Geneva number plate. Don't forget to tell him that."

During the day, and especially after the events of the early morning, a trip to the post box appeared safe and secure compared to a large Italian thug waving a Magnum in your face. As the mail boxes were emptied, normal letters, bills and supermarket promos were all that came out. Momentary relief was the mood of the day.

20

In response to Jack's latest call, Didier Grass confirmed he was busy, hard at work with the chateau situation. Jack always detected Grass was so close, keen to say more but, like a lawyer, also trained to hold back when not at a stage to give specific details. He always updated his friends immediately after the calls. Arno was extremely bitter.

"I can't believe he was here again, in our hands and we let him escape. Did the lawyer tie those guys into the Geneva businessman, Jack?"

"Oh yes, he was sure they were hired goons connected to him, most likely to protect Crappy whilst he got out of the chateau."

"So if we survive this, does it mean Crappy goes free and we get busted? Not exactly modern-day justice."

"Arno, I keep getting the impression Grass is moving on something big, but he's cautious, like a good lawyer should be. He's going to protect his own backside first, then ours."

"What the hell, Jack. Never been in such a dam complicated load of shit in my life before. Someone should write a book about this."

"Crossed my mind too, but I need a clear head to do that. One day ..."

"Listen, Jack. You and I can always talk frankly together, we're close. Think it would do us both good to play some golf, take our minds off this place. They know me at the Evian club. What do you think? We need some fresh air, they can screw us but they can't take the life out of us."

"It's early, a beautiful day. Sad to see you end up the loser, but yeah, let's get away from here."

Within half an hour, the Panamera was hitting one-eighty. Soon the autoroute would split, south towards Chamonix, north to Thonon-les-Bains, then onto Evian-Les-Bains, the golf course overlooking the lake of Geneva.

"What do you think? Pretend we don't have a care in the world, play eighteen holes, or shall we get real, play nine and drown our sorrows in Au Bureau?"

"Don't mind, Jack. Every ball I hit I'll imagine it's Crappy's head. A good feeling."

As Arno manoeuvred his Porsche into the golf club parking and clicked his boot open, both men felt more relaxed. It was a good idea to get out for the day. Both were determined to talk about anything other than the mounting problems at the chateau.

After registration at the clubhouse, Jack tossed a coin to decide who would tee off. Arno won, threatening Jack with a mean game.

By the end of nine holes, Jack had proved his point. He was the superior golfer by far, Arno showing more brute force than touch style. As they'd made their way around the course, the conversation had ranged from cars to stock markets, and the old days in Holland. The chilled water bottles now empty, both men felt ready for a cold beer. Evian was in full summer tourist mode, the parking difficult but it was always possible to find a space in the Casino parking if the tip was big enough. Arno thought twenty euros more than generous.

Jack checked in with Carly. All was ok. Arno moaned about the lack of seats on the terrace, inside being the only place available. The first cold beer went down quickly. A second was ordered.

"Sorry, Jack. Know we have a sort of silent code here, but it's on our minds day and night. What will you do if this goes to the wire? Your boys I mean ..."

"Depends on how far they take this. If I loose the penthouse, it's a lot of money. Maybe they sell it at some corrupt auction, somebody gets a dream home, I end up with nothing. As they know about everything we own, there's no place to turn. And you?"

"Steph wants to go back to Holland. We have a big family but, like you, if we lose this big investment and they talk to the Dutch tax office ... what do they say about being in something up to your neck?"

Jack hated the pending impact for his family more than anything else. He wished Arno had left the subject alone, but he found himself staring at the bar TV. Arno carried on talking, but Jack had switched off.

The second beer was drained almost as quickly as the first. Arno lifted his hand to attract the barman.

"Hold on, Arno, put your arm down."

"You mean that's it for today?"

"No, look, the TV."

Arno turned showing little enthusiasm.

"That's him, Lasalle, the guy Grass told us about."

"So what are they doing with him?"

"Barman, can you turn that up?"

"Everybody is asking that today. Don't you know the story? It repeats every half an hour. Another capitalist falls. Ha ha ha..."

Jack left his barstool for the quietest corner he could find. Arno was now fixed on the screen.

"Didier Grass, please, it's Jack Rafter."

"One moment, sir."

"Are you watching a television, Mr Rafter? There are some interesting reports today."

Grass suddenly came across as a smug fixer, a top lawyer for the first time since the relationship began.

"I'm in a bar in Evian with Arno Van Bommel. What's happened to Harvey Lasalle?"

"From what I understand he is in deep trouble, under arrest. They caught up with him in Paris. There's a long list of demeanours from being involved in a prostitution ring to blackmailing clients into submission, hacking computers for his own gain, a terrible chap. Just today alone, a long list of people have come forward with serious grievances. I think we can assume his business days are over. By the way, did you see the clip about the beautiful woman also arrested at her home in Evian this morning?"

"Um, no, but if it's the one who came here to steal our computer files, I hope the bitch will go to jail for the rest of her miserable life. So, ok, but where does this leave us? The tax office still holds our documents. Even if Lasalle is out of the picture, he's managed to leave us on the hook ..."

Jack's initial enthusiasm struggling.

Grass sighed. "That's a hard one. We need to prove he set this thing up. This could go on for years, I'm afraid. In the eyes of the tax office you have been doing your best to avoid paying tax, and that's going to be an uphill struggle."

Jack's mind was taking the usual roller-coaster ride.

"So we wait, and wait, until they decide to take everything."

"We are doing our best, Mr Rafter, really."

Jack gave a polite "Thanks, goodbye" and walked back to update Arno.

The drive back to the chateau left both men dazed, the good news that Lasalle had been arrested, and especially his hacker, overshadowed by the pending tax attack. Dan was called to meet at Jack's for an update.

At the gate, Jack and Arno checked their post-boxes. Both were void of anything surprising.

21

A NORMAL DAY for employees at the tax office came nowhere close to exiting, even the expectation of unusual events would be hard to imagine. So as Nathalie Fouchard turned into her private parking space beside Annecy's Central Tax Bureau, it seemed like any other working day. Her aging Citroen croaked and died.

Upon arriving at her office, the secretary informed her about an urgent call from Paris. She *must* be ready and prepared for the 10 a.m. caller.

As if to be insulted by such punctuality, she felt the urge to enquire more about the reason behind it ... or should she remain professional, like it's just another petty administration matter. What else could it be?

"Did the caller mention anything specific? You know how busy I am these days. We're living in challenging times, everybody wants a delay. I too have performance targets to achieve ..."

She felt she had said more than enough. At the back of her mind many issues tangled her thought process. Harvey Lasalle's arrest. Could this be the reason for the call? Perhaps it was the growing village gossip about her husband's gambling addiction, or the Chateau Montjan dossier. She was backing herself into a corner, the walls getting smaller by the day, yet to avoid this call would be impossible. Over her crowded mind she realised her secretary was still talking.

"Sorry, a lot going on lately."

"No problem, Madame Fouchard. I only said the caller will be a man, Mr Volat. His secretary insisted you must be available. You must receive the call in the privacy of your office as the content will be very important. That's it."

Nathalie Fouchard desperately wanted to exchange roles with her secretary this day. She was aware of the name Volat, but this was a man so senior, his name often quoted in official government documentation. He gave views on the country's tax situation. Why would he make a personal call to her office?

She had already suffered a sleepless night after watching countless repeats of the Lasalle arrest. Now this punctual call. She could only consider the stupid reckless day she met with a shady Swiss businessman and agreed to go along with his plan. It had appeared safe at the time: he was so powerful, offers of so much money, her personal problems solved forever.

As she closed her office door, glancing at her watch, seeing a little over one hour remained before the call was due, a bulging grey file at the back of the cabinet caught her eye. She recalled a chilling meeting with a British man a couple of years earlier. He had made the poorly calculated short-term decision of running a full-time chalet business in the mountains. A magnificent twenty-bedroom place. But he decided to pretend he remained fiscally resident in the UK. The place was busy every winter, more than forty guests when full. His downfall. Local jealousy, the internet, followed by the tax office checking on local supermarkets, ski schools, bank accounts. His story of having a very large family, *who loved to ski,* fell apart immediately. During the process, a meeting had been arranged by the man's lawyer at Madame Fouchard's office. It was obvious from the initial handshake and the aggressive glare on the man's face that he detested his situation, even more the people who brought him into it. He made veiled threats of shopping local people.

"The truth is always hidden in this country. Everyone hides behind one another who were also cheating the taxman."

Madame Fouchard had tried her best to ignore this, but the man had become more incensed by the moment. Banging the table, she had considered asking her secretary to call the police, when suddenly the man had stood up, shaking a fist at her.

"People like you always get paid back. Some way, some how you will hurt one day. Wait till they come knocking at your door, then see how it feels ..."

With that the man left alone, probably for the airport. He was never heard of again. She often chose to blank out the more aggressive meetings, but this one was coming back regularly to haunt her.

Five minutes to ten. She could not remember ever checking her watch so often. After one hour at the desk she'd managed to consume five cups of coffee. Her secretary's face showed more surprise at every refill, any knock at the door immediately rebuffed with a short "Busy, much later."

The well-worn phone touchpad held her attention like never before. She checked with her assistant, making sure she was glued to her post. Ten a.m. came and passed. Could this be a joke? No, not at the tax office. Jokes did not exist. Five past ten. Maybe the important man had other more pressing issues, changed his mind, perhaps changed his plans.

Clouds were gathering over the lake of Annecy. Was this a subtle sign for the future? Ten past ten. Something was wrong. Why had there been the pressure of having to be ready for a ten o'clock call?

Her nervous system was on high alert; too much coffee mixed with stress.

She raised herself out of her leather chair to reach for the window, needing some fresh air instead of the cool breeze pumped into the office. At full stretch, her desktop phone ringing caused her to fall back into the chair. She stared, momentarily frozen, looking at her right hand, almost willing it to pick up the receiver.

"Yes."

"Madame Fouchard, I have your call."

Her voice was shaking, but she had to hide it.

"Nathalie Fouchard."

"Good morning, Madame Fouchard, I have Jean-Claude Volat for you. Hold on please."

Many seconds passed. She directed her heavy breathing away from the mouthpiece.

"With Jean-Claude Volat. Madame Fouchard?"

"Yes, I was expecting your call earlier."

"Really... Well, we are both busy people, so let me stop wasting your time and come quickly to the point. I have taken over control of the Rhône Alp's region and other departments. That makes me your new chief, but we will probably have little contact. I'll appoint someone soon to deal directly with you, but in the meantime some changes will occur, and quickly. Later today a team will arrive from Paris. They will report to me concerning your entire department until I decide otherwise. From this moment you are to halt any activity whatsoever with regard to ... a certain Chateau Montjan and its owners. My team will be given all, and I mean all documents you have on this matter, computer files, everything. Is that clear?

Well, Madame Fouchard?"

"Very clear, Monsieur Volat."

Nathalie Fouchard shook in her seat, she nervously tapped her fingers on the mousepad. Any moment the name Harvey Lasalle would come into the conversation, she was sure.

"I am also considering moving your function to another office. Lyon, maybe Marseille. I'll decide on this soon. You've been far too long in one place. Do you have any questions?"

Something had changed dramatically. She felt weak, fragile, her life turned around in one short phone call.

"No questions, Monsieur Volat."

"Maybe you should prepare for my team's arrival, all files ready. They have a tight schedule. My secretary will update you on the matters I mentioned. Goodbye, Madame."

Within thirty seconds, the secretary announced a call from Monsieur Fouchard.

"Can you come home, darling? I'm out of money. Is there more coming from what's-his-name, Henry Lavelle, the Swiss man? Please, can you come?"

The smell of alcohol was almost coming through the phone.

"I'll be home sometime, sometime."

Each and every moment of every day the remaining chateau owners saw bears about to devour them. Was the postman lingering longer at their mail boxes? Could the service personnel be bailiffs in disguise? Knocks at the door were checked through the spy hole before opening. The press offered no comfort at all. Every day a new headline high-lighted the rich being targeted, politicians promising any form of tax avoidance from the largest corporations to the local shopkeeper. *Your days are numbered.*

Jack had good and bad days, swimming in the local lake with his boys and Dan lifted his spirits. But as soon as he sat in front of his com-puter, his mind drifted off to that place he so often visited in the middle of the night, half asleep, half awake, the negative winning over the posi-tive. Daytimes were not getting easier.

Arno invited his friends to a barbeque in the garden one evening, his attempts at humour made in respect of poor Henry.

"So fellow chateau owners, I now know my future. Spoke with Hollywood this morning. Actually they're chasing me."

His friends already showed broad polite smiles.

"They're offering me a big film role. No, seriously, could be one of two titles, either, *Fat Iron Man* or *Taken, reluctantly, but rapidly given back when it got light*. What shall I go for?"

As always, Arno drew laughter and shakes of the head. Everybody knew Henry could have told it better.

Jack was busy with the barbecue. "Anybody care to eat? The meat looks good and tender"

A flurry of activity prepared the table and poured generous glasses of wine. A toast to everyone's health. The atmosphere, for a short period, hid the real lives of the chateau owners.

As the wine flowed, conversation bounced from the positive: Dan considering a trip back to his birthplace, Carmel, Jack seeing the mar-kets somewhat improving, to the negative: more expense on the chateau accounts due to the departure of three apartment owners. As dessert was served, a tasty concoction of strawberries, Häagen-Dazs ice-cream and small berries from the local markets, Arno spotted someone at the main gate.

"Strange, it's nine in the evening. The bad guys don't normally work this late."

Jack, Dan and Arno all stood, showing animal-like instinct as if to protect the family. They walked towards the black gate. The man peering through the metal bars stood firm. As they drew closer, the man became uncomfortable. No one smiled, only fixed stares from those on the inside. Jack took out his keys, ready to open the small side gate.

"Good evening, gentlemen. So sorry to bother you at this time."

A very suspicious Jack responded. "What do you want exactly; we are all well insured ..."

"Oh, nothing like that. I have a letter for Jack Rafter. If he's not available, Arno van Bommel. If ...

The man was cut short by Jack. "I'm Jack Rafter; you can give it to me."

"Sorry, gentlemen, I may sound vague. I work in a local lawyer's office."

The mood chilled immediately.

"No problems really. This letter arrived today from one of our offices in Paris, by courier, with a simple instruction to deliver it to this chateau. That's why I'm here tonight. Just finished work. Sorry, I can't tell you more."

The three men remained suspicious, thanked the messenger and returned to the barbecue.

"What do you think, open it now or at the table? What could it be?" Arno whispered to Jack and Dan.

"I'm so fed up with waiting for the next bomb, let's just do it here, together," said Jack.

> This coming Friday, a very important meeting needs to
> be held, all owners should be available in the chateau, say
> around eleven am, gather in one apartment, Thank you.

No signature or other clue gave the letter's author away.

22

Harvey Lasalle managed to post bail. The one million Swiss Franc bond hardly damaging his wife's account. She didn't know the man anymore; just as long as he kept paying, she would play along. He knew his time was limited. The prosecuting vultures would soon prove the many charges against him. He had to tread carefully. What he could do to stay a free man challenged him every waking moment.

"Madame Fouchard, you know who this is. I have left several messages. Please call me back. I need to speak with you urgently. Everything is ok. I will explain."

Since the arrival of the new team from Paris, files had literally closed in front of her and there was still the pending threat of being moved to another office far away. Nathalie Fouchard was adamant she would never speak with Lasalle again. She currently took full advantage of the much-abused French social security system, calling in sick on a regular basis. Her husband was now a true basket case. She also gave in and joined him for an early glass of wine, sometimes from 9:30 in the morning as it seemed to ease the anxiety.

"Madame, you know who. I will keep calling, you know I will."

Lasalle sat low in his office chair wearing jeans, Gucci loafers and a polo shirt as if on holiday. Now his views towards the French Alps appeared further away. Employees faked respect, as if they knew he would soon disappear for a considerable number of years. The newspaper headlines were on full display at the company reception. Now a very large clock ticked away on his own life. He made call after call, searching for the source of his predicament.

"Of course you remember me, Lasalle Harvey. Like to offer you lunch. Need to catch up on a few matters. How soon can you make it?"

The replies were always the same. "Sorry, far too busy these days. Let me get back to you."

He even called the dirty back-street lawyers, promising every form of bribe in his armoury.

"Use of a luxury yacht, Europe's most desirable ladies, a gift, the latest Lamborghini?"

Something blocked his old information trail and nobody was prepared to walk this trail for any price.

Anna Tina Geisinger deleted every message he left. All traces of her contacts with the man were erased from both computers. Deep in her heart she knew her fate. Somebody with powerful connections had set them both up. The evidence overwhelmed her. How could so much detail come to light?

Her life had turned full circle in a few small weeks. Now she was a small cog in the wheel. Her boyfriend making regular excuses to cancel the next date. The long mirrors now ignored, soon she would appear in court. Why did looks matter any more?

Didier Grass was unaware of the changes at the tax office. He decided to play things low key until Lasalle was safely behind bars, taking days off, long weekends, and benefitting from the summer temperatures.

Carlo Frascati remained silent. Grass felt fine about his actions regarding Lasalle. However, for his chateau clients, he remained powerless. Apart from the legal process barriers, playing for time, incorrect documents from tax office errors, he could see no way to help them.

Gerard Crappy signed for the hire car, ignored the, "*Pleasant day, sir*" wishes from the Hertz girl and flew towards the parking lot, throwing his small leather bag at the back seat. Within half an hour he would be in Antibes. The anticipation of becoming a yacht owner as opposed to arranging the finance for other people caused him to smile. A cold false smile that showed little concern for what may be happening to his old neighbours. As he arrived at the Sun Seeker offices, the smile became broader.

23

THE CARMILLON COLOURED TGV pulled into Chambéry main station at 10:15, perfectly on time. A mix of tourists gazing bewilderingly from left to right, and office workers pushing through the bemused arrivals, glued to their mobiles, children screamed as granny and granddad held out their arms to greet the tiny relations.

One person seemed oblivious to it all, marching through the crowd, firmly pulling open the door of the dark red Audi taxi.

"Chateau Montjan, directly. I don't need a tour of the city."

The Moroccan driver nodded in approval, whilst taking a shifty sideways look at the interesting passenger on his back seat.

Jack had proposed his place for the mystery Friday morning meeting, making a quick visit to his post box beforehand. There was still no sign of evil proceedings. By 10:30 everybody had arrived. Jack was pensive.

"It's not the lawyer, the tax offices don't work this way, a bailiff... well no, Crappy, no bloody way. Any other ideas who's coming?"

Heads shook around the room.

"Maybe it's this Lasalle creep, as he's now out on bail, offering us a deal."

Dan was clutching at straws.

More shaking of heads.

The chateau gates opened for the Audi taxi, the driver ordered to proceed slowly.

"Don't make any unnecessary noise..."

Jack persisted with his theories.

"Maybe someone else knows about the water flowing under here. Someone's going to offer us mega millions for the place."

"Sure, Jack, then they can turn this into a film. We'll become top box office stars, move to Hollywood."

Arno was pacing, twitching, and showing his discomfort.

Dan looked around the room.

"Maybe we should have chosen Hollywood over the Alps."

Jack brought the exchanges back to firm ground. "We should be perhaps a little more serious. Nothing pleasant has happened to us for months now. Why should this be better?"

Boris again offered any assistance he could dream up. "Would you like me to record the whole thing, high quality disk, in case we need evidence? You've been kind enough to let me take my summer holidays here. I'd love to do something useful for you guys."

"Just stay close, Boris, sort of in the background, but be ready for action, if you know what I mean," requested Jack.

The warm summer sun gave the chateau wives a chance to lounge on the penthouse balcony acting as if they didn't have a care in the world, their conversation also mostly directed at who was coming at 11:00 this morning.

"Jack's acting more like the old Jack these days. Nick and Simon are pestering him. That's good for his mind. I think he even sleeps through the night and the humour's far more like him. What else can he do?"

Carly was refreshing the cold drinks.

"Arno has mood swings, he always did. I hope today he swings to the happy side." Stephanie watched the red Audi depart through the chateau gates.

The guys inside the apartment declared a quick, *"all the best* "with their coffee mugs to whoever, whatever was about to happen this morning.

Jack checked the TV.

"Almost eleven and the markets are doing a Friday bounce. Good sign."

The door buzzer gave two firm rings. All eyes in the room flashed from one to the other. Jack managed a tense smile whilst moving to the hallway.

"You know what they say; life all comes down to a few minutes ..."

His friends placed the mugs on the coffee table and rose, staring towards the door.

Jack tried peering through the security hole, but it was dark. He took a deep breath, head back, pulling the door open with a firm left hand.

"Somewhere in the back of my mind I thought this could be possible, but ..."

The familiar broad smile, perfect cosmetics. Eva looked wonderful. Jack thought he saw a tear in her beautiful green eyes. She held two Champagne bottles high in each hand.

"Am I the fortunate fellow?"

"I'm back, darling. Perhaps invite me in?"

Jack embraced Eva warmly with both arms.

"First things, first, Eva. We missed you. This feels good."

"For me too, Jack, been far too long. So sorry."

Arno, Boris and Dan looked like three happy teenagers.

"You're back..." they declared in surprised unison.

The balcony now empty, all eyes focused on Eva as she entered the lounge.

"Could I join you in one of those?"

Three large guys watched by wives all crushed towards the coffee machine, Eva's request a priority.

She took a deep breath, clasped her hands across her stomach and sat in the furthest corner.

"You know, for the past weeks, even on the train this morning, I played and replayed this scenario over and over in my head. How do I explain this? You all probably thought I'd had enough, get out, and leave them to handle it alone?"

No reaction came from the faces fixed on Eva, not even a small shake of the head.

"I knew we reached the point where something had to be done, and I was powerless here. I became so angry, hatred was building in me."

Eva was slipping into a mix of accents: French, English and somewhere halfway to Moscow.

"At first I was scared, thinking how I can pull this off. Then the anger returned, red tape can always be broken. I intended to do just that."

Jack surveyed his neighbours. Even during his most intense meetings, when a client was about to entrust his life savings to an opaque company located on a small island thousands of miles away, never had he seen such expectation.

Eva continued. "I know you have all been through hell, especially you Jack and Carly. How you managed with your boys ... I can't get my head around that. The heartless bastards behind this deserve a miserable end. I can't guarantee that, but I can tell you one important thing. It's over, yes you heard right, it's really over. You will never hear how, don't ever ask me that question please. All that personal information we lost is by now shredded, gone forever, as if it never existed. People have been removed. I hear that Swiss dog will soon be in jail for many years, his hacker also. We can continue our wonderful life here. No, I'm not joking..."

Never before had such large egos been so silent, from the ski teacher to the car dealer, the financial man, even the tech genius. All remained in shock, mouths moved, grunts came and went. Slowly Jack stood up.

"Eva, how can we ever repay you? I was wondering why the whole thing became delayed, checked my post box daily, wished a miracle could happen, then gave myself a reality check."

Arno also managed to speak.

"Can I propose a pretty disgusting celebration tonight, all of us? I don't care if I empty my wine cellar, hangover for a week, doesn't matter."

Carly noticed Jack staring at nothing in particular, but his face said everything. He'd become ten years younger during the morning.

Eva sat back in her chair, comfortable with her presentation, but had to ask, "one major question, what's happened to that piece of human garbage, Crappy? My contacts have no angle on him. Any ideas?"

Jack slapped his hands together.

"Saw him back at the chateau a few days ago. He was trying to leave very early with his gear. I kicked him to the ground. The guys were ready to help me put him in the cellar. But two heavies appeared from nowhere, waving a large handgun in our faces. They took him away. Guess he's long gone, far away in hiding, probably never see him again. He let all this happen, set us up, happily gave our most personal information to his paymaster. What he set up on Nick and Simon ... wonder what his cut was for that?"

"We're never gonna know, but he deserves some kind of justice. It's just not right that he walks away a free man. We know the law will do nothing. I could happily strangle him for his friends attack in the celler. Henry should be with us today."

Annabel dropped her gaze to the floor as Dan stopped talking abruptly.

"I'll speak with the lawyer, see what he thinks. He's well connected; maybe he can turn up some data on where he's hiding. A trail. Come to think of it, Boris, you keep offering. How about his computer?" Jack winked hopefully at Boris.

"I have his old codes, assuming he hasn't changed anything. Worth a try, let me get to work."

Boris immediately left for the comfort of his bedroom.

An air of surprise remained throughout the day in Chateau Montjan. The residents all returned to the comfort of their own apartments after the breaking news. The big remaining questions that filled their heads being. *How could Eva do this, what possible contacts could simply make this disappear? Was it really over, had Crappy left their lives for good?*

Jack decided, for the moment at least, to keep the news between the owners. If he told the lawyer it was almost a guarantee things would be made more complicated, that's what lawyers do. Moreover, the residents needed some time to recharge, without any more doubt or questions. However, a simple request for the lawyer to try finding the whereabouts of Gerard Crappy would be good, despite the reservations from the wives.

"Leave it alone now, he's out of our lives and that's the most important thing."

Jack, Arno, and Dan felt violated, cheated by a disgusting individual. This moment came and went but their anger remained. He'd come close to destroying what they had built; and without Eva he would have succeeded. The wounds were too fresh to simply forget about the man.

24

Boris spent hours alone, both inside the chateau and around the grounds, his laptop always open with a ghostly trance fixed on the ever-changing screen. Something was complicating his life and the chateau males were getting concerned about their Dutch friend.

"Sorry, Jack, Crappy or some specialist has changed a lot. It's very hard to get into his machine. I even checked with an old university friend in Brussels. He's employed by the Eurocrats to protect their equipment, top notch guy. He's got an idea how I can get in but I can't hassle him. He's always under pressure and earns like twenty thousand a month..."

"Keep trying, Boris, you can do it."

"What will you do if I find him?"

"Don't know. I'd have to discuss that with the guys. Dan and Arno feel extreme about him. If they get their hands on him ... well, plus he could have scarred my boys for life. He has to pay for that, it's on my mind daily."

"Is it worth all this?"

"I think so, but it's so tricky to bring him to justice. If we open that can again it's guaranteed our tax issues could come up."

"A hit man?"

"Arno knows those types in Amsterdam, but I can't drag my family into that situation."

"So maybe an accident?"

"Now you're talking. That appeals to me, the guys too. Just find him first ..."

"Hope he's still in France?"

"I've got a meeting. Have a good day, Boris."

Anna Tina Geisinger had done a pretty good job of protecting Gerard Crappy's computer. She used her considerable expertise to ensure all suspicious access was virtually impossible, except of course via her codes.

As she gazed across Lac Léman towards Lausanne, she felt her day could have begun better. An official recorded delivery letter thrown on the desk confirmed that she must appear in court in Thonon Les Bains in one month. Her lawyer should see this immediately but she had no enthusiasm. To show him would only generate another large bill and her income stream had stopped as soon as Lasalle was arrested. The pattern with her boyfriend continued.

"Sorry, too busy to meet this week."

Surely he had another girl. The bastard ...

Caring for her stunning looks was a thing of the past. She now stayed alone in her small rented apartment, eating takeaway pizza and drinking cheap supermarket wine. At least a kilo had been added to her once tight waistline. The girlfriends she lost to concentrate on a wonderful future had now moved on. How could she explain this cage that she now lived in to them? Another dead end.

A downright disgusting thought that played around constantly in her spinning head was the recent invite from Gerard Crappy to spend time on a yacht in the south of France. This made her even more depressed.

Why him? Nice guys did exist, but in another world. Not hers anymore.

As the days went by her computer remained the only close companion. The more she considered the misery that was now virtually guaranteed for the next few years in her young life, the more the resentment grew towards the characters that put her in this place. She began a short mental list of her most hated people.

First Harvey Lasalle, but he was going to jail, what could she do to him?

The chateau owners, but they were just innocent puppets she had played with and used for short term gain.

The Swiss mafia. The vague gossip was that they were behind her downfall but she wouldn't be so stupid to try harming them.

Gerard Crappy. He treated her like a cheap hooker, available if required, dismissed when the job was over. Yes, this is her most hated person. She's awaiting a judge, Lasalle is all finished, but Crappy's as free as a bird.

As the growing hatred consumed her she opened the second bottle of sweet white wine. The more she drank, the better it tasted. It was rubbish but her head saw more and more logic by the hour, Crappy had to pay for her downfall. She could enter his computer but how much deeper could she sink if he discovered her to be the culprit. Someone else had to help and the last glass from the second bottle told her who. She had kept the email addresses of Jack, Arno and Dan.

Gentlemen, don't bother replying to this mail, it won't work, and you will never find me. But I believe you have a tech guy working with you, we almost met once in our private cyber world. I need to speak with him, only him, let him have this mobile number. I promise you will not regret it. Maybe one day we will meet in person.

"What do you think, real or fake?" Jack read the email to Arno.

"I checked with Dan. We all got the same. Must be the bitch who hacked our systems."

"Thought the same, Arno, but what's the harm in Boris talking with her? He's smart, we can't pull this off, they live in a different world. One strange nerd term she knows we're not Boris."

"Let's ask him. Where is he?"

Boris was in his favourite place, a cosy green hammock, in one of the small forests, hidden from all, listening to music totally unknown to the guys. Eyes closed, his body made nervous movements to the rhythm.

Dan almost pounced on the relaxed Boris.

"Boris, sorry to bother you, man. We need to speak with you about something ... well ... weird."

"Sure, Dan. Where are the guys?"

"Behind me. Here they come now."

Boris jumped to the ground, quickly surrounded by his friends.

"Take a read of this, we all got it this afternoon."

"She wants to talk to me, why? Thought she was arrested, pending a possible jail term?"

"We have no clue, we can't call. What if she talks computer tech? Only you can do that."

Jack gave a look of confidence towards Boris.

"Okay, I'll do it but when ... where?"

"Here looks good, feel ready?" Jack acting as if he was closing a new deal.

"Wish me luck, guys. Never met a geek with her looks before."

A soft Swiss German accent greeted Boris after three rings.

"Hallo."

"Um, hi, this is Boris. Hear you want to talk to me."

"Ah Boris, the man I almost met recently in our secret world. Think you took the wrong route, but you came close."

The third bottle was taking its toll on Anna Tina. Boris noticed her slurred speech.

"Yes, sorry about that, face-to-face would have been my preference."

Anna Tina began feeling flirty.

"Good things happen to clever boys, you know."

Boris felt compressed, three men almost rubbing heads with him and still not hearing everything.

"Well, I called, like you asked. Tell me why?"

"Naughty Boris, you're asking me to be a bad girl."

Boris thought, go for it.

"If you want to be a bad girl, that's ok by me."

Jack began to wonder what he had done. This was turning into a simple dirty phone call. Arno moved away to hide his giggles.

"Today I decide, decide, decided, oh whatever, to be a very good girl, although not for Mr Crappy."

Suddenly the guy's mood became frosty. Eyes shot from one to the other. Did they hear that name right?

"Here is a code for you, Boris, a code, a very nice little code that I think you would like to tell your friends about. Are you ready ... Boris darling, are you ready?"

Boris seriously wished he could have met this contact without the aid of technology. He played the image of Anna Tina in his mind and took a deep breath.

"Okay, I got it, for sure, looks fine. How can I thank you?" Boris was getting hopeful.

"Just come to see me in jail, bring me nice things."

Boris glanced at his friends, as if asking, what now?

"Keep her talking," whispered Jack, "maybe she has more..."

As Boris pressed the phone to his ear, he heard a large intake of breath followed by a yawn.

"Whoops, now I have to change my blouse."

"Why?" asked an innocent Boris.

"Wine everywhere, silly girl. So long, Boris. Call me some time."

The disappointment showed on Boris's face, unlike the upbeat smiles on his friends.

"She's a bad one, Boris. Don't forget what she got up to here," said Arno, feeling the urge to protect his Dutch buddy from a disastrous meeting.

"Why the hell did we not go for Skype?" asked Boris.

"Sorry old chap, too late for that now. The code ..."

Jack's face showed stress as he tried to make sense of the numbers on Boris's tablet.

"Let me go back to my main machine. This code looks like the perfect fit, the one I've been missing for the last few days."

If Boris ever dreamt of having an entourage, he'd just found it. The three men followed him like puppies behind the pack leader.

Anna Tina braved a quick glance in the mirror. She detested what she saw: baggy skin under her once large green piercing eyes. They were now misty; the sharp see-all concentration had now become a lost stare. As she opened the fridge door taking the last bottle of sweet white, she missed her step, turning and falling on to the small couch next to her desk.

So what, she thought.

I don't need a glass. Even film stars drink from the bottle.

She again considered her actions. Had she made the right decision? It was too late anyway. After two large gulps, the bottle was put somewhere on the floor. Anna Tina felt tired. This day was now over.

Boris crashed onto his office chair, wriggling himself into a comfortable position, Jack, Arno and Dan took chairs from the next room, placing them around the table, all vying for the best view of his screen.

"It's always such a mystery to me how you guys type so quick." Dan showing he was more outdoor man than tech lover.

"Simple. I love this work. My parents spoilt me with tech gifts from a young age. It was the only direction I could go in."

"How long do you think?" Jack was getting impatient, rubbing his hands together.

"If the code is good, just hold your breath."

Apart from the tiny click-click-click, the office remained silent.

Boris was biting his upper lip.

"Holy shit, I'm in..."

A collective, "yea," sounded around the room. Arno desperately wanted to offer everyone a drink to celebrate, but at the same time could not pull himself away from the changing screen.

"Here we go, his recent emails, he has been ... busy. Car hire, hotel bookings, new one every couple of days, whole slew of requests to stop mail coming to this address, marine insurance offers ... strange why? Nothing heart-stopping yet. Changed his mobile number. Hold on ... can you see this one? Sunseeker Yachts Antibes. Confirmation he will be arriving to pick up his new yacht, *Fisc Attack,* what the hell. You believe this?"

The mood in the room changed from interest and expectation to instant anger, aggression showing in all eyes, including Boris's.

"This dirty stinking little bastard. No doubt his pay-off for what he did here." Arno pushed his chair back so violently he crashed into a book cabinet, shaking with rage.

"Please try to stay calm, Arno. Can you imagine how many times I sank to an all time low because of this parasite?"

Jack, as always, was doing his bit to bring the meeting back towards control and inject some reason, but could still not resist punching the wall with his right fist.

"This rotten little fucker calls his yacht what..." Jack was more incensed than his friends had seen in a very long time

"Sorry, Jack, this cannot happen. Just not darn right. I can't live with this." Dan stood, hands in pockets breathing heavily, staring towards the Alps.

Jack surveyed his close friends, even after all they had been through, the current mood in the room was different. If Crappy was still in the chateau he would be torn apart, treated like a target for a street gang. The damaged inflicted over the last months had turned into pure anger and hatred for the man. Maybe Anna Tina should have stayed quiet.

Boris quietly printed and copied to the USB key what he guessed to be the most important data. Due to the tinderbox atmosphere in the room he decided to hold off with the yacht specs and some other stuff that would have caused explosions during the evening. Very little conversation flowed between the men. Each and every one created mental images of how they would harm Crappy, which blow would do the most damage, how his face would change when he realised his end was near. Slowly they excused themselves, heading back to wives and apartments for another night with little prospect of sleep.

Jack rose early; his boys now well into the long summer holidays. He felt tired but owed it to them to make the best of summer, suggesting a lake swim. They eagerly agreed but Carly insisted they must have breakfast before they leave. This gave Jack time for a fifteen-minute treadmill workout to bring his sleepy head up to speed. As he walked down the second flight of stairs towards the gym, Eva opened her door. Jack felt a twinge of embarrassment. With last night's anger they had forgotten to inform the most important lady who had sorted out their worst nightmare.

"Can I come in, Eva? Need to update you."

"Of course, Jack, welcome anytime. Coffee?"

"Why not. Was heading for the gym, but this is more important."

"I'm intrigued, Jack, please tell."

"I'll try to keep it short. A kind of strange sequence of events."

"Think I can handle that, Jack."

"Well ... emails arrived yesterday for myself and the guys."

"Typical in this country, females always come second."

"Sorry, not my way. The hacker girl wanted to speak with Boris"

Eva now moved closer to Jack, nodding and staring expectantly, knowing this would be interesting.

"Boris spoke with her, although she did sound a little drunk."

"Drunken people tell more, Jack. No surprise."

"She did indeed tell more. The missing code to get into Crappy's computer – she gave it to Boris."

"And he used it, it worked? He got in?"

"Oh did he. We saw ... well, apart from Crappy being a busy man on the move. Sit tight, Eva. He's just taken delivery of a luxury yacht, in Antibes. Seems he picked it up a few days ago.

This is the ultimate insult; he's called it, *Fisc Attack*."

Eva began to use the language heard in Arno's apartment before she had disappeared to Paris. Jack stared at her, shaking his head.

"Please don't leave for Paris again. Think we need you here."

"No worries, Jack."

Eva went Eastern European again.

"There is no way I can pull that stunt again, it was a one-off. This new situation has to be handled in a different way."

"Your input's always appreciated, Eva. I'm sure the guys are all trying to dream up the perfect pay-back for this creep, but we're not there yet."

Eva came back quickly.

"It's August, the South coast is full of yachts, but, I'm sure with the help of a pretty face and some charm, he can't hide from us ..."

"This is moving quickly, Eva. I can see a bizarre holiday plan in the offing."

"Exactly, so let's move, and quick."

Jack was determined to make the swim with his boys. Dan had joined them. After the customary races, the men sat under a large ceder tree, cold beers in hand, a serious discussion about to take place.

"Looks like we need her again."

"Guess you mean Eva."

Dan shook his head watching Jack's boys clowning in the water.

"Always Eva. I told her about last night's discovery."

"Was she pissed off?"

"Same Eva. Went all strange accent, angry eyes, but she's not leaving for Paris this time. She has, I guess, stunning girlfriends who can help us in the south."

"Help us as in partying? That's a memory for me ..."

"Sorry, Dan, happily married man. Eva thinks the right girl can find out where Crappy is. Most likely via the yacht broker, the mooring. Maybe he's still doing tests. If they look anything like Eva, that won't be difficult."

"And then?"

"Chatted with Boris the other day. He asked just that. What would we do when the grubby little bastard is in our hands?"

"This reminds me of my old times, Jack, in Iraq. We knew the objective, all planned to perfection, but that moment of taking someone out. Even in the military you've always got someone looking over your shoulder. This has gotta be done the right way."

Jack's sons were hungry on the way back to the chateau. He called his neighbours to propose an evening dinner meeting in the garden. Some big decisions needed to be taken.

Diplomacy dictated that Eva always sat with the wives, the men staying a reasonable distance away. Heaven forbid too much affection was displayed to the lady who saved them. This would be akin to trying the Pamplona Bull Run in ski boots. Only a matter of time before you were cornered and gored.

The men had decided to present a holiday plan, a celebration in the Sainte-Tropez area now all the problems were behind them, although the only female up to speed was Eva. If they were lucky enough to find Crappy, plans would be made at the time, although the sea accident idea brought a sickly smile to their faces every time it was mentioned. So many diversions were available. It was the perfect place to occupy the family whilst tracing their nemesis.

"So who's in?" asked Jack, raising his glass in the air, expecting a positive response.

Annabel was the first to nod her approval, her expression almost as if she knew what the boys were planning. Dan put his head to one side like, *dumb question.*

Arno lifted his eyebrows thinking, for Nick and Simon alone, the bastard deserves this.

Boris looked doubtful, his expression asking, *can I come too?*

Eva offered to show the other ladies one of her favourite beachwear shops in Port Grimaud.

Arno offered to book a nice hotel, plus a couple of restaurant reservations. Boris looked a little daunted. Would his summer shirts be up to the pending fashion parade?

They agreed on an early night with plans to be finalized the next day. By Wednesday they should be four hours away from paradise.

Boris was already packing his most powerful computer.

Eva called old girl friends in Paris asking for their help in the South of France. "A bizarre, but rewarding short holiday." No one said yes. Eva could not let her friends down ...

Boris set his alarm to make the proposed early workout with Dan. He found his body firmer and his shirts tighter since he'd become a new neighbour at Chateau Montjan.

Enjoying a last yawn, he began to drift away, but the high pitched hum from his mobile brought him back quickly.

"Boris, do you remember this voice?"

If it was who he thought, she was far more in control now than the last time they spoke.

"Anna Tina, is it you?"

"Good man, Boris, you're sharp. Just the way we have to be in our profession."

Boris became rapidly focused on every word he was about to hear. This was the same girl he had observed working in Crappy's apartment. Not at all the drunken mess who had passed on the code.

"It's nice to hear from you again, but I can't imagine that at this time of night you have another code for me."

"Boris, after I passed you the code, I reflected long and hard about what I had done. This may sound sort of limp, maybe too late even. I hope not, but I never felt comfortable taking the information from your friends at the chateau. They all appeared to be ok people, worrying ethics about their tax declarations, but a special type of person. That's rare in this world. However Crappy, he looked upon them all as a cheap ticket to get what he wanted, to take full advantage and get out when he destroyed them."

"Well, I'm trying to believe you, Anna Tina, but please imagine we all look upon you as a big part of the problem."

"I know, of course I did it, but thinking back to the times when Crappy stroked my arm as I tried to work, almost made me vomit. Now, I am trying to stay out of jail and he's lying around on a brand new yacht."

"You know about the yacht?"

"Boris darling, I gave you the code, but I didn't destroy it. I'm also following his new life in the South. Too sick for words, and this is why you're hearing from me tonight."

Boris was sitting bolt upright in bed. The moon shone into his room but something told him a late night surprise was just around the corner.

"Let me come directly to the point. If you and the owners are planning what I think you are, I could be a very important asset to you down there. Let me help, promise I will follow whatever instructions Jack Rafter, Arno Van Bommel or you give me. Crappy once bragged about how he arranged the beating up of Rafter's boys to frighten the owners out of the chateau. For that alone he deserves to pay. Am I in or out? I won't let you down."

"Would seem I have to wake a few people up in the chateau tonight. Can I call you back after our chat? It's not only up to me"

"I sleep late, Boris. Make it work, I want to help."

Within five minutes Boris was presenting a bizarre action plan to the sleepy group. Although suspicion filled their minds, they could not ignore the fact that this was by far the best way to get close to Crappy. He could never quite capture Anna Tina but this could be his chance. They really had no choice but to say yes.

"You're in, Anna Tina. How, when and where will follow tomorrow. Sleep well."

As he checked the spacing around his new mooring, quickly dismissing the young deckhand with a twenty euro tip, Gerard Crappy was the happiest man in France. His new Predator looked splendid, more than twenty meters, the stainless steel fittings shining in the evening harbour lights. He had dreamt for many years about owning his own yacht. Now this was all his. What he did to earn it could not worry him less. Those foreigners at the chateau could go to hell for all he cared; he would never see them again. His new life was to be more sea-based than land. He took another selfish look back at his new baby.

25

CARLY PREPARED A light breakfast for the holidaymakers on their round balcony at seven sharp. Leaving around eight would mean lunch could be enjoyed at whichever restaurant Arno had chosen.

Boris raced from door to door. He'd never been to the south of France before. He was so glad that he had once worked for Van Bommel Motors. The Rafter boys were pestering him about the pending release of *Call of Duty Ghost*. Could he hack a sneak preview for them?

Jack, always the attention to detail business man, took Boris towards his office.

"So you've spoken with Anna Tina. She knows where to meet us?"

"No problem, Jack. I get the feeling she is a real professional, dedicated"

"Think we know about her professional qualifications ..."

"I thought about this for hours before I could fall asleep. We all saw how much she hates Crappy, but he can be putty in her hands. We need her, Jack. She's smart, a cool operator. If he see's us it's over ..."

"You know Boris; we trust you and your judgement. Let's hope she can give him something special from all of us."

With that Jack stood up and made a final check on his email.

Arno and Dan confirmed departure was imminent.

"We're all packed, four cars, enough to stay a month."

Carly nodded a sheepish ok.

Wish I could do that for her, thought Jack.

Only Stephanie noticed the breakfast atmosphere. It was happy and positive, and why not? But the way the guys exchanged glances at one another reminded her of a pending business trip, the pressure of deals to be done. Why did they flip from smiles to worries? Arno would be carefully interrogated on route.

The mid-week traffic flowed well. The small convoy stayed close together, Arno always the racer, Stephanie the brake. After Avignon things bunched up.

"Remember lunch in Megève, honey?"

"Of course, why?"

"Saw a weird glaze over your face that day."

"You know why, that laptop."

"Saw the same this morning over breakfast, but no laptops around..."

"Don't know what you mean."

"Arno, please..."

"Come on, Steph. We've been through a lot lately. Allow me an odd reflection moment. Lost a lot of sleep these last months, still can't believe it's over."

"Okay, you're off the hook for now, but you know me, Van Bommel."

Arno made a mental reminder to inform the guys their movements were probably being monitored.

Boris loved the company of Dan and especially Nick and Simon. They'd been friends from the beginning.

"Really never been to the south before, Boris?" said Dan, staring in surprise at the rear-view mirror.

"No, first time, and what a lucky guy to do it with you all."

"If we can't find you a future wife there, then we can't find one. The beaches are full of potential."

Nick and Simon curled their heads towards Dan. "Girls, hey?"

"Really guys, Boris needs a girl in his life. You have time"

Dan often took the Rafter boys with him. Jack and Carly had confidence in everything about him, even considering his murky past, although that was not his fault. But he did his best to help them through the ugly period of late taking the boys for regular ski trips, and their style was now truly impressive. Anything to leave their parents thinking time. They would be friends for life.

"Check this idea out, guys; I should talk to the girls first. If they're pretty, clean and wealthy, then maybe you can also talk. Deal?" Dan saw two pained expressions behind him.

"Yea, Californian boy, sure."

Jack signalled his buddies the need for a fuel stop. A motorway sign showed a large service area coming up, five kilometres away.

Jack fuelled up first whilst the ladies went inside. As he parked in the shaded area outside the shop, his mobile announced a call from Boris.

"Jack, Anna Tina called. She's there, in Nice, and ready to go to work. Thought I'd tell you while the girls are in the shop."

Jack scanned the windows. Carly was deep in the cookie section with the boys. The queue at the check-out would ensure she needed at least another five minutes. The others were still fuelling up behind.

"Thanks Boris. You're right; our wives will never buy this situation. She'd better stay low key for the moment."

The line went dead as Arno pulled the door open.

"Leave that bloody phone alone, you're on holiday, man."

"Listen quickly, Arno, that was Boris. Anna Tina's arrived in Nice. Due to meet Eva at the car hire. She sounds keen to do this."

"Well, she'd better be fucking serious this time. If she really hates him as much as us, our thank you to him will taste better."

"Let's talk later. Boys at the bar tonight and make it clear to her."

"Okay, take it easy. Two hours to go."

Carly and Stephanie found it strange how quiet their husbands were while heading for such a beautiful place.

Gerard Crappy had pure satisfaction written all over his face. The technology in his new yacht was working like a dream, the lounge TV boasting a range of five hundred channels. This morning only one took his interest, Swiss news. Daily coverage of the latest problems for Harvey Lasalle and the occasional mentions of a beautiful female hacker who had disappeared ...

Pity, thought Crappy, I would still like to welcome her on my yacht. How I stopped myself groping that wonderful body still surprises me.

As he surveyed the marina, several pretty girls were busy on small and large craft, making preparations for the day. He focused on a powerboat two moorings away. He began stroking his chin, the Swedish lady unaware of his interest. She constantly bent over showing a perfect bottom, her large breasts falling out of the black mini bikini. She was too intense on tying a rope to care. Slowly she turned towards Crappy, breasts still uncovered. She stroked her nipples as if she knew he was looking, and then gradually replaced her top. Crappy decided his Predator was missing an important optional extra.

The Hotel Amarante shone like a palace high above the golf domain of Ste Maxime.

"We're back."

Jack grinned, cruising cautiously down the narrow slope towards the hotel reception.

As requested, the rooms were all on the eighth floor, side by side, each having views of the golf course and onto the bay of Saint-Tropez. Jack took a suite to accommodate his boys. At the end of the corridor, the final two rooms would be occupied by Eva and Anna Tina. The men were most interested as to how this chemistry would work.

Arno announced lunch had been arranged at a nearby restaurant, but he forgot the name. Stephanie told him his pronunciation was so bad he'd best forget what the place was called and just show everyone the way. There was no resistance.

A truly old days feeling came over the friends. Jack the organiser, Dan the cool gentleman assisting the ladies with seating, Nick and Simon talking with a cute girl from New York who needed some serious attention. Her new iPhone rather too full of icons. Their newly acquired tech skills impressed her. Jack and Arno lingered at the bar reflecting on how Anna Tina could assist them.

"So Eva takes her to Antibes tomorrow morning and Anna Tina tries to get the whereabouts of Crappy's Predator."

Boris placed his hands on the shoulders of Jack and Arno.

"Sorry to interrupt, the ladies are ... well, they asked me to get you."

"We're coming. Had a chance to check on Crappy's movements?" enquired Jack.

"Took a quick look at the hotel and here. He's very happy with his new yacht. Several mails to old maybe girlfriends, inviting them to enjoy his company on the Med. Sad little creep."

"Well, if we can find him, Anna Tina should sort that problem out."

With that the men joined the table, Arno's choice of restaurant making everyone happy.

The reception staff at the Amarante were used to seeing all forms of arrivals, from rowdy Italian football teams to bizarre musicians brought in to play on a Russian billionaire's yacht. But the two ladies who stood in front of them promoted a slightly uncomfortable atmosphere.

Eva and Anna Tina could have been related. Both one meter eighty-five, long well-cared for shining dark hair, oversized breasts, perfect dress coordination and even with close to perfect French accents. Odd words appeared more from the East.

The young man behind the reception felt his colour changing. He wanted to say so much, but his mouth froze. He slid the registration forms to Eva.

"I guess our friends checked in some hours ago."

The young man had taken full advantage. Whilst the ladies filled in the forms, he had gazed at their wonderful breasts. Now he paid the price. He glowed like a firework about to explode.

"Yes, Madame, all checked in. They left for lunch and should be back anytime. Can I help further?"

Eva smiled politely. "Just get somebody to bring our cases."

"I'll do it," blurted the boy, hoping his enthusiasm would be rewarded.

Boris found alcohol to be quite pleasant. Since his new friends were regular drinkers he found it impolite not to join in. His whole life had changed.

"Try the Daiquiri? That's a nice drink."

"Really," replied Jack, "don't mind if I do."

While the ladies headed off to the pool area for some afternoon sun, Jack and Boris waited in the bar for the guys to join them.

Eva tickled Jack's back.

"We're here."

Boris could not restrain his nervous first impression whilst doing his utmost to keep his gaze high, directly into the eyes of Anna Tina.

"You must be Anna Tina?" Jack stretched out his hand cautiously.

"That's me. Great to meet you, Jack, especially under these more balanced circumstances. Now I can help to put things right."

Eva shook her head. "Most things have been put right. It's only a slug on a yacht that needs our attention now."

Arno and Dan filled in behind, closely followed by Boris. The group moved to a corner table with stunning views over to Port Grimaud. Boris insisted Daiquiris should be enjoyed by all.

"Okay, here we are. Still positive?" Jack glanced from left to right.

"More than positive, we owe him. He thinks he can walk away, play with a new toy and leave us to rot. He's wrong." Arno had his meanest look on.

Eva complimented Boris on his choice of drink.

"Early tomorrow, Anna Tina and I will leave for Antibes; do our best to find out where he is. Soon as we know that, we arrange some sort of chance meeting with Anna Tina. If you're sure he can't swim, let's go for the drunk overboard routine..."

Anna Tina came across as a new enthusiastic team member, taking in the serious faces around her. Her work at the chateau had to be repaired. She sat close to Eva, a faint smile showed her confidence. Otherwise she showed little emotion for what was being asked of her.

Jack and Arno both being competent sailors offered to check out the power boat rentals so when the time came they could be close to their quarry. But the question in all of their minds was, *what exactly do we do when we find him? Could they really pull this off?*

All rose early the next morning with the exception of Arno and Stephanie. Jack caught Eva and Anna Tina leaving the breakfast room and wished them, "good luck."

Everybody did their own thing, golf, pool, beach. Anticipation was heavy awaiting the return of the well endowed ladies.

"That's the type my old boy friend bought."

Anna Tina stood in front of the receptionist at Sunseeker Antibes pointing to an open brochure showing a glossy presentation of the latest Predator 68. Unfortunately for Anna Tina, the equally large-chested reception girl was not impressed by her charms.

"So Madame, how can I help you?" The bored girl hardly bothered to lift her head.

Eva stayed in the hired Renault watching Anna Tina from behind large sun glasses, hoping like crazy a man would show up.

"My friend, Gerard Crappy, took delivery of one of these a few days ago now. I came to surprise him."

The receptionist cocked her head to one side, raising her large dark eyebrows.

"Sorry Madame, we don't give out any information about our clients. Yacht owners are very private people ..."

Anna Tina felt the girl had already seen her script.

"I only want to know where he is. We go back years. Surely you can help me?"

"Madame, I could lose my job if I give that information away. I don't know you."

Anna Tina considered coming back later when the girl left for lunch, but just as she was about to excuse herself, a tall dark suited Italian man entered from behind the reception.

"Bonjourno, Senorita."

Anna Tina beamed at the new arrival, the receptionist glared at her.

"Maybe you can help me. I'm just trying to catch up with an old friend who bought a Predator 68 from you recently. Nothing more than that."

"And his name?"

"Crappy, Gerard Crappy."

Determined to maintain her control, the receptionist stood between Anna Tina and the handsome Italian.

"I told her we don't give out such information."

"I don't think such a beautiful woman could be a terrorist. Why don't you help upstairs, the new brochures need sorting out."

The girl left with a large sigh, her heals clicking rapidly, narrowing her eyes at the only man in the room.

"Mario Rossetti, Head of Sales for this region. I arranged the Predator deal, and I can tell you he's a very happy man."

Anna Tina moved closer to the counter ensuring her tight T-shirt took over the salesman's concentration.

"I just want to find out where he is. Surprise him. We're old friends from Paris."

"He's a lucky man. I love surprises like you. Can I invite you for a test sail; the whole range is ready for me"

"Thanks, but Gerard is ... well, an old flame. I know how happy he will be when he sees me."

"Yes, I have no doubt about that ..."

The tall Italian could not understand his invite being turned down for a small nervous Frenchman, but felt the odds were against him.

"Okay, we arranged a mooring for him in Sainte-Maxime. We offered this area but he didn't like the price. Check with the harbour master there. You'll find him. Oh and he insisted on a strange name, especially these days, the craft's called, *Fisc Attack*."

Anna Tina gave a surprised "thanks," shook the man's hand and turned towards the door.

"If he's not there, I'm here every day."

"Won't forget that."

Anna Tina never really liked slimy Italian men.

The hotel pool was crowded. One of the world's largest private yachts, Russian owned, was hosting a party the following night. The owner a keen football fan. Unsurprisingly Arno and Dan were fixed on the athletic couple at the shallow end.

"Bet she's a pole dancer."

"So what's he?"

"A pole holder I guess ..."

"He'd better hold her tight tomorrow night; Russian money might tempt her away."

Suddenly most of the males around the pool turned towards the glass entry door. Eva and Anna Tina made the pole dancer look cheap. Who could also not resist a quick turn of the head. Jack and Dan plunged in, and just as quickly leapt out of the pool eager to hear the news from Antibes.

"I kept this area all for us."

Boris was determined to impress Eva, but more so Anna Tina. He dreamt of the day he could talk tech in in a quiet corner with his counterpart. Huddled close together, the chateau guys waited for the girls update.

Eva began.

"You won't believe where he is guys, you just won't believe."

"Close if you say it that way." Jack stretched his legs to block an interested Swedish couple from moving too close by.

"Clever man, Jack. This little bastard has a mooring here, in the marina. Thanks to Anna Tina, she got the information."

The guys smiled proudly at the ladies, all thinking, wondering, how Crappy would react to Anna Tina suddenly appearing in Sainte-Maxime. Could this really work?

The golf carts were parked in a neat row, electric cables tangled behind charging up for the early start the next morning. Above on the terrace a table for twelve was perfectly set awaiting the most interesting group staying at the hotel. Seating was a challenge, the single men edging towards the single girls, the married men seeking safety next to their wives. Boris felt himself the man of the evening after Eva invited him to sit between herself and Anna Tina.

"It's great to be here. The problems are all behind us now. To a wonderful long life together."

Jack's toast was eagerly accepted by all around the table but Stephanie still caught quick glances being exchanged between the males of the chateau.

As the conversation flowed the men knew that somehow a visit should be planned to the marina the next day. Arno reminded the wives about Eva's promise of a visit to the best beachwear shop in the area. This was eagerly accepted. Relief was evident. Now the men could continue the search for Crappy's mooring. Strangely Eva's friend, Anna Tina excused herself from the beachwear shopping trip.

"I have cupboards full of beachwear. Think I'll sightsee around Sainte- Maxime."

As the Predator's vibration-less twin MTU motors became silent; the owner stretched his neck in the direction of a powerboat two moorings away. The Swedish lady was enjoying a close embrace with a much older man.

"Certainly not her husband," murmured a jealous Crappy, as he looked up and down the rows of resting million-dollar yachts. Couples and families were all celebrating after a fine day at sea. He tapped his sleeping laptop back to life. Outlook announced only three mails, two from lady friends, who sadly could not make his wonderful offer of cruising the Mediterranean.

The third was from an unknown source, referring to a model bikini photo shoot at the marina the next morning. As hard as he tried, the internet confirmed nothing. He decided to remain in port the next morning anyway.

Tomorrow could finally be his lucky day.

26

As he peered through the apartment window, Harvey Lasalle's stare fixed on the squeaking tram arriving seven floors below. His mind shot back to the happier times he had spent in the place some thirty years ago. Girls would come and go like an ever-revolving door, so many he found it difficult to recall their names. He snapped out of the past as his mobile announced a call from the Geneva office. He hesitated, should he bother to pick it up? Voicemail was his preference these days. No good news had come his way for several weeks. As the last ring sounded he felt compelled to know, his hand shot towards the Blackberry.

"Yes."

"Sorry to disturb you, Mr Lasalle."

Lasalle recognised the voice of his long serving accountant, Jean-Michelle Pac.

"I can't imagine you have any good news for me. What is it?"

"Something unusual I just picked up."

"So tell me..."

"Better not over the phone. Can we meet for coffee this morning?"

"If you think we have to. Where?"

"Café park, on the ..."

Lasalle interrupted. "I know the place. One hour ok? Be on time."

"I'll be there."

Lasalle reflected on a previous conversation with his chief accountant. Pac was instructed to clear up any loose ends, offshore accounts buried or at best well hidden, destroy any incriminating documentation to distance Lasalle from anything that could cause him more misery.

But his mood deepened. He could only hope Pac had not discovered more potential pain for his old boss.

Selecting a straw summer hat, baggy denim shirt and sandy cotton trousers, he felt sure he could go unrecognised, the wrap-around sunglasses ensuring another layer of disguise. He chose the backstreet walk to the café. His old contacts rarely took these routes; the larger the boulevard the more they could be seen. These days he hid more than ever before.

His accountant was never late. Lasalle could not remember a single day when he arrived first in the office. As he surveyed the small café room, he saw only two ladies, probably tourists, and a mother and small boy were inside. No man with a file under arm, eyes darting nervously caught his sight. He shuffled towards the darkest corner he could find, ordered a small coffee and checked his mails.

"Sorry, very sorry."

Pac burst into the café like a man running down the platform hoping to jump onto a departing train.

"Calm down," whispered Lasalle, the waiter already flashing him looks of, *where do I know that man from?*

A small coffee was brought over for Pac. He was a regular.

"I hope this is not a waste of time. You know how unpleasant my public life is these days. I don't know how long I will stay a free man."

"Just felt it's something you need to know." Pac looked uneasy.

"I hope it's not more bad news?"

"That's for you to decide ..."

Pac thrust his left hand into an old brown leather case. He shuffled a few papers back and forth as if looking for something special.

Lasalle looked worried staring at the nervous hands of Pac. So many bad things plagued his life these days. What more could come out of that worn briefcase?

The accountant slowly took out what looked to be a bank statement. Lasalle vaguely recalled the name at the top. One of the many holding companies he set up, but when? He had no idea. Pac held the paper between his thumb and forefinger in the direction of his pale ex boss.

"You see the problem?"

Lasalle slowly scanned down the statement. Deep in his mind he recalled this company being under the control of Gerard Crappy, simply a shelter fund to pay the likes of Anna Tina Geisinger, the three workers in the cave, or anybody else Crappy thought worthwhile, to ensure Lasalle gained control of the chateau. The last figures at the bottom of the statement showed a dismal balance of minus two hundred and fifty Swiss Francs.

Pac looked eager with anticipation. He sighed, taking deep gulps of air towards Lasalle.

"Remember I never felt good about him, tried to warn you... He always had a bitter look in his eyes, like the yachts should have been his not the clients."

"Could you elaborate?"

"I knew him years ago when he worked for that Italian yacht broker. Remember you met him when you bought the Benetti?"

Lasalle nodded slowly, looking worn and thoughtful. Better he say nothing to his accountant about the long relationship with Crappy.

"I prepared this file for you. It's too complex to go over here, but I think when you read it your feelings for this man will ... be strong and ... well, just read it."

The two men shook hands and parted in different directions. Pac was happy he could still serve his boss. Lasalle gripped the file like his life depended on it.

The whisky with ice tasted far better than the morning coffee. Lasalle was in two minds about opening the pale grey file on his lap. Good news failed to exist for him these days. After one more sip he said to himself, "What the hell," as a slight twinge of doubt entered his mind concerning the disappearance of Gerard Crappy.

Spreading the bank statements across his low lounge table, his eyes kept fixing on signatures, ones that looked very much like his own. Every paper he checked showed another transfer from his catacomb of offshore companies to the one Gerard Crappy controlled, Geneva Core holdings. At one stage several million Swiss Francs bloated the account.

Every new page he turned showed another injection. The final statement for August brought the balance to minus two hundred and fifty Swiss Francs. The third whisky was quickly downed. Harvey Lasalle's head was a mess, his business deviations so complicated; he failed to recall the names of all the large and small corporations he had set up over the years. The last month had caused him to block out so many grey moments from his business career.

Holding the glass to his mouth, he slid his forefinger down the July statement. His eyes became wide, painfully so. The glass slid from his hand, tiny particles exploding across the wooden floor.

A transfer of ten million five hundred and fifty thousand euros had been made to a unknown account in Antibes. Harvey Lasalle stared at the statement until his head ached. He then made phone calls, so many, determined to speak with the eager young man from the military.

27

KISSES AND SPEND-SPEND-SPEND, but please-think-of-the-plastic, jokes were exchanged as the wives left with Eva for her favourite shop.

The men had planned a, *fishing trip*.

Within seconds they were in the elevator descending to the garage. Anna Tina waited behind Jack's black Range Rover.

"Um...um...um," stuttered Boris, while the other men stared with obvious pleasure. Anna Tina looked, well ... different. She wore a short red mini skirt, no bra, a thin tie-at-the-waist white blouse, and heels that allowed her to look Boris straight in the eye. Two ageing Belgian golfers passed, shaking their heads, wishing they could shed at least thirty years and lose twenty kilos.

Jack considered the cosmetic surgeon must have been very pleased with his work.

"I'm ready."

"You're not kidding, Anna Tina. Hope we can protect you. You may get ... well, let's say, appreciated walking around Sainte-Maxime like that."

Jack gestured her to the rear door of his car. Now the last minute planning had to be taken care of.

Arno followed Jack's Range Rover with Boris. Jack touched the screen speaker icon; Dan looked motivated and keen to commence the operation.

"Suggest we park along the road a little, out of town in case Crappy is walking around, then split up, following Anna Tina towards the marina. Boris, anything to add?"

"Yes, Jack. My idea about the bikini shoot got him interested. He searched the net all over the place, so it looks like he'll be around the marina hoping to meet his dream bikini girl."

Jack noticed Anna Tina raising her eyebrows. She was taking long last-minute glances towards the Mediterranean, very deep in thought.

Crappy does not deserve this, Jack considered.

All of the men wore baseball caps, large sunglasses and bags slung over their shoulders. Anything to cover up should Crappy appear.

"Don't forget, some sort of simple accident if possible," Jack whispered into Anna Tina's ear before she strode away towards the marina. Several divorces could be initiated that day. Men were falling like flies.

Crappy checked himself in the reflection of the sliding glass doors; his tan was sufficiently sailor-brown. The white Saint-Tropez motif shirt and shorts combination would, he hoped, be enough to lure the right girl in the direction of his craft. Having been the owner of such a beauty for one week now, it was high time the first lady came on board. As he bounced down the rear steps he smiled, two young, well formed crew girls were polishing a gleaming sail yacht with a US flag across the wooden walkway, but they continued to polish as if he were a local garbage collector. Look as he might, no bikini shoot was taking place in the marina. He decided to take a coffee across the road, grunting his order at the waiter he began to fall into a deep mood, staring down at his skinny legs.

"Bloody useless internet," Crappy looked depressed.

"Excuse me, is this seat taken? You remind me of ... yes it's you Gerard."

Anna Tina bent forward slightly towards the Predator owner, offering a cheek kiss. Crappy's open mouth showing the image of a man who thought he'd just won the Euro millions jackpot.

"Yes, yes, I mean no ... it's really not taken. Please. Is it really you Anna Tina, I thought you were in deep trouble?"

She shook her hair back which caused her breasts to swing slowly left and right. The buttons on her white blouse under pressure. Crappy was mesmerised.

"Yes, it's really me. I walked past a couple of times. Just could not make up my mind if it was really you."

"It's me and you look truly wonderful..."

"Well, I'm taking a short holiday. Putting my problems behind me for the moment."

"Well then ... can I offer you something?"

"Is it too early for a glass of wine? After all, I am trying to relax."

"Of course, I'll join you. *Garçon.*"

Crappy flicked his fingers, but the waiter only came over to check on the new arrival, ignoring the small man.

"Bonjour Madame, something special for you?"

Crappy could not resist taking a shifty look at Anna Tina's breasts.

Fifty meters away and more, a group of serious men were seated in cafés holding newspapers high, moving them left and right and keeping an eye on their prey.

"How far away is our hire boat? This may move quickly, he's so taken seeing her again." Dan spoke softly to Jack.

"It's close. I guess one hundred meters or more from his yacht."

"Okay, so we follow them and..."

"We take this stage by stage. I still love the accident-at-sea idea but it's in Anna Tina's hands for the moment."

Crappy suddenly became the most polite man in the south of France. He was so keen to invite his dream lady in the direction of his Predator, but what if she refused? What if she hated boats? Sailing? His nervous system was running at overtime.

"Did you ever go back to the chateau? I just walked away from the place."

"I would prefer not to talk about that mess if you don't mind. We're both here. Let's keep it pleasant." Anna Tina looked displeased.

Crappy was determined to dance to her tune.

"Another glass, Anna Tina? What a coincidence meeting you here ..."

She slid her right forefinger slowly down between her breasts, shaking her head.

"I don't know, you seem a nice man. You always were, but there are so many stories of nasty men taking advantage of innocent ladies in this part of the world. Well, what should I do?"

She so wanted to glance at her capable bodyguards, hopefully not far away, but knew this could jeopardise the whole plan.

"I promise I am a one hundred percent gentleman, Anna Tina. The worst things you will ever hear from me are compliments. I am a good guy, the chateau thing ... well, like you said, all in the past, forget it."

Anna Tina gave a warm smile, but Crappy missed what her eyes were really saying behind the dark sunglasses.

"Okay, why not. I was dreaming about taking a walk around the marina. Would you believe I love yachts? Not those boring busy sailing yachts but powerful yachts with mega engines. Girls dream I guess ..."

Crappy was torn between showing his Predator keys, ordering a new drink, if the waiter responded, and babbling about his similar love of powerful yachts.

"So you are not only beautiful, but a girl who knows what a real yacht looks like."

"Like I said a dream. One day maybe." Anna Tina took a deep breath, Crappy was hypnotized.

Jack and Dan made a quick detour behind the café where Crappy sat, heading towards their hired powerboat. Boris and Arno chose to walk through the car park. Within two minutes the four were on board checking systems. Boris watched Anna Tina's progress with binoculars. Crappy fidgeted like a school boy on his first date. Anna Tina was moving her upper body to the sound of *Take That*.

The other men in the café flashed jealous stares at the small sailor muttering, "can't be her boyfriend, just can't be."

"You know, Anna Tina, please don't think this a line but I love beautiful yachts, and I ... actually own one. Never mentioned it before, but ..."

Anna Tina cocked her head to one side, faking surprise.

"You really own a yacht, really?"

"A brand new one, a Sunseeker Predator. Took delivery just one week ago."

Anna Tina had to keep up the act, but it was difficult. She would never win an Oscar for her performance, but the growing hatred towards Crappy and her new found affection for the chateau owners gave her the motivation to put matters right, whatever the cost.

"Oh ... what colour?"

"Grey and black, more than twenty meters, forty-five knot top speed, almost as beautiful as you."

"She's doing a great job, poor girl. He's crumbling."

Boris updated his friends.

"Does it look like they may be moving towards his yacht?" Jack pulled his black baseball cap lower as two German tourists surveyed the intense looking men.

"Not yet, Jack. I think Anna Tina is making sure he's convinced she's a simple yacht-loving geek beauty, who is amazingly back in his life again."

"Hope she doesn't have to do anything ... well, sexual with him, poor thing." said a concerned Jack.

Arno felt his contribution was now required.

"Don't worry guys. Not the first time for her, but maybe for him. She'll forget it by tomorrow."

"Thanks Arno, that puts it all in perspective." Jack felt for the safety of Anna Tina, his fatherly instinct remembering what had happened to his boys.

"Where is your beautiful craft?" Anna Tina was trying her best to be amazed at her luck.

"Just over there, in the marina. Would you like to see her? I have a splendid bar on board."

Now it was time to make him work.

"Maybe not today. I don't even have a bikini with me."

Crappy's hands started moving at electric pace gesturing around his head. He could not contain his excitement.

"If that's all you need, we can pick one up here, two doors away. My treat."

"Oh, you are such a persuasive man. I knew there was something special about you the first time we met. How can I say no?"

The shop owner smiled and shook her head whilst checking out Anna Tina's perfect bottom. They both knew it would take a miracle for her to fit into that bikini.

Walking side-by-side to the yacht, they passed within ten meters of Crappy's old neighbours. With or without their cover-up clothes he would not have noticed. His only thought was how Anna Tina would respond to the sight of his shining new toy.

"Grey and black, you said. This must be yours. Wow... So beautiful"

Crappy took Anna Tina's arm as she took off her heels. His heart beat increased as she held onto his shoulder for support, her clothes hid little, and she was almost on his yacht. He also thought the bikini would never stay on.

She was determined to ignore the yacht's name.

Arno pushed the red start button. The Volvo V-8 roar made him feel good; close to a powerful engine again.

"Think we have enough power here, guys. We can outpace him easily, fifty knots at least in this baby."

"Okay, let's give him space to leave."

Jack thought about Carly and his boys. The next few hours could change life for all of them.

Crappy gave Anna Tina a quick tour of his yacht, doing his utmost to linger in the master bedroom, almost insisting she change and put the tiny bikini on, but she kept him busy.

"Can we please go out to sea? I never thought today would be like this. A handsome old friend, a yacht. Shall we have a drink, a toast to a beautiful day?"

Crappy took a quick crafty glance in the mirror. She was lucky; he was a handsome man, owner of a yacht, and a bulging bank account. His right hand nervously pulled out a bottle of Krug from the glass bar and within a few seconds the cork blew high above the predator. Anna Tina gave a false giggle. The four men on the other side of the marina swore.

"I will try that tiny bikini when we get away from here. I'm not so keen on all the staring faces so close in the marina."

She was in full control. Crappy had no idea how to handle this lady. If she told him to roll over and put one paw in the air, he would surely oblige.

Slowly the Predator eased away from the mooring. Anna Tina poured their second glass of champagne, resting her hand on her new boyfriend's shoulder. He felt like a Hollywood A-lister, smirking as he passed smaller craft, stretching around Anna Tina and touching the button to open the sliding roof. The four men in baseball caps pulled up the side protectors one hundred and eighty meters away, watching Crappy leave the harbour.

The Gulf of Saint-Tropez was busy. Massive yachts mingled with Jet Skis, sail boats, ferries, but the red power boat followed the wake of the Predator like a shadow.

Crappy desperately wanted to put an arm around his dream lady, miraculously back in his life, but was so scared to make a wrong move. She was his perfect woman, physical, beautiful, tall. He decided to do whatever she asked. The day would go well for him, no doubt.

"Shall we open another bottle, Gerard? You did say the bar was full."

"Of course, my darling, whatever you like."

Crappy felt a little light in the head. He took a deep breath. Whatever she wants, he thought, this is getting better.

Boris focused his binoculars and observed the second champagne cork fly high into the air.

"She's doing a great job of getting him pissed. He won't be able to find his way back to the harbour."

"Maybe he won't need to," whispered Dan, casting his mind back to Henry's last day.

"Now we're far away from the harbour I will keep my promise. Where did I leave that bikini?"

ALAN WATSON

Crappy turned towards Anna Tina. Several yachts were close by. His normally alert nervous system was now alternating between on and off. He glanced back at the controls. All ok, his glass now recharged again.

"To the smallest bikini you will see today. Cheers, darling, back in five minutes."

Crappy downed the glass in one go.

His heart was thumping under his teeshirt, rubbing the glass across his lips. He had never drunk so much by this time in the morning, but he had also never come so close to such a physical beauty, and on his own yacht. His life was improving by the minute.

"If I know much about drinking, and you guys know I do, Crappy is well on his way."

Arno rested the binoculars on the windscreen, smiled a wicked smile and passed them to Jack.

"You're right, Arno, it's not the waves, it's Anna Tina's work. He never has an empty hand, she's really doing it."

"She's been gone now a while, what do you think?" asked a concerned Jack.

"Changing probably. Got to keep him boiling." Arno's typical direct humour never failing.

"He'd better keep partially alert, it's busy today. We don't want our plan to go off track." Now Dan looked concerned.

The Predator slowed to a drifting pace. Crappy shook his head as if to clear the mist. She was taking a long time, or did he lose track of the last five minutes? His face became serious.

How could such a stunner, especially Anna Tina be on his craft? She never appeared that interested back at the chateau.

She reminded him of Eva, but Eva never even offered him the customary French cheek kisses. Now he was alone with a woman who turned all male heads, even the married family men. He suddenly felt a touch of unease, suspicion. Was this a dream?

"So, nice bikini? Darling."

His jaw dropped, he licked his lips, breathed in deeply and slowly nodded his head.

"Well, darling, say something, is it ok?"

The nodding became faster.

"Yes, yes, it's the most wonderful bikini I've ever seen."

Anna Tina stood motionless. She knew the slightest movement could cause the top to slip, a pleasure Crappy did not deserve. They both stared at one another.

"Lucky little bastard, take a look at this."

Arno passed the glasses to his friends. The comments were the same from each one; typically male appreciation of a very attractive woman.

"Shall we take some sun, darling? On the front cushions."

"I guess you have a pair of Speedos somewhere close?"

Anna Tina sarcastically lifted her eyebrows towards Crappy's shorts.

"I do. I'll change now."

He almost fell down the polished stairs, thinking I can do this in thirty seconds.

Anna Tina hoped like hell that the bikini would stay in place. She was almost afraid to breathe; every small movement of the yacht caused her to adjust the frail material. She imagined her new male friends arguing over the binoculars, and wondering what would happen next.

Crappy felt so challenged. The bedroom mirror showed a skinny accountant's body, and the Speedos were too tight. But the alcohol level in his veins played tricks. Maybe he did resemble someone in a famous action movie, but which one? The only way to keep his frail act in place ... another top up, then he would feel calm again.

As he edged along the deck towards his dream woman, mustering full concentration between two full champagne glasses and the motion of the craft his head became tight. The full summer sun was strong. His dream woman was just three meters away. As Anna Tina stretched out her hand to take one of the glasses, her left breast slipped out of the miniscule cotton top. Crappy reacted and pretended he had missed the moment, doing what he thought a decent guy would do and quickly raised the glass to his lips.

"Cheers, my darling."

The champagne dripped from his mouth, trickled down his chest and onto his red Speedos. Anna Tina turned away towards the sun and eased her magnificent breast back into the top.

"To a wonderful man, yacht, and day."

Another bottle appeared from under the front deck dining table to top up Crappy's half-empty glass. His eyes were now glazed; the movement of the yacht causing him blurred vision. The last time he'd drank so much was at his brother's wedding so many years ago, and girls like Anna Tina were not on the guest list.

In the distance, a group of five Jet Skis came blasting across the bay of Saint-Tropez. They would pass close to the Predator in no more than thirty seconds. Now Anna Tina's mind began racing, she had to seriously focus for the next few moments.

The guys on the powerboat also picked up the Jet Skis pending arrival, most likely between their two craft.

"These guys look crazy. They almost hit that sail yacht."

Jack directed the binoculars between the Predator and the crazy ones.

"Arno, let's move, quickly, something's wrong here."

As Crappy held the glass to his mouth, wondering how much more alcohol he could force into his small body and still remain upright, Anna Tina bent down, arms stretched out as if starting an exercise routine. As she stood up her large breasts were free and pointed towards a man who had no idea what to do, his only reaction to lift the glass to his lips again.

"Um, cheers."

"I knew this tiny thing would not stay on," Anna Tina cursed softly.

She moved close to Crappy, he swallowed hard, causing more champagne to flow into his feeble body.

The old neighbours were now cruising dangerously close to the Predator.

"Um, darling, what's wrong? Shall we go inside?" asked a confused Crappy.

"I like it here, the sun feels good."

Anna Tina was determined to maintain control.

She was now a few centimetres away from the small man's chest. He stared, his eyes wide. This moment had never happened before in his life.

The Jet Skis could be heard clearly now bouncing over the wake of a large sail yacht.

Her nipples brushed against his chest, his body was moving backwards as if he needed to escape the situation. As she pressed even closer his behind pushed against the yacht's safety rail.

"Was this not what you wanted?"

Anna Tina gave a confident superior smile, with her naughtiest look over the sunglasses.

"Yes, but I ..."

She arched her back and with a quick thrust of her breasts pushed him backwards over the safety rail. His glass smashed on the wooden deck.

As he hit the water, head first, a wave eased the Predator away. Before he surfaced, the craft had moved a good ten meters further.

"Arno, watch out you'll hit those bloody lunatics ..."

Dan held onto the wind shield staring aggressively at the first rider.

Anna Tina stretched forward over the safety rail pretending to be so concerned, boat hook in hand.

"What can I do, darling? I don't know what to do..."

The mix of alcohol and salt water stopped Crappy from shouting back. He was coughing violently, spitting seawater. His old neighbours stared at his panicking body in silence.

The first Jet Ski thudded into the back of Crappy's head, the sound like a hammer hitting dense wood, the water around him immediately turning red. His body became lifeless, only moving up and down with the motion of the small waves. A second Jet Ski bounced across his back.

Arno just managed to avoid a collision with the last rider. Insults were screamed, but the guys had no idea about the language. The last Jet Ski veered almost out of control and glanced off the bow of the Predator. Anna Tina was drifting helplessly. The Jet Skis were now hidden behind the craft. As she stared at their water jets firing high in the air she saw what appeared to be small machine guns strapped on two of the rider's backs.

"Stay calm. Just take my hand."

Dan stretched out his arm to help Anna Tina off the Predator's rear platform. She fell into Jack's arms.

"Are you ok? We saw what happened."

"I don't know. You saw I pushed him over the edge, but ..."

"We have no idea who they were. They rode like maniacs, almost as if on a mission. Try not to look at the water."

Jack surveyed the number of craft in the same stretch of water. He was sure someone must have seen this disaster."

A chopper flew uncomfortably close by, returning to its platform on a nearby yacht.

"Keep your caps low, guys."

Arno gently piloted the powerboat away from the drifting Predator. Anna Tina kept her head covered with arms and hands. Despite Boris and Dan checking the area thoroughly with the powerful binoculars, Crappy was gone. His new toy drifting gradually out into the Med.

The Jet Skis were quickly checked and loaded into the garage. The five young men looked up confidently at the man in expectation, their military tattoos clearly visible on the upper arm. He ignored them, only showing interest in watching the Predator, now a dot on the horizon, float away. Thinking to himself that his Benetti Vision was a far more impressive craft.

"The mission is fulfilled, Sir. You promised immediate payment on completion. We want to leave now ..."

Lasalle turned and focused on the tall Russian, his colleagues forming a neat line behind him as if they were preparing for a military parade.

"Not so fast. I would like to see the body. Is that too much to ask?"

Lasalle gave a forced smile.

"It would be wise not to mess around with us. The mark is dead, just like you contracted for." The tall Russian's cold blue eyes fixed on Lasalle's.

One of the group turned his focus away from Lasalle towards the back of the salon where an open safe caught his attention. The man closest to the tall Russian leaned forward whispering a short sentence in his ear.

"My team thinks we could have been seen today. It's busy, that's bad for us. The price is now one hundred thousand each."

"That's not what we agreed. It would be unwise to abuse my generosity; I am a well connected man..." Lasalle sniggered at the tall man.

"We also have special contacts, so you pay the price now, or else."

Lasalle fully understood his position was difficult. If he could stall and move back to the wall safe, a hand gun would improve his bargaining power.

"Let me think for a few minutes. We can find a solution."

Lasalle edged gradually backwards, sliding his left hand along the polished salon dining table. Now only three meters away from the open safe, he began to turn and stretch out his arm.

The AKS-74U fire-burst hit his back, his crisp white shirt instantly turning red. His head glanced off the safe door as he crumpled on the shining wooden floor.

The captain and crew members had been given strict orders to stay below deck in their quarters until Mr Lasalle gave his ok. But the sound of men running back and forth to the yacht's garage could no longer be ignored. There was a faint recognition of an unusual language, maybe Russian.

Within three minutes, five Jet Skis were heading full power towards the open sea.

"Mr Lasalle, Mr Lasalle, is everything ok? Is something wrong?"

As the Benetti captain cautiously entered the main salon, he first spotted the open safe. As he moved closer, the lifeless body of Harvey Lasalle took his attention. A large pool of blood surrounding the motionless body. A maid screamed, dropping a tray of glasses at the far end of the dining table. As the captains eyes moved from Lasalle to the wall safe, he stared and wondered why would someone of Harvey Lasalle's stature leave a safe open with nothing but a small hand gun inside?

28

THE FRONT PAGE of the local morning papers told a grim tale of a drunken yacht owner who had fallen overboard, his death caused by serious head trauma.

A typical summer marine accident, most likely a passing craft.

The police appealed for witnesses and useful information, promising an urgent and full investigation. Strangely the newspapers were void of any coverage on Harvey Lasalle's demise.

Breakfast was a mix of cheery conversation, the ladies discussing yesterday's purchases, and the things they fortunately did not buy. Then awkward periods of silence. The men reflected on a day they would never forget, constantly finding excuses to visit the well-stocked buffet together.

Eva and Anna Tina were nowhere to be seen, sending excuses that Anna Tina had taken too much sun and needed a quiet day alone.

Carly proposed a day at the beach. Jack agreed.

"But only after a round of golf, please."

The women, together with Jack's boys, left for Nartelle beach. The men descended to the golf club.

"Dan, you're an ex military man. What do you think actually happened yesterday?" Jack was carefully inspecting his driver.

"Looked real professional to me, they controlled those things like pros. Anna Tina said something about small machine guns on their backs, but why Crappy? Who else knew he was here?"

"Guess we may never know, which could be a good thing. Thank god Anna Tina got off safe. Any thoughts, Arno?"

"Little bastard deserved what he got. But the idea of Anna Tina getting him drunk, falling off, and well, pissed man drowns. I didn't calculate this end. Sorry can't help further. Perhaps he crossed someone else. Those guys came at him so full of intent, then left so quickly, professional hit if you want my opinion."

"Let's hope nobody will recognise us. It was bloody busy out there, even with our gear on."

Jack drove off determined to only concentrate on his golf.

Later that morning, pulling out of the garage en route for the beach, Eva's divine form could not be missed leaning into a taxi.

"Hey, Eva, everything ok?" asked Jack.

"Not exactly. Anna Tina wants to go home."

Leaning into Jack's car, Eva whispered. "Maybe this was not her forte. She keeps telling me how she saw the guy's head literally explode in front of her."

"Tell her, we're very sorry and that we're still trying to put the pieces together. Give her our best wishes. Thanks may not be the best word at this time."

"I'll leave tomorrow, Jack. See you all for dinner tonight."

The afternoon at the beach went well. Jack, Dan and Arno often staring at far off Jet Skis, but no team of five was spotted, especially with such exceptional riding skills.

After three more days, the short holiday was over. Eva had returned to the chateau via Nice, the remaining neighbours planned an early start to ensure they arrived home by mid-day.

"So, darling, did the break live up to your expectations? You seemed to be very much occupied with the guys."

Carly gave a serious stare at Jack, almost demanding a reaction.

"Loved it, after what we've been through, think we all needed this."

"You're sure it was a holiday? The fishing day really tired you out. That evening you all looked wrecked, plus you didn't catch anything."

"It was just for fun. None of us are really fishermen."

Jack hoped so much that Carly would soon begin reading, anything but this line of questioning.

As Carly opened her book, Stephanie was about to start her own answers-please routine with Arno, one car ahead.

The Chateau Montjan looked as beautiful as ever. The gardener was finishing off trimming the lawns, the end of August sun still strong. A warm feeling came over Jack as he gazed up towards the third floor. Eva watched the cars arrive and descend to the parking.

Everybody was keen to catch up on business and personal matters. Carly and Stephanie went shopping and Jack had to answer Omran Abdulla's ten-question email headed, *why am I invested in banks and trend followers?*

Later in the afternoon Jack sauntered down to the gym, needing a workout after the heavy meals and wine consumption in the south.

"Dan, Arno... Am I seeing this right, it's a gym you know?"

"Oh, I know, but life has to change after the stress we suffered. We need to take more interest in our bodies," smiled Arno.

"With you all the way. Let's go."

Dan bounced onto the treadmill.

"Shall we agree, this nightmare is over? No need to keep going back over old ground now," proposed Jack.

The other two men nodded, said nothing. Half an hour later the short workout was over.

"Any sign of Eva?" asked Jack as he held the door open for his friends.

"No, strange, thought she would be around, at least say to say hi," said a puzzled-looking Dan.

That evening the chateau remained calm. After the most mind-blowing *holiday* for many years, it was obvious that the owners intended to stay in the privacy of their own apartments, needing family time or time alone to ponder how life would move on from here.

Eva made daily calls to check on the health of her new friend Anna Tina. She seemed to be over the experience and had a new boyfriend showering her with gifts. However she quickly refused his kind offer of a weekend sailing in the south of France."

At 9:30 sharp, Eva's mobile showed a call from Paris.

"Eva, my beauty, how are you?"

The Minister was sounding worse for wear, maybe a little drunk, possibly just tired. "I am ... fairly fine really. Back home now after that experience in the south."

"That's why I'm calling. I'm quite sure it was Lasalle behind this. But looks like the Russians he contracted to do it got greedy, killed him and emptied his safe. And the Swiss have demanded no media coverage so he must have been so close to someone who needs protecting."

"Really, this gets complicated." Eva showing concern.

"We are certain he was aware of Crappy's theft. As for the rest, who knows..."

"So we have to keep this between us. They have no idea who really did it, but they fear someone saw them"

"Perfect. Say nothing to those you live with, Eva, you do under-stand? I mean nothing. I want them to stay living under this pressure. I just received a number of ... well, close to perfect photographs taken by a passing chopper that day. Even with those silly baseball caps I could easily identify your chateau neighbours. From this angle it looks like their red powerboat did the evil deed. Stupid fools. And if you have a weak moment, remember, I can always bring the tax office back to life ..."

"You need to know, these are not bad people..."

"Eva, when you sell your soul to the devil..."

"I know that, I know. It's like I never left the service."

"One day, maybe soon, maybe later, I will have a project for your new team. Keep them alert, fit and ready."

"You know I will, like the old days."

"Call me the next time you're in Paris, Eva. I miss you."

© Alan Watson 2014

Printed in Great Britain
by Amazon

17915362R00147